THE MIDDLE OF THE END

THE RAEK RIDERS SERIES

THE MIDDLE OF THE END

THE RAEK RIDERS SERIES
BOOK 5

MELANIE K. MOSCHELLA

ISBN: 979-8-9891986-8-9 (paperback)
IBSN: 979-8-9891986-9-6 (e-book)

www.melaniekmoschella.com

For my LGBTQIA+ friends and family. Your strength inspires me.

NOTE TO READER

Dear Reader,

This series addresses serious, potentially upsetting topics. For a full list of sensitive subject matter, please visit my website: melaniekmoschella.com and select the Content Warnings page. I hope you will join my characters in finding the strength they need to overcome their struggles. However, if you feel any of these topics might be detrimental to your well-being, I encourage you to pass on my books and find your reading bliss elsewhere.

With love,
Melanie

THE MIDDLE OF THE END

1

MEERA

Meera lay as still as she could, waiting impatiently for the sun to rise. The raek fires she kept burning illuminated her immediate surroundings but not the tree canopy overhead. Kennick, Shael, and Linus were visible—motionless on the pine needle forest floor—but beyond their cozy sphere of light was a realm of menacing shadows. The dark shapes of branches and leaves rustled on the periphery of Meera's shifting firelight, and she stared at them, wide-eyed and incapable of sleep.

She was too agitated—not because of the possibility of what lurked in the dark beyond her fires—but because of what paced and twitched within her; she was thrumming with the need to act, desperate to jump at her spirit's call for atonement. She had left her dungeon cell to start making amends for her mistakes, and the pull to start right away pounded in her head and buzzed in her blood. It was an itch creeping all over her skin that she needed to scratch. Sleep wasn't an option for her—only torturous stillness and seemingly endless waiting.

Ever so slowly, the leaves above her lightened from deepest black to greys and blues. Then, as her heart ticked by the unhurried minutes, they warmed to the yellows and reds of fall. The sun was finally rising. Birds chirped their good mornings and fluttered from their nests. The whole world seemed to awaken around her —ready for the new day—and she could only blink and hope that she was also ready.

Meera had long-since squirmed away from Kennick to avoid disturbing his sleep. Now she wriggled against the ground, trying to get comfortable and resisting the urge to spring from the forest floor and pace until she could actually do something—something meaningful, something good. Rolling onto her left side, she found Linus facing her, his eyes also open. For a moment, they just stared at one another. Then Meera grinned; she still couldn't believe Linus had come with them.

Like a log, she rolled several more times across the ground until she and Linus were face-to-face, collecting pine needles on her already grimy clothes. "Did you sleep okay?" she asked quietly, aware that Kennick and Shael were still breathing in deep, even rhythms.

Linus shrugged the shoulder he wasn't lying on. "To think I could have slept in an actual bed last night and woken up to Cook's breakfast," he replied.

"Yes, but you're free now!" she said, searching his eyes and hoping he didn't regret his decision. "I'm glad you're here," she added, reaching out and poking him in the stomach.

Linus grinned at her. "Do you remember the day we met?" he asked.

Propping her head in her hand, Meera nodded. Of course, she remembered—every detail of that day had been etched into her mind by fear; she had been so scared approaching Cerun to feed him for the first time. She remembered the Captain's anxiety and how he had all but run down the grassy hill to the canal. She remembered the smell of the bodies and the flies buzzing around her. She remembered Linus crying, staring at his dead brother. She didn't know why he wanted to reminisce about that day now.

"You went back in for the bodies even though no one told you to—no one expected you to," he murmured. Meera shrugged. "I thought you were some sort of angel, you know," he added, huffing a quiet laugh. She chuckled with him, still unsure of why he was saying all of this but glad of a reason to laugh, nonetheless. "But you weren't. You were just a person—a braver, better person than the rest of us," Linus concluded.

"No," Meera argued. "I was stupid and impulsive."

"Maybe at first, but you went back for the bodies when you didn't have to—Why?" he asked quietly.

She shrugged again. "You looked upset. I figured one of them was important to you, and I figured I was the only person who could get them," she answered dismissively.

"Yeah, but you didn't even know me. You just did it because it was the right thing to do. Most people ... most people wouldn't have done that—I wouldn't have done that," Linus said. "I guess I —I guess what I'm trying to say is that I want to be the kind of person who does the right thing even when it sucks."

"Even when you have to sleep on the ground?" she asked, smiling and raising her eyebrows at him.

"Even when I have to ride on a feathered monster," he replied, grimacing.

"Rough flight?" Meera asked with another little laugh. It was light enough now that she could see the strain around Linus's eyes and how rumpled his hair was. She supposed flying for the first time in the dark of night would be terrifying, and it hadn't been a short flight.

"I'm out of rum," he replied humorlessly.

"Good," she said unsympathetically. Rolling onto her back, she gazed at the colorful leaves overhead and wondered how much longer she would have to wait until she could actually do something. Then, on a whim, she asked, "Linus, what ever happened to the captain of the guard—the one I knew? Does he still work at the palace?"

Linus didn't answer at first, and Meera rolled back to look at him, stomach lurching. When she saw his face, she knew. "No!" she cried, forgetting to be quiet. "No! No!" Leaping from the ground, she tangled her hands in her filthy hair. Him too? The captain too? How many people had died because of her?

Linus scrambled up after her and put his hand placatingly her arm. "Meera, he's fine. He's fine," he kept saying.

She didn't believe him. "He hanged. Didn't he?" she asked, her voice oddly high and strained. She couldn't seem to draw in a full breath, and the sound of her short, ragged inhales grated in her ears like nails on slate. The raek fires around them suddenly bulged and went out. Then Kennick was in front of her, putting his hands on her shoulders and trying to move her away. She didn't budge; she was busy searching Linus's face for answers.

"No, Meera. The captain is fine—he retired is all. I haven't seen him in a while, but I'm sure he's fine," Linus insisted.

Meera didn't believe him. "The guards? The guards that were there that day—did they hang too?" Kennick put his hand lightly on her cheek and tried to turn her to face him, but she ignored him; she only had eyes for Linus. She needed to know—she needed to know how many lives she was responsible for ruining.

Linus shook his head in answer, but Meera knew he was lying. Brushing Kennick aside, she took several steps away, just trying to breathe. Shael stood nearby staring at her—they all were—and she hated how concerned and scared they all looked. Shutting her eyes, she breathed, counting her inhales and exhales until her heart rate steadied. After one last deep breath, she opened her eyes and announced, "We're all up, so it's time to find Duchess Harrington!"

The three men standing before her were all silent and wide-eyed for a moment. Meera might have found it comical if she wasn't trying so hard not to fall apart. "Meera, slow down. We do not have any food or supplies. We need to collect ourselves and make a plan first," Kennick said. His dark eyes were so full of love and sympathy that she had to look away from them. She couldn't stand to think of their shared loss; she just wanted to start doing something—something good, something to make up for her mistakes.

"I—I need—" she tried to say, voice trembling.

"You need a bath, Meera! You stink! Your knell men might be too polite to say it, but really, you can't go anywhere or talk to anyone until you wash yourself," Linus interrupted, making a face.

Meera choked out a laugh from her tight chest. She felt like she was teetering at the precipice of her sanity, capable of laughing or melting down at any slight sway of conversation. After she laughed, she nodded; she knew Linus was trying to distract her, but he was also right—she really was filthy.

"Okay, so we need food, soap, and rum. Who has money? I'll go into town!" Linus declared.

Kennick and Shael both glared at him, not nearly as amused by Linus as Meera was. "We're not buying rum," she told her friend. She assumed Kennick had money, although he and Shael hadn't brought any supplies with them; they had thought they would be returning to the border right away. Meera cringed inwardly, hoping they weren't too upset by their change in plans.

"I will go into town and get us supplies," Kennick offered.

Linus barked a laugh. "You can't go into a Terratellen town," he replied, looking Kennick up and down pointedly.

Meera agreed, but she and Linus—the humans in the group—both had recognizable scars. "It'll have to be Shael," she said. "He's the least conspicuous looking."

"Let me go! I'll just hide my stump," Linus argued.

Meera opened her mouth to answer, but Kennick beat her to it: "You are not going anywhere. I do not trust you." Shutting her mouth, she glared at him. "Meera, for all I know, he came with us to try to get you recaptured. I do not know him, and I do not trust him—not with you. Shael will go into town, and the three of us will stay here," Kennick added, seeing her face.

"That's fine, but we can trust Linus," Meera replied, rubbing her eyes and wishing she had gotten a little sleep. She had thought she would start looking for the duchess right away, but instead she was doomed to more waiting.

Linus proceeded to recline on the ground, apparently unconcerned by Kennick's mistrust. Meera, Shael, and Kennick devised a list of supplies, and Shael put his riding jacket over his knell-style shirt to look more human for his foray into town. Before he left, he reached into the pouch he wore around his waist and handed Meera a bar of soap. "You need this more than I do," he said, wrinkling his nose in jest.

Meera took the soap and rolled her eyes at him before watching him walk away into the trees. "Going to go take a bath," she announced to Kennick and Linus, and without looking at either of them, she turned and walked into the woods in the opposite direction of Shael.

She had only made it ten feet into the trees, however, when Linus trotted up next to her. "I'll join you," he said.

She smirked, knowing he didn't want to be left alone with Kennick. "I don't remember inviting you to join me, but okay," she agreed, continuing to meander through the unfamiliar woods.

"Where are you going? Isn't the ocean that way?" he asked, pointing.

"I don't need the ocean. I'll just make a bath wherever I feel like it," she replied.

"Okay ..." he said, not asking her what she meant by that.

A few minutes later, Meera stopped. "Here looks good," she announced, proceeding to shape a large rectangular hole into the ground and fill it with water. She heated the water with her raek fire, and bending down to untie her boot laces, she glanced up to find Linus looking shocked and a little alarmed. His expression made her titter another small laugh. "I can shape raek fire, air, rock, water, and metal," she told him.

"How?" he asked, swallowing.

"A wild raek gave me the powers—Shaya, my raek," Meera explained. "Don't worry, they aren't contagious," she added, noting Linus's furrowed brow. Then she hopped down into her bath fully clothed, seeing as she didn't have privacy. It didn't matter; she needed to wash her clothes as well, anyway.

After a moment, Linus seemed to recover from his shock. "That looks nice," he remarked, peering into the steamy bath. "Mind if I join you?" He didn't wait for her to answer, however, before kicking off his boots and splashing into the warm water. Sighing, he leaned back against the lip of the makeshift tub.

Meera might have argued, but she was glad not to be left alone with her thoughts. She merely scrubbed her clothes and body with Shael's soap. Linus had the decency to avert his eyes when she reached under her shirt and into her pants. Meera spent a long time scouring her scalp, and after she rinsed the suds from her filthy hair, she shaped the water out of the tub and refilled it. She felt so dirty; she wanted to keep scrubbing and scrubbing, but she passed the soap to Linus instead and watched him half-heart-edly clean himself.

He eyed her across the water, tossing the soap onto the ground between them when he was done. His usually honey-brown hair hung dark and wet on either side of his face. Meera was still getting used to how much older and more grizzled he looked now. "What's the deal with your husband?" he asked, scratching at his beard.

"We never actually managed to get married," Meera admitted, avoiding the question.

Linus raised his eyebrows at her, and she knew what he was thinking even if he didn't say it. "Yes, I got pregnant without being married," she said in irritation. She didn't want to think about the pregnancy. "Do you need a lesson on the finer points of concep-tion, or has your mother covered that for you?" she asked snarkily.

Linus laughed. "Don't worry about me. I don't attract many ladies these days."

"Is it the general's uniform that scares them away or the drink-ing?" Meera asked, feigning obtuseness.

"Must be the uniform," he replied, casually lifting his left arm out of the water and pushing back his wet sleeve to reveal his stump. Waving it around, he added, "This is a big draw for the ladies. It's only good for one thing, you know."

Meera gaped at him a moment before throwing back her head and laughing—really laughing. It felt so good to laugh, too; for those few seconds, she forgot everything. The creeping figures at the edge of her mind disappeared, and there was only Linus's grinning face and the sunshine filtering through the leaves above. Then she wiped the tears of mirth from her eyes, and reality settled back over her.

2

LINUS

Linus regretted his comment at first—he was used to being around men and the kind of bawdy humor they digressed into to avoid talking about their real lives—but when Meera laughed, he smiled and relaxed. He supposed woman or not, she also needed distraction from the cruelties of life, and he was happy to provide some for her. Although, after her loud burst of laughter, his concern about her knell man rose to the surface again. "Seriously, Meera. If your fiancé finds me taking a bath with you, is he going to kill me?" he asked. He hadn't liked the look the red-haired man had given him earlier.

"Kennick won't hurt you," Meera replied unconcernedly. "Besides, I handle the killing just fine on my own," she added, and suddenly, her face changed; she was no longer smiling, and she was no longer looking at him. Picking up the bar of soap that he had tossed onto the ground, she began scrubbing her hands, arms, and neck all over again.

"Meera?" Linus asked, watching her movements turn more and more frantic. She didn't look at him. She kept rubbing and scratching at her skin, her big eyes round and panicky on her face. "Meera!" he cried, moving through the chest-deep water toward her. He caught one of her wrists in his hand and tried to use his stump to block her other arm, but just when he touched her, Kennick appeared at the edge of the bath. Linus immediately raised his arms and stepped away.

Meera seemed to come back to herself then. "I'm okay, I'm okay!" she said, looking between Linus and Kennick. She put the soap down with a shaking hand and disappeared under the water's surface. For several seconds, little bubbles trailed up from her, then nothing.

Linus stared at the reflective surface of the water and waited, holding his own breath. He watched and waited until his lungs forced him to suck in air. He took a step toward Meera, but he hesitated, glancing at Kennick uncertainly. He wanted to get her, but he didn't know what her knell man would do. Kennick was also staring at the water with a look of strain on his bizarrely angular face. Finally, Meera emerged, wiping water and hair from her eyes. She didn't even gasp for air; she just gripped the edge of the bath and hopped adeptly from the water.

Linus followed her out much less gracefully, and as soon as the cool air hit him, he regretted getting in the bath to begin with; his skin prickled with goosebumps all over. The next thing he knew, the bath was gone. The ground where it had been looked freshly churned but otherwise level with its surroundings. Suddenly, warm air buffeted him from all directions. He jumped and made a stran- gled noise, but then he realized that Meera was doing it to both of them—drying them. Supposing it was better than dripping dry and freezing, Linus stood stoically and tolerated the strange magic.

Kennick hovered near Meera, and when she stopped drying them both and reached up to touch her long—clearly matted—

hair, he stepped forward. "Let me," he said, pulling off one of his bracelets and turning it into a comb. Linus stared wide-eyed at the comb for a second, but then he blinked and looked away, trying not to draw the man's attention. He considered retreating into the woods, but he didn't want to leave Meera alone with Kennick—engaged or not, Linus wasn't sure what he thought of the knell man.

While Meera sat and Kennick started the tedious process of working his comb through her snarled hair, Linus plopped onto the ground and very slowly began pulling on his boots and gathering his hair behind his head. He always left his boots tied loosely to slip on and off, but he struggled with his hair; tying it back was one of the few things he often needed help with. He considered asking Meera for help but was too proud to do so in front of Kennick, so instead, Linus did the best he could, looping his pre-tied leather thong around his hair several times. He was sure it didn't look great, but it would do.

Meanwhile, he watched Meera as Kennick worked through the many knots in her hair. It looked to Linus like he was being exceedingly gentle, and yet, her face was slowly fracturing, her eyes filling with tears. Helplessly, he watched as her breathing became rapid and shallow. He tried to catch her eye, but she was staring at the ground before her like her life depended on it. Finally, her face shattered. "Enough!" she shouted, reaching her hands back and grabbing her hair. Linus saw a flash of light, and the next thing he knew, Meera was holding a large clump of hair in front of her, looking startled. "Oops!" she said quietly before whipping her head back to face Kennick. "I didn't burn you, did I?"

"No," the man said softly. He looked like he was in pain, but he stayed very still. Linus couldn't blame him—he wasn't sure he would risk touching Meera if she was burning things and saying *oops*.

"I—" Meera started to say, staring at the hair in her fist.

"I will fix it," Kennick told her.

Meera nodded and incinerated the hair she was holding. Kennick proceeded to detangle the remainder of her snarls. Linus wasn't quite sure what was happening. He thought maybe he should leave, but he hated the look on Meera's face. "Bartro made the captain retire after you freed the raek. The captain wasn't happy about it, but they had a ceremony for him and everything. I was still recovering and couldn't go," he told her. He was lying: Bartro had hanged the captain and the two guards who had failed to prevent the prisoners from escaping.

Meera's eyes slowly traveled up to his face and focused on him. "Really?" she asked, sounding small and vulnerable.

"Oh yeah! I heard Bartro even made a whole speech about the captain's service. He had a way about him, didn't he? Bartro? He could really make a person feel special," Linus replied. He didn't know what he was saying; he was just trying to talk—to distract Meera from whatever was going on in her mind.

"Did he make your stump tingle?" she asked, a fresh light gleaming in her eyes.

Linus laughed. "He certainly tried. He gave me a ring—said if I was only going to have one hand, I might as well make it as impressive as possible ... I lost it in a game of cards. Did he give you anything?" he asked. He hoped he wasn't stumbling into upsetting territory.

"He gave me a pen—a nice carved wooden one," Meera admitted. "It's at the bottom of a lake."

Linus nodded. He wondered vaguely whether Meera and Bartro had had a physical relationship, but he didn't ask. "He knew how to manipulate people, that man," he remarked. "It was all him, you know, Meera. The duke, the three boys—it was all him. He knew what he was doing."

"It doesn't matter. I played my part," she replied, still calm.

Linus's eyes shifted to Kennick, who had just finished detangling Meera's hair and formed a pair of scissors out of more metal from his body. Linus watched as the knell man proceeded to cut and even out Meera's mangled hair across her shoulder blades. Then he looked back at her face. "So, what exactly is the plan here?" he asked.

"I just want to talk to Duchess Harrington—to offer her my assistance with anything she might need. I just want to help her if I can," she said quietly.

"What if she demands that you do something ridiculous? What if she insists you should die for what you did?" Linus asked. He thought this was an incredibly stupid plan, and his mood was turning; he was growing hungry, and his head throbbed as the rum from the night before drained out of him.

Meera sighed. "I'm not going to blindly do whatever she tells me to do. I haven't lost my senses," she said defensively.

Linus wasn't so sure about that, but he didn't say so. "Then what?" he asked. He was starting to wonder what the hell he was doing there. He had wanted to do something good—something Meera would do—but he was a one-handed eighteen-year-old without magical ability and had no idea how he was supposed to do anything at all.

Meera shrugged. Kennick finished cutting her hair and began braiding it down the back of her head. "Then I'll go back to Levisade and do whatever I can to help Darreal end the war," she said. "You can come, or I can help you get settled somewhere else," she added, eyeing him.

Kennick finished Meera's short braid and tucked it under, fastening it into a nub at the base of her neck. Linus didn't bother answering her; he didn't know exactly what he was doing there or what he would do next. Instead, he stood and averted his eyes when Kennick tenderly kissed the side of Meera's face. He supposed the knell man didn't seem all that bad.

Together, they made their way back to the clearing where they had slept and waited for Shael to return with food and supplies. Meera paced the small area, and Linus and Kennick sat down and watched her. Linus wanted to keep talking—to distract his friend from her thoughts—but he couldn't think of anything else to say. His own situation was gradually settling over him as his sober brain realized that the life he'd known was behind him. It was both a comforting and unsettling thought.

When Shael returned, they all ate and deliberated their next move. He told them that the Harrington's house was unmistakable and nearby, and Kennick had to prevent Meera from immediately leaving to find the duchess. Then the red-haired knell man persistently coaxed her to eat until she had finished her small portion of food. Linus ate quickly and reclined on the bare ground, fiddling with the pine needles under his hand.

While the others argued about who should go to the house and when, he tried not to listen. He didn't much care what they did in Harringbay. He thought being there at all was a mistake; Meera couldn't possibly get anything out of talking to the family of the man whose death she had caused. Linus suspected the other men felt the same way, and yet, they were all going along with it, hoping Meera wouldn't lose her shit again.

Drinking some of the water Meera had magicked into his flask for him, Linus wished it were rum. He didn't think this plan would go well, and he didn't look forward to witnessing any of it. A part of him wondered if he should just leave—set off on his own to start a new life—but he didn't. He stayed. Meera was the only friend he had at the moment, and he would stick out this foolish plan with her ... Then he would help her knell men pick up the pieces when it was a disaster, he thought with a sigh.

Eventually, he heard them decide that they would all go to the estate together the next morning, prepared to flee if need be. Kennick was going to spend the rest of the day scoping out the area, and Shael was—apparently—going to babysit Linus and Meera. Linus lay back and shut his eyes, ready to doze through the rest of the day. He hadn't gotten many days off as a general and was going to consider this a vacation. He was at the beach, after all, he thought with a wry smile.

He had never seen the ocean, but he didn't bother rousing himself to go look at it. There wasn't much in the world he was especially interested in seeing. There wasn't much he hoped to do with his life at all—though he supposed he wouldn't mind sleeping with a woman before he died. He hadn't been joking earlier when he had told Meera that women weren't interested in him and his stump. There had always been prostitutes hanging around the war camps, of course, but Linus had found them too sad to touch. He would rather be with a woman who actually wanted to be with him—not that he held out much hope for that. He had loved Meera once, and she hadn't loved him back. Now he was crippled and unsightly. Besides, not everyone was Meera— most people were horrible.

Meera called his name, but Linus kept his eyes shut, feigning sleep. He was one of those horrible people, after all. He was under no illusion that he was a good person; he knew who and what he was. He may have impulsively—and drunkenly—followed Meera out there to do something good for once, but unlike Meera, he had no false hope that he could make up for his past actions with a few good deeds. He kept his eyes shut and pretended to sleep, doubting he would actually get any sleep without alcohol in his stomach. At the next opportunity, he was going to find rum.

3

MEERA

Meera called softly to Linus to see if he was sleeping. When he didn't respond, she and Shael moved into the woods to avoid disturbing him. After meandering for a bit, they settled on a downed tree, and it took all of Meera's willpower to sit still. She wanted to keep pacing—run even—but she saw how everyone kept looking at her, and she didn't want to alarm them. She wasn't happy about waiting until morning to find the duchess, but she acknowledged that the others were only there to support her and wanted to respect their opinions.

She and Shael sat in silence for a long time while she tried not to jitter her legs, endeavoring to appear sane. Finally, she glanced sideways at her friend. He looked troubled in his usual stony sort of way. She hated to see it, considering how well he had been doing when she had left Levisade, and she hoped she wasn't the cause of his unhappiness. "Shael, you don't have to be here," she told him. "I wish you hadn't broken your oaths for me. I bet Hadjal would forgive you if you went back ..."

His dark brows furrowed when he gazed back at her. "Of course I broke my oaths for you, Meera! When I read Darreal's letter I—" he choked off, his voice full of emotion.

Meera looked down at her feet. She wished she hadn't caused everyone so much pain. Everything she ever chose to do seemed to hurt people. But rather than apologize to Shael and add to their seemingly endless string of apologies to one another, she reached out and took his hand, squeezing it. She was selfishly glad to have him there even if she wished he were somewhere else, happy. Shael squeezed back. "Meera, I hope you know the baby—losing the baby was not your fault," he said quietly.

Meera pulled her hand away and swallowed. She didn't want to talk about that—she didn't want to think about it. She wasn't ready yet. Every time Kennick looked at her, she saw his grief and was reminded that she had caused it. It was too much. She wanted to deal with one thing at a time, and the first was making amends for the duke. She needed to shed at least a sliver of her bone-crushing guilt. However, in avoiding her feelings, she knew she was leaving Kennick alone with his, which only added to her shame. "Shael, I need you to be there for Kennick. I—I can't right now," she said. She felt disgusted with herself for saying it, but it was true; she was barely standing on her own two feet and didn't feel like she could let anyone else lean on her.

"I will always be there for Kennick, but ... I do not think I am the person he needs," Shael replied, and she knew he was right. "I mean, Kennick and I are friends, but you two have the whole true mates thing and all," he added, nudging her with his elbow.

Meera grimaced at him, embarrassed by her weird raek trait. "You know, I think that just means he and I are fertile together," she said dismissively. She loved Kennick, but their love wasn't always easy. True mates or not, Meera often found herself doing the wrong thing in their relationship; she always seemed to be running away when she shouldn't and was probably doing it again now. Still, she needed to run—she needed to put one foot in front of the other or risk crumbling to the ground.

"Do you mean that?" Shael asked, suddenly staring at her with piercing intensity in his green eyes.

Meera looked back at him in surprise. "Sure, I mean, I love Kennick, but I think maybe the true mates thing is just something that happens between raeken that will produce a lot of eggs together. I mean, I don't really know, but Shaya didn't make it sound like it had anything to do with love. I'm not sure raeken love each other that way," she said, and thinking of Shaya opened another burning pit in her stomach. Meera had shut her raek out in her despair, but she still wished Shaya had cared enough to fight for her.

Shael bumped her knee with his, drawing her attention back to him, and she was a little alarmed to find how intently he was gazing at her. "Meera, did you love me as much as you love him?" he asked. His eyes were full of hope and pain, and he pushed at his already sleek hair in agitation.

"Shael—I" she started to say, not even sure how she would complete the thought.

"Meera, I love you! I have always loved you, and when I thought you were hurt, I would have done anything to get you back. Then we found you, and I realized I wasn't really getting you back—I had to stand there and watch Kennick hold you and kiss you when I wanted to, and I know you love him ... But if there is some chance you love me too—I have to fight for you this time like I should have fought for you before," he said in a jumble.

Meera stared into his eyes, at a complete loss for what to say. Her heart clenched seeing Shael so vulnerable, and a part of her wanted to hug him and shout with joy that he was finally valuing himself enough to fight for his happiness, but the rest of her sank with dread because she was going to have to break his heart. She loved Shael—she had always loved Shael—but she wanted Kennick. True mates or not, baby or not, she still wanted Kennick. She didn't know what to say; she didn't know if the truth or a lie would be kinder, and she was so damned tired of hurting people.

Finally, she took a breath and said very quietly, "Shael, I think I did love you as much as I love Kennick, but it didn't work. I chose him, and I still choose him. You'll find someone else to love too." She hoped that was true so that they could go back to being friends. She didn't want to live her life without Shael, but now she wasn't sure she could spend time with him knowing he was pining for her.

Meera looked into his eyes expecting to see pain or stony indifference, but instead, she was met with an unanticipated determination in their green depths. Suddenly, he leaned forward and brought his lips to hers. She hesitated, unsure of what to do. She shouldn't kiss him, but she didn't want to pull away and hurt him either—she didn't want to hurt people anymore. Uncertainly, she leaned into the kiss, and when Shael nudged his tongue against her lips, she opened her mouth to him. He touched her face and kissed her with so much passion that her stomach jolted, and for several seconds, she let herself be distracted by his touch. Then she remembered herself and pulled away.

Shael let her, and when she stood and wandered wraithlike into the woods, he didn't follow her. Meera meandered through the trees until they thinned, then she walked onto the rocky bluff between the woods and the beach. There was no one in sight, so she crossed the rocks, removed her boots, and stepped out into the sand. The soft sounds of the crashing waves brought her back to her childhood; it had been many years since she had seen the ocean and swam in it with her father.

She walked toward the water until the wet sand sucked at the soles of her feet, and the ends of the waves kissed her toes. The salt water stung the small abrasions on her feet, and she tried to focus on that minor physical pain rather than let herself feel everything lurking within her. Tears she couldn't staunch slipped from her lower lashes, and she clutched her arms, cold from the breeze off the ocean but unwilling to use her magic. Her raek fire had burst unbidden from her hands earlier, scaring her. She knew why—she knew she needed to work through her feelings—but she didn't think she could release all of the emotions barricaded within her. She wasn't sure she would survive it.

As Meera stood battling down her grief and guilt, Kennick walked up beside her. He didn't say anything; he just stood next to her, feet also bare, staring at the Cerun Sea. Meera didn't look at him. She couldn't believe how stupid she had been. She had returned Shael's kiss to avoid hurting him, without even considering how it would hurt Kennick. She was a monster, a child-burner, a flaming pit of destruction! "I kissed Shael!" she blurted, not bothering to explain or defend herself. Then she finally glanced up at Kennick, heart in her throat and tears still in her eyes.

"I saw," he said calmly, looking down at her with his liquid black eyes. "I could not bear to be away from you."

Meera supposed Kennick had been silently observing for a second time that day; she had known he was watching her and Linus that morning. She couldn't blame him—she was always running, after all. She was always ruining everything and destroying everything. All day, she had been spending time with Linus and Shael and avoiding Kennick, who she loved most of all. She knew it wasn't right, but she felt like she would crack wide open and spill apart every time he touched her—he seemed to bring all of her emotions to the surface, and she wasn't ready for that. Even so, she couldn't keep ignoring him; she wouldn't keep hurting him if she could help it. "I'm so tired of hurting people," she said bleakly.

For a moment, she hung her head, then she studied Kennick's face, wondering how much she had destroyed him. As usual, he was the epitome of composure; his hands were in his human-style pockets, and he smiled at her reassuringly. "I can go kiss Shael if it will make you feel better," he offered. His dark eyes glinted, and his pointy canine tooth showed on his lower lip, making Meera smile automatically.

Slowly, she registered what he had said, and she laughed "Don't! I'm afraid I might enjoy that, and I don't think my human sensibilities could handle a three-person relationship," she admitted.

Kennick laughed with her. "Just a traditional marriage for you?" he asked.

"Just you for me," she replied, taking his hand and gazing up at him.

"Just you for me, too," he agreed, and he bent down and kissed her softly.

Meera wanted to fall into the kiss, but she was afraid; she was afraid of coming undone. Kennick wasn't a distraction from her life—he was her life; he was her life and her home, and she had killed their baby and ruined everything. After only a moment, she pulled away and squeezed her eyes shut—pushing down her emotions and blocking out her pain.

Kennick nudged her with his elbow, and she reluctantly opened her eyes to meet his gaze. "That was a beautiful ceremony. Should we call ourselves married?" he asked, repeating what she had once asked him.

Meera grinned despite her inner turmoil. "I think we can do better," she rasped—her voice tight with her repressed feelings. They had long lives ahead of them, and she didn't see any reason to rush. If Kennick still wanted a big wedding, she would give it to him. She cleared her throat. "I don't have my tiara," she reminded him.

He grinned back at her. "Do you think you can walk on the ocean?" he asked, raising his eyebrows.

"With you I can," she replied, offering him her hand. Together they walked out onto the ocean, jumping the short waves as they rolled to shore, and for a long time, they stayed on the water—not talking, just being together. Kennick seemed to sense that Meera wasn't ready to face their loss yet, and he didn't push her. While Meera, in turn, offered him the support of her presence, finding she didn't need to feel strong or steady to love him—loving Kennick was easy.

4

SHAEL

When Meera walked away, Shael knew there was no hope. Even when she had kissed him back, he had known ... Even before he had kissed her, he had known. Meera's rejection hurt, but Shael also felt pleased with himself; he was proud of his actions—for trying, for putting himself out there and fighting for what he wanted. For once, he had not let the fear of pain or his own self-doubt dictate his behavior. He felt oddly calm and settled—that is, in the moment before Kennick sat down on the tree next to him. Shael's heart jumped into his throat as he looked sideways at his friend. "I'm sorry. I had to try," he said, swallowing.

"If you had to try, then do not be sorry," Kennick replied. He looked weary but not angry. Seeing his normally tall, confident friend slumped on the tree next to him made Shael feel awful. Kennick had just lost his baby, and he had tried to take Meera from him, too. What kind of a person was he? He had been feeling good about himself for breaking his oaths to find Meera—he had been feeling proud for sharing his feelings with her—but now he felt like raek dung.

"Be forgiving with yourself, Shael," Cerun reminded him from where he and Endu sheltered on the craggy bluffs nearby.

"You are right," Shael replied mentally before returning his attention to Kennick. "How much did you hear?" he asked.

"Everything. I never went to the Harrington's house. I tried, but I could not leave her. I came right back—then I did not wish to interrupt. I shouldn't have listened, but I could not seem to walk away," Kennick explained.

Shael nodded. He understood. "Then you know Meera loves you and chooses you and is worried about you even if she is struggling to show it," he said.

"I know," Kennick replied.

"Go get her," Shael told him. He knew Kennick did not want to be sitting there with him.

"Will you be okay?" he asked.

"We will all be okay, eventually," Shael replied. It was not like him to be such an optimist, but he actually believed it.

Kennick squeezed his shoulder and left to follow Meera. Shael rose and wandered back to their clearing to keep an eye on Linus. He did not trust Meera's human friend not to use their supplies to try to buy alcohol in town. He could not quite decide what he thought of Linus. Shael felt bad that Cerun had caused him so much pain—mangling his arm and killing his brother—and yet, Linus was a general, not an innocent teenager anymore. He had clung to Shael in terror on their flight to Harringbay the night before, and Shael could not figure out what had motivated him to make the journey.

When he returned to the clearing, Linus was still lying on the ground where he had last seen him. Meera and Kennick did not return until morning, so he and Linus spent an awkward evening together in which they made as little conversation as possible and yet were never out of one another's sight. Shael could only hope the next day would not be completely devastating for Meera and that they could return to Levisade right away.

THE NEXT MORNING, Meera and Kennick wandered back into the clearing just after the sun rose, and they all ate a quick breakfast together. Shael did not know what to say to Meera after their kiss the day before, so he fell back on his old habit and said nothing. She did not mention it either—or look at him—but Shael got the feeling her behavior did not have anything to do with him. Her hands kept clenching in her lap, and her one foot jittered like she could not wait to get going. She was the only one anxious to approach the Harrington's house; Shael could tell that Kennick—and even Linus—thought it was a bad idea. Meera would not be dissuaded, however, so after breakfast, they walked out of the woods.

"You know, you still don't look normal," Linus said, eyeing Shael and Kennick in their human-style clothes. Shael had on new pants and a shirt, and Kennick had tucked his simple shirt into his already human-looking pants. Meera was still wearing her knell attire—she had refused to wear a dress, and no one had argued with her since they might need to fly away too quickly for her to change.

"The Harrington's are no friends of the Crown, and I won't let anyone hurt us," Meera assured him.

Linus did not look reassured, and Shael's anxiety was growing as well. "Meera, this is not going to go well," he warned her, finally breaking their mutual silence.

She just looked at him and shrugged.

"Why don't you just leave a pile of gold on their doorstep or something?" Linus asked.

"Because I'm going to apologize," Meera replied. She looked determined, and Shael knew she would not be deterred from her mission. They were in it now.

He led everyone to where the large house stood on the outskirts of town. It was white-painted brick with blue shutters and a well-kept front garden. He assumed it was the Harringtons' house because the rest of the town consisted of relatively poor-looking little houses and makeshift shacks set up for the fishermen to sell their wares. The Harringtons' house sat close to the beach on the southernmost edge of the bay. It was a pretty house in a pretty spot. Shael could picture his parents vacationing in a place like this.

Still, he approached the house's front doors with extreme unease; he had no idea what kind of reception they would receive, let alone how the duchess might react to whatever Meera had to say. Meera was the only one who did not hesitate at the door; she stepped forward with palpable energy and clanked the large brass knocker down three times—the knocker, he noticed with curiosity, was shaped like a whale's tail. After her third knock, Shael held his breath for a moment, wondering whether Meera would just keep pounding on the door, but thankfully, she stepped back and waited with the rest of them.

Shael glanced aside at Kennick. His hands were in his perfectly tailored pants, but Shael could see the tension in his friend's shoulders. They had left their weapons behind. Kennick had also removed his visible jewelry, though Shael knew he would still have plenty of metal stashed on his body. Not for the first time, he wished that he had a magical ability to fall back on without his sword. He supposed he had his half-knell strength, and that would have to do. Then he glanced at Linus, who looked perfectly at ease, and he studied the human man for several moments, only feeling more baffled as to what he was doing there.

Linus noticed his attention, smiled, and belched loudly. Meera elbowed him, and just after she did, the front door swung outward. A man in a servant's uniform gaped at them, momentarily forgetting to greet them. "Uh ... H—hello. How may I help you?" he finally asked.

"We'd like to speak to Duchess Harrington," Meera announced, all but bouncing on the balls of her feet in agitation.

"Is the duchess expecting you?" the man asked with furrowed brows, clearly already knowing the answer.

"No," Meera replied simply, not even trying to explain herself.

The man opened his mouth, then hesitated with it hanging open, unsure of what to do. Shael thought maybe he should smile to ease the man's discomfort, but he could not manage it; his bowels were cramping with nerves. He did not want to see Meera as broken as she had been on the dungeon floor again. "Very well," the man said after an overlong pause, standing aside for them to enter. Leading them to a drawing room, he left them there, but Shael heard him flag another servant in the hall to alert the duchess of their presence so that he could guard the door of the room.

Shael sat down rather stiffly, and Meera perched at the edge of the sofa next to him, legs jiggling. Kennick positioned himself on her other side and put a hand on her knee. Linus proceeded to meander around the room, looking at the various bits of fishing memorabilia on the walls and pulling books off of the bookshelves. When he noticed a drawing of a pirate, he laughed. "Hey Kenny, think you can make me one of these?" he asked, pointing to the pirate's hook hand.

"Maybe later," Kennick said tersely. Shael thought his response was generous.

"What's a man gotta do to get some refreshments around here?" Linus called loudly. Shael scowled at him. He could not see what Meera found so entertaining about the man.

"Sit down and be quiet," she told Linus, barely looking at him. Linus obeyed, sitting in a large leather chair to the right of the sofa.

For several minutes they were all quiet before the door opened again, and a woman entered. She was slight with reddish-brown skin, straight, slicked-back hair, and a purple dress. The woman appraised them under half-lowered lids. If she was shocked by their strange appearances, she did not show it; she looked disinterested—drowsy, even. Standing in front of them all, swaying, she said, "Well?"

Meera rose to her feet, and the rest of them followed her example. "Duchess Harrington, my name is Meera Hailship. I came to speak with you about your husband," she said, fidgeting with her hands. She looked so vulnerable and hopeful that Shael had to look away; he studied the nautical rope pattern edging the blue and white carpet they stood on.

"My husband is dead," the duchess replied.

"Yes …" Meera said. "Your Grace, I would like to apologize for contributing to your husband's death and to offer you my services for anything you might need."

The duchess stared at Meera for several long moments as if digesting her words. Shael tensed, ready to act if necessary— ready to run. Cerun and Endu were as near as they could get while remaining hidden in the bluffs, waiting. Finally, Duchess Harrington laughed. Her laugh seemed to startle her, and she stumbled slightly. "Silly rug," she said to cover her stumble. Shael wondered if she was drunk or medicated.

The duchess looked back at Meera. "The king killed my husband, girl. How did you contribute? Did you warm his bed?

Wipe his royal bottom? Whatever it was, if it wasn't you, it would have been someone else. The king killed my husband, and the king is dead—struck down for his wickedness. My husband has been avenged," she said bitterly. Shael could only assume the king's death had not brought the duchess any comfort. He released his held breath, grateful to the woman; he thought that had gone about as well as it could have.

However, Meera did not look quite as pleased as Shael felt. "I informed the king about your husband's plans to cross the Cerun Sea, Duchess Harrington. His death is on my conscience. Please, is there anything you or your daughter need? Is there anything I can do for you or the people of Harringbay? I have abilities, I—" Meera said, but Kennick grabbed her arm and cut her off.

"We need for nothing, and death will find us all as sure as the tide comes in," the duchess said morosely. Then she turned and left the room.

Meera looked like she wanted to follow her, but Kennick held her back. The manservant entered a moment later to escort them out, and he stared at Meera with enough curiosity for Shael to know he had listened at the door. He thought they had better leave quickly in case rumor of their visit spread through the town. As they exited the house, Shael took a deep breath of cool air; he could not believe how well that had gone, and he hoped Meera could now put this behind her.

5

MEERA

Meera walked with wooden steps out of the Harrington's house, feeling like a dry twig that might catch and burn any second. Duchess Harrington had been a ghost-like imposter of her former self. She had seemed utterly lost and devastated, and Meera had done that to her—Meera had taken away the love of her life. She wanted to apologize more, get on her knees and beg for forgiveness, but the duchess hadn't even cared about what she'd done.

Meera slowed, wanting to turn back—to try again—but Kennick put a gentle, coaxing hand to her low back and encouraged her to keep moving. Linus whistled a tune as they walked across the cobblestone front courtyard, and she tried to focus on his whistling rather than attempt to decipher the thoughts hurtling around in her head. She kept imagining what more she could have said or done or how else the situation might have gone. She considered returning over and over again but couldn't make up her jostling mind. Kennick's hand kept leading her away.

They were about to step onto the street when a voice called,

"Wait! Stop!" and Meera obeyed; she stopped and turned hopefully, even as Kennick, Shael, and Linus tensed, ready to run. There was a young woman in a pale pink dress striding toward them. She had copper-toned skin and thick eyebrows over hazel eyes. Meera could tell instantly that she was the duke and duchess's daughter—not just by her appearance but by her bearing. As she hurried toward them, she kept her back very straight and her white-gloved hands clasped in front of her. Two maids followed after the young woman, looking harried and calling, "Lady Emmaline, please wait! Please, Lady Emmaline, let's go back inside!"

Lady Emmaline stopped fifteen feet away from their group and appraised them with a much sharper eye than her mother had. "It was you who spied on my father and informed the king of his intentions?" she asked Meera.

"It was," Meera replied. She had lived in Levisade long enough to lose her patience with titles and formalities. Now that they were outside, she felt she could dispense with such things.

Lady Emmaline was slighter and shorter than Meera, but the young woman still managed to look down her nose at her. "I heard you offer my mother your assistance with anything we might need ..." she said searchingly. At this point, her maids caught up to her and were trying to usher her back inside. "In a moment," she told them, holding up a gloved hand. Her pink dress was frilly and girlish, but her voice was firm and commanding—not childlike in the least.

"I did," Meera confirmed. "Is there something I can do for you?" she asked hopefully. She took a step toward the lady, but Emmaline flinched and took a step back. Meera held up her hands. "Please, I feel awful for what I did to your father. I just want to try to make up for it in some way."

"Come inside, and we'll discuss what you can do for me," the lady replied, proceeding to turn around and glide back toward the house, her maids scurrying after her.

Meera saw Shael and Kennick exchange a pained look, but she ignored them and followed the duke's daughter. She didn't know what Lady Emmaline could possibly want that her money couldn't buy her, but she supposed she was about to find out. Whatever it was, she would do it; she was ready to do anything that would make her feel even the slightest bit better. Her hope lightened her steps and quieted the flames licking under the surface of her skin. She practically skipped back into the Harringtons' house.

Lady Emmaline led them inside and instructed the servant who had answered their knock earlier to lead them to a dining room. As they followed him further into the house, Meera heard the lady's maids entreating her to go lie down and thought it was strange as the lady had looked perfectly well. However, she simply followed the man to the dining room and sat down where he gestured. They were all clustered at one end of a long table, and another servant appeared moments later with refreshments.

Meera ignored the food and drink put in front of her even though she hadn't eaten much in the past two days. She was too anxious to eat; she sat on the edge of her cushioned seat and waited for the lady to return. Linus, on the other hand, poured himself an overlarge glass of wine and began to drink it quickly. "Behave yourself," she hissed at him. Having Linus around was beginning to feel like leading around a poorly trained dog, and Meera didn't have the energy for it. He merely grinned at her and drained his glass before reaching for some cheese and crackers.

Meera stared fixedly at the door and ignored him. Eventually, the lady entered the dining room and sat on the far side of the long table. She was holding a rolled bit of parchment and handed it to one of her maids to walk over to them. The maid then handed it to Meera, looking terrified. Meera took the parchment but never glanced away from Lady Emmaline. "What is it you want me to do?" she asked. She couldn't wait any longer; she needed to know what her atonement would entail.

Lady Emmaline's maids looked affronted. "You will address the lady by her title," one of them told Meera. Meera didn't acknowledge her.

Lady Emmaline studied Meera down her nose like she was the most vile thing she'd ever seen. Meera could sense Kennick's irritation next to her, but she ignored him. Linus continued to eat and drink like none of the rest of them were in the room. Finally, the lady said, "If you were the spy that informed on my father, then you know he was trying to find a captain to take him to the place torn from that map," gesturing to the parchment Meera was still holding.

Meera didn't bother looking at the map; she knew which land the lady was referring to. She had seen it on the maps in Levisade. "You mean, Kallanthea?" she asked.

"You know the place?" the lady asked. Her eyes briefly widened, but she quickly regained her composure.

"Not really," Meera replied. "I know what it's called from being in Aegorn. I don't know why King Bartro killed your father for wanting to know about it." She glanced at Kennick, but he didn't offer any information about the land.

"Kallanthea," Lady Emmaline said to herself like she was tasting the word for the first time. "My father's ancestors came from this land. We believe the Crown has attempted to remove it from the minds of Terratellens because there is magic there."

That would make sense, Meera thought; Terratellen royals had a long history of hating magic. If they could pretend Aegorn didn't exist, they probably would. Instead, they were attempting to fight and kill the magic in Aegorn. "My father's ancestors also came from across the Cerun Sea," she said thoughtfully, wondering if she, too, was a descendant of Kallanthea.

"You told my mother you have abilities?" Lady Emmaline asked, ignoring her comment.

"I do," she said vaguely.

"Is that how you spied on my father?" the lady asked disdainfully.

"No. I didn't have abilities, then. I just ... followed him," Meera replied. "What is it you want from me?" she asked again, beginning to lose her patience. She would apologize, and she would perform an act of service for the lady. She would not, however, be toyed with.

"My father was trying to reach this land—Kallanthea, as you call it—because he was trying to save my life. Before my grandfather died, he spoke of magic from his ancestral land that could cure any illness. I have been ill my entire life. My lungs cannot handle sickness. The mild coughs and colds that others recover from easily put me on my deathbed. It's only a matter of time before one of them takes my life. My father wanted to find this land and bring back their magic for me," Lady Emmaline explained with straight shoulders and a smooth face.

If Meera could feel any worse for getting the duke killed, she would. He was a kind man who had loved his wife and had been willing to do anything to save his daughter. Emmaline still hadn't answered her question, however. "You want me to go to Kallanthea?" Meera asked.

"I want you to take me there," the lady replied, her strong voice finally faltering slightly.

Meera thought about that. She wondered whether the raeken could fly all the way to Kallanthea in one go or whether it was too far. Then she wondered whether the journey would be worthwhile for the lady. "Our friend in Levisade heals with magic. We should take you there," she said, thinking of Soleille. She didn't know what kind of magic they had in Kallanthea, but Soleille might be able to help Lady Emmaline.

"No," she replied. "My father thought my best chance was across the sea. They are my people, and they might know what's wrong with me and how to fix it."

Meera felt skeptical, but if the lady's father had died to get her to Kallanthea, she supposed finishing the job was the least she could do. Finally, she unrolled the map she was holding and looked at it. It was a basic map depicting Terratelle, Aegorn, Cesor, and Arborea. The edge of Kallanthea showed where the map was torn on the right side. "Can Endu fly that distance?" she asked Kennick.

"It would be too risky to find out. There may not be anywhere for him to land if he needed to," he replied.

Meera stared into Kennick's eyes, wondering what he thought of this idea. He gave her a small smile, and she knew he would follow her anywhere. "Do you have a ship?" she asked Lady Emmaline.

"I have a ship, and I have a captain. The difficulty is getting past the Terratellen naval forces," she replied.

Meera shrugged. She could shape the wind to blow them away, she could turn the ocean's tides, she could halt their cannonballs in their tracks—she was her own force and could keep the navy at bay. "I can handle them," she said. "Looks like we're going to Kallanthea!"

"To Kallanthea!" Linus shouted, raising his wine glass and draining it. Meera laughed in spite of herself. She wasn't eager to get on a ship, but she was glad to be able to finish what the duke had started.

Lady Emmaline looked a little nervous, and her maids appeared downright horrified. "How exactly will you get us past the navy?" she asked. Meera saw her eyes flicker fearfully toward Shael and Kennick. She suspected the lady had been putting on her bravest face for them.

"Magic," Meera told her. "I can control the wind and the water."

Lady Emmaline swallowed visibly and didn't ask any follow-up questions.

"I've never been on a ship," Linus said to no one in particular.

The lady frowned at him. "Will it be necessary for you to bring your ... companions?" she asked Meera.

"Yes," Kennick said, answering for her.

"Emmaline—can I call you Emmaline? Knell don't really use titles," Meera said. Emmaline raised her dainty eyebrows at the word *knell*, but she nodded her head stiffly. "Emmaline, this is Linus, Kennick, and Shael."

6

EMMALINE

Emmaline watched the strange visitors cross the front courtyard from her bedroom window. Her maids thought she was lying down, but she was really just trying to catch her breath. She couldn't believe what she had just done ... Not only had she bid the woman with the scar—the professed former spy for King Bartro—to take her across the Cerun Sea, but she had also told her and her companions to meet her at the dock in three days' time to depart!

Emmaline had never left Harringbay—now she would be leaving in three days with strangers on a ship that didn't yet have a captain or a crew! Removing her gloves, she rubbed her eyes. Maybe she *should* lie down, she thought. What was she thinking? Who was she to journey across the ocean to an unknown place? Then Emmaline took a deep breath and put her gloves back on. She was her father's daughter, descended from people who had crossed that same ocean. Besides, she thought; she could make this journey and try to find a cure for herself, or she could spend the rest of her short life in her house, wondering if each day would be her last.

Walking to her wardrobe, she pulled out a jacket; she had a captain to find. Sneaking quietly through the house to the front door, she hurried across the courtyard. Then she walked the road into town. When she reached the busy streets of downtown Harringbay, she tied a kerchief over her mouth. She rarely went into public, and when she did, she had to take such precautions; any small sickness could overwhelm her feeble lungs and kill her.

Emmaline had been living with her imminent death for as long as she could remember. Caution and precaution were her way of life. She wore gloves, she covered her face, and she stayed away from people whenever possible. She could not remember being hugged or kissed by either of her parents, who had always kept their distance out of love for her—out of a desperation for her to make it to another birthday.

For a long time, each birthday had felt like a triumph, like Emmaline had truly accomplished something in living one more year. Her latest—her eighteenth—however, had felt like a bridge she had never expected to cross. She had never been meant to survive childhood, and yet, she had—she had grown into a teenager, then a young woman. She felt as if she was standing on the precipice of adult life, wondering what came next. She had never dared to dream that she might have a life—a family of her own, even—and now she was so close to that possibility that she dared to hope. Her hope made her bold.

Emmaline wove through the teeming streets of Harringbay, looking for the bar her maid had told her about. Though she hardly knew anyone in the town where she had spent her entire life, many of the people around her greeted her with dips of their chins and tips of their hats. She was notorious; her father had been beloved, and everyone had been aware of his sickly daughter. Emmaline forced herself to walk with her back straight and her head held high, meeting the eyes of each person who greeted her and nodding her head in return.

All the while, she searched for the sign she was looking for. She knew only one ship's captain, after all: Captain Mel had traveled to Harringbay for her father's funeral, and rather than travel all the way back to Altus, he had set up a bar in town—so her maid had told her. Emmaline was looking for a sign with a fish on it—a ridiculous task in a fishing town. Almost every sign had a fish on it, but as far as she knew, she was looking for one with a fish and nothing else.

Finally, she found what she was looking for—at least, she thought she did. The fish was rather poorly painted, but it was the only sign she had found without a shop name. While she had only met Captain Mel once, he was distinctive looking, so she would know him when she saw him. Staring at the red door in front of her, she hesitated. Against all odds, strange people had come to her house offering to help her, but that offer wouldn't matter if she couldn't provide them with a ship's captain ... Emmaline feared her hope would be for nothing; she didn't have enough faith in the world to think that the woman with the scar knocking on her door meant anything. Life had disappointed her enough times for her to know that she might be disappointed again.

Even so, she took a deep breath from behind her kerchief and clasped the door handle in one of her white-gloved hands. Entering the small, dark space, she peered around to find a smattering of tables and a makeshift bar. There were two men sitting alone at tables drinking, and Captain Mel stood behind the bar wiping out glasses. His white beard shone brightly in the dim space and against his dark brown skin. Emmaline released a shaky breath in relief; she had found the captain. Now she needed to convince him to set sail with her—something her father hadn't managed to do. Chin raised in false confidence, she approached the bar.

"Be right wit'cha!" Captain Mel called before looking up and doing a double-take. "Lady Emmaline! What are you doin' in the likes of this place, my lady?"

"Hello, Captain Mel," she replied nervously.

"Jus' Mel now, my lady. 'Scuse me for askin', but should you be out 'n' about like this, my lady?" he asked, putting his glass down and scratching his chin under his beard.

Emmaline thought Mel's little bar was probably the filthiest place she had ever been, but she didn't say so. "I wanted to ask you something ... Mel," she ventured, unsure of how to ask the incredibly huge favor.

"Ask away!" he replied, forgetting formalities in his bafflement.

"Well, you remember of course what my father had traveled to Altus to ask you," she began. The captain's smile faded, and his eyes grew wary. "Captain Mel, I have found people who assure me they can get me safely past the navy if I provide them with a ship and a crew, and ... well, I'm hoping you'll captain that ship," Emmaline said. The small space was quite warm, and she was starting to sweat under her jacket and kerchief. Her forehead tickled with perspiration, but she didn't dare wipe it away after touching the bar's front door.

"I—Lady Emmaline, I'm retired! I'm a barkeep now, not a captain. Besides, what you're suggestin' is too dangerous. Your father would toss in his grave if he knew I was endangerin' his daughter—to be sure," he replied.

Emmaline felt tears start to press at her eyes, but she forced them down. "Please, Captain Mel. I think there might be magic there that can cure me. That's what my father wanted—to find a cure for my illness," she said, leaning toward him to whisper. "There's a group of knell willing to come and to keep us safe." At that the captain looked truly startled, so she kept talking: "I'll pay you whatever you want, and you can keep the ship when we're done!"

"I don't have a need for money or a ship, my lady. I'm sorry, but I can't help you," he replied, shaking his head and making his long beard waggle back and forth. "And I hope you will see reason and change your mind about this trip."

"If you don't have need of a ship, then why did you stay in Harringbay?" she asked insistently. "You miss sailing, don't you?"

"Smelling the salt air again, I admit, was a balm to my old soul. I decided to stay rather than make the trip all the way back to Altus and live in the shadow of the man what did strike your father down, but I don't 'spect to sail ever again," he answered, but despite his answer, she thought there was a small glimmer of hope in his cloudy eyes.

"I'm going to go no matter what, Captain Mel, but I would feel safest in your hands," Emmaline said, her last desperate means of persuasion.

The captain sighed at that and removed his hat to rub his balding scalp. Several long moments passed in which Emmaline thought all hope was lost. Then Mel hung his head and asked, "When do we set sail?"

"In three days!" Emmaline cried, unable to contain her excitement. "Can you find a crew?" she asked.

"In this town? I 'spect I can," Mel replied. He sounded tired just thinking about it, and she hoped he was up for the journey.

Emmaline told him where to find the ship in the shipyard, and he agreed to get it out of storage and meet her at the main dock in three days with a full crew. She knew she was going to have to steal something from her house or sell some of her jewelry to pay them all, but she didn't care. For once, she was living for the future and not just that day. She was living, and in three days, she would set sail to try to keep living.

———

EMMALINE SPENT the following days making more preparations. The captain had told her where to go to get supplies for the ship, and she bartered for the first time in her life—surprisingly well, too, she thought with satisfaction. Then she packed and repacked her own trunk, fretting over what she might need for a long sea voyage and an unknown land. In the end, she packed almost everything she owned—it was her ship, and she could fill it if she wanted to.

Her maids constantly pestered her to change her mind and stay at home, but they were loyal and didn't alert her mother to her plans—not that she would even notice her absence, Emmaline thought; her mother acted like she was already dead most of the time. Ever since her father had been killed, she had withdrawn and stopped talking to Emmaline or even looking at her. It was like she had chosen to lose them both all at once instead of one at a time—except that Emmaline was still there. She was still alive.

The day they were to depart, she snuck out of the house with her enormous trunk. Some of the servants helped her—the ones she knew she could trust. Emmaline had left a note to her mother with her maids, explaining where she was going and saying her goodbyes, just in case. It hadn't been difficult for her to write; she had been writing similar farewell letters to her parents periodically over the course of her entire life. She had always liked the thought of leaving them last words of love when she died. The letters were all piled in a morbid little box under her bed, ready for the day when she finally succumbed to her illness. Emmaline had always planned for her death, but she had never planned for a life. What if she lived? What if they cured her?

Hope spurred her to the dock where her father's ship, the *Lady Emmaline*, was to set sail. She took one of her family's carriages, and Adam, the coachman, unloaded her trunk, dragging it to where the ship stood swaying gently in the early morning light. When she thanked him, he gave her a conspiratorial wink and wished her well on her journey. Emmaline held her chin up and tried to look confident even though her stomach was rioting with nerves. Turning her attention to the ship, she found that Captain Mel was already there with his crew, loading supplies. She smiled to see them at work, some of her nerves turning to excitement; this was really happening! She was really going to sail to Kallanthea!

Emmaline's anxiety quickly returned, however, as she stood on the dock and waited ... and waited. Her knell protectors were nowhere to be seen long past when the ship was ready to sail. The sun rose steadily into the sky, and the possibility that her mother would notice her absence and come to retrieve her increased with each passing breath. But despite her growing concerns, Emmaline did not pace or fidget or tap her feet; she stood straight-backed and still, and she waited.

From time to time, she could sense Captain Mel's eyes on her, but she didn't board the ship to speak to him; she wouldn't know what to say. Could they still make the journey without magic to protect them? Emmaline didn't know much about what the scarred woman could do, but she had seemed so sure, so confident. Was this all some sort of elaborate joke? Getting a chill from the breeze off the ocean, she began to fret about her health. Should she really be making such a journey this time of year? What if they ended up sailing back in the winter? Could her body handle that? She reminded herself that she would hopefully be cured when they sailed back, and she continued to wait.

Finally, the strange group approached the ship. They were walking down the dock, arguing loudly, and the pale, dark-haired man seemed to be holding up the one-handed man. When they got closer, Emmaline could see that the one-handed man with the scruffy beard was drunk, and she crossed her arms in agitation. She didn't know why these knell were dragging around such a useless human, but the scarred woman, at least, appeared clear-eyed and ready to go—not that the group as a whole had any luggage.

"Sorry we're late," the woman said when they neared. "One of us disappeared to go drinking in the middle of the night, and we had to search the whole town to find him," she added, shooting the drunk one a nasty look.

"You should have left him," Emmaline replied tersely.

"That is what I said," the dark-haired man agreed, looking irritated.

The drunk man laughed and stumbled precariously close to the side of the dock. Emmaline almost wished he would fall in and drown, so he wouldn't get in the way of her plans any more than he already had. She needed the knell and their supposed magic, but she had no use for a drunk. He didn't fall, though—the scarred woman grabbed him and shoved him toward the ship.

Meanwhile, Emmaline appraised the woman's other companions: the dark-haired man appeared normal and reasonable enough, but the red-haired man was wearing metal decorations on his ears and stood with his hands in his pockets, looking unnervingly calm. They were both rather well-muscled and eerily inhuman ... Swallowing, she averted her eyes to the ship. She hoped these people could do what they claimed and weren't pirates who would rob her, rape her, and ransom her back to her mother.

Together they boarded the ship, and Captain Mel gaped at the newcomers. "Captain, this is our protection," Emmaline said—she couldn't remember any of their names. She turned to the strange group. "This is—"

"Captain Mel!" the scarred woman interrupted her. Emmaline stared at her in surprise, wondering if she could read minds or something. Then she remembered the woman had spied on her father and would, of course, know who the captain was. "How did the lady convince you to do this, Captain?" she asked.

For a moment, Captain Mel just looked confused, clearly wondering if he should recognize the strange woman. Clearing his throat, he replied, "Same way she convinced you I guess, Miss." Then he proceeded to turn and shout orders to his men, apparently accepting the newcomers.

Emmaline released a breath she hadn't known she'd been holding; she was really doing this! They were really setting sail! She edged up against the side rail to keep out of everyone's way while the ship slowly started to move and pull away from the dock. Despite growing up in Harringbay, she had never been on the open ocean before and watched the dock slide further and further into the distance with an odd feeling in her stomach. Then she turned and faced the sea, and her breath caught in her throat. Wind whipped her, and salt water sprayed her face from a breaking wave. The ship rocked precariously, and she gripped the side rail, gasping for breath and suddenly wishing she were home —safe in her bedroom.

7

MEERA

Once they left the dock and the crew settled down, Meera approached the captain to ask if there was anything they could do to be of assistance. She was glad to be helping Emmaline get to Kallanthea but didn't relish a long sea voyage of sitting around and waiting for something to happen. She needed to keep busy—keep herself distracted. She still wasn't ready to face her grief even though she could feel herself slowly losing control of her shaping. She still had *enough* control, she told herself.

"There's always work to be done aboard a ship," Captain Mel assured them. "Don't s'pose any of you can cook? I couldn't find a proper cook on short notice."

Meera jumped on the job, offering to cook whenever she wasn't needed on deck to divert nearby ships. Kennick said he would be lookout—his knell eyes would catch movement on the horizon far before any of the crew could—and Shael proceeded to point to the different riggings and working of the ship and ask the captain a lot of questions. Meera tuned him out; she had no interest in ropes and sails so long as they got her where they were going. Taking Kennick's hand, she led him to the railing to look out at the Cerun Sea.

Kennick put his arms around her, and his solid body at her back with the wind in her face felt almost like flying. Meera sighed and leaned into him for a moment. Then her mind started to churn, and she quickly pulled away and peered around the ship, searching for diversion. She didn't know where Linus had gone, but she didn't much care as long as he didn't fall in the ocean; she was so mad at him. They had woken up in their clearing with no idea where he was and had had to wander the town for hours to find him. Meera didn't like his drinking, but she didn't know how to stop him either. She could only hope there wasn't much alcohol on the ship—not that that was likely.

Kennick seemed to sense her unease and pointed to where Shael and the captain stood to redirect her thoughts. Shael was clearly still asking questions, and Captain Mel looked both annoyed and frightened at the same time. Meera laughed at the sight. "I didn't know Shael was interested in sailing," Kennick remarked.

"He had a dog named Flotilla as a boy," Meera told him, remembering the painting she had seen of them in Shael's parent's house. He had been so happy in that painting ... Meera hoped she hadn't crushed him too badly with her rejection.

"Really?" Kennick asked, smiling.

"Yes, but apparently Flotilla couldn't swim," she added, recalling what Shael had told her.

Kennick laughed. "Looks like Shael will have plenty to keep him occupied on the journey," he said, watching their friend start to work with the crew.

Meera was glad to see Shael smiling and keeping busy, knowing what kind of dark depressions he could fall into. "Maybe when we get home, we should get him a puppy," she suggested. "We could name it Fleet!"

"What, like a consolation puppy?" Kennick asked, giving her a skeptical look.

She supposed it wasn't the best idea ... but it wasn't the worst. "Think about it: a dog might even be better company than me—it would run with him, cuddle him in bed at night, and wouldn't be able to fly away or burn him!" she said, grinning.

"Maybe I should get a dog," Kennick replied, his pointy canine tooth showing over his lower lip.

"Hey!" Meera shouted, pushing him playfully. But then she caught sight of Emmaline standing a ways behind Kennick and got distracted; the young woman's face looked strained, and she was gripping the railing like a lifeboat.

Kennick glanced behind him to see where she was looking. "Don't you have a job to do, sailor?" Meera asked him. He smiled at her in understanding. She kissed him briefly and walked toward the lady.

Meera knew she might not be the best person to comfort the duke's daughter, but there didn't seem to be anyone else to do it. "Are you alright?" she asked.

Emmaline immediately straightened up and released the railing. "I'm just not used to the wind," she replied.

Meera shaped the wind to still around them. "There. Is that better?" she asked.

Emmaline gaped at her. "You really can control the wind ... H —how? How did you get these abilities?" she asked.

"After I spied for the king, I set Shael free from the palace. He took me to Aegorn—" Meera began.

"The dark-haired one?" Emmaline asked, looking past Meera toward where Shael was working.

"Yes. Then in Aegorn I met a wild raek. She gave me the abilities in exchange for my help ending the war," Meera explained briefly. She thought Emmaline might ask where her raek was or how she planned to end the war and dreaded both questions.

However, Emmaline surprised her; looking out to sea, she simply said, "You've done a lot in your life."

Meera supposed that was true but didn't think Emmaline had anything to be jealous or sullen about. "When I think about my life, I think about my friends and family—all the people I love," she responded. She left out that she also thought about the people she'd killed. "Your father is dead, but he loved you. And you have your mother," she added, seeing the sorrow in the other woman's face.

"My mother acts as if I'm already dead," Emmaline admitted, looking down at the waves below them.

Meera sighed. Kenna Harrington had seemed changed by her husband's death. Unbidden, Meera thought of her own father— who was there but not all there—and she wondered whether he was waiting for her in Levisade or just too caught up in his research to notice her absence. Then she attempted to shake the dark mood creeping over both her and Emmaline: "You're still alive, and look at you!" she said, gesturing around them. "You're on an adventure!"

Emmaline gave her a small smile, but Linus suddenly appeared on Meera's other side. "Don't feel good!" he moaned before promptly vomiting over the side of the ship.

"Serves you right," Meera replied testily. She hoped he would think twice before getting that drunk again.

"Not the rum—the ship," he said, swaying. He really didn't look very good.

"Where can I take him to lie down?" Meera asked Emmaline, who had moved away from Linus and looked repulsed—not repulsed but scared, Meera realized; she looked scared because she was afraid of getting sick. "He's just seasick," she assured the lady.

Emmaline explained where their quarters were, and Meera led Linus below deck to find him a bed. When she opened the door Emmaline had instructed her to, she laughed; it was a small room with a tiny round window and two sets of bunk beds. "Cozy, huh?" she asked Linus.

He only managed a groan in reply, and she shoved him down onto one of the lower bunks. She had no sooner tracked down a bucket to leave next to him when Kennick appeared in the doorway. "Ships," he said simply.

Meera saw him take in their new room, and she laughed again. "Do you want the top or bottom bunk?" she asked, following him back down the narrow corridor and up the stairs leading to the deck.

"Whichever you will be in," he answered in a low voice.

Meera felt a little jolt through her core. They hadn't spent that kind of time together since being reunited, but she wasn't sure she was ready for it—true mates being extra fertile ... Not to mention, just a kind touch from Kennick threatened to pull her emotions up from where she was stuffing them down inside herself. "I don't think our roommates would appreciate that," she replied briskly before reaching the deck and assessing the ship's situation.

Walking to the rail where Captain Mel was standing, she looked out over the water with him. There were two ships in the distance that the captain was peering at through a spyglass. "Are they navy?" Meera asked him.

"Don't think so," he replied.

In that case, Meera left the ships alone and contented herself shaping extra wind into their own sails to speed their progress. The captain looked alarmed at first by their sudden change in momentum, then he eyed her. "Godspeed and all that," she said, grinning at him.

"Is that what you all are? Gods?" he asked.

"No," Meera said. "We're just people."

"Mmmhmm. You know, I didn't recognize you at first, but I do now. I know you were there that night I met with Ned. I remember. You best do right by Lady Emmaline, you hear?" Captain Mel warned with a sharpness in his old eyes.

"The girl or the ship?" Meera joked, but the captain didn't laugh or smile. "Captain Mel, I'm here to make up for that," she told him.

He regarded her for a long moment then nodded. "You'll have two boys to help you in the galley," he replied before turning and barking out orders to his crew.

Meera looked around and noticed for the first time that the men of the crew were all rather old or rather young, and those in between bore some deformity or other. "I suppose there aren't many men left in Terratelle," she remarked to Kennick, who was loitering nearby.

"There are—they are just at the border," he replied.

She grimaced; she was supposed to be ending the war, not leaving her responsibilities on the horizon behind her. The trouble was, she didn't know how to do that.

"I am sure we will think of a way to send them all home soon," Kennick assured her, seeing the look on her face.

She gave him a small smile even though she didn't share his confidence; it was still good to know she wasn't alone in her seemingly impossible task. On impulse, Meera hopped onto the railing next to Kennick and pulled him toward her for a kiss. Both of them had their hair braided tightly back, so only the wind whipped their faces. At first, Meera forgot all of her troubles, reveling in the way Kennick's mouth could always turn her to liquid metal. Then she pulled away—she could never forget for long. When she saw the concern in his dark eyes, she averted her gaze.

Some of the nearby crew members were leering at them and others looked scandalized, so Meera let herself slide down from the railing. It really was a rough crew, she thought—ragged and thin. She supposed these were the desperate men willing to take their chances against the Terratellen navy and sail with knell toward an unknown land. They looked hungry, so she decided it was time for her to get to work. With one last brief kiss, she left Kennick to find the galley and start cooking.

8

MEERA

Preparing three meals each day for the crew turned out to be ample distraction for Meera; cooking ate away at her time and focused her mind on something other than her troubles. Everything was smooth sailing in her new job—except for the boys. Captain Mel had assigned two young boys to help her—Doug and Freddy—and they continually reminded Meera of the boys she had killed. When they laughed and talked, she wondered how the three she had killed had sounded. When they discussed their hopes and dreams, she wondered what bright futures she had cut short.

Meera began to lose control of her abilities more and more often—not in any large way, just little things. She frequently shaped wind into the ship's sails to speed their progress and occasionally stirred up such high winds that Kennick would come running down to the galley to tell her to stop, that she was going to tear the sails and knock the crew overboard. She felt her flames licking under her skin almost continually and lived in fear that she would lose control of her fire and burn someone. Her fear only made her shaping more precarious.

In the galley, she shaped to make the kitchen work easier—filling pots with water, heating food quickly, putting fires out ... The boys had been afraid of her abilities at first, but they grew to enjoy seeing her use magic. More and more, however, she would go to fill a kettle or shape a heavy pot from a cabinet, and nothing would happen. Meera didn't tell anyone about her misfiring magic because she didn't want to scare the whole crew; her abilities were meant to get them safely to their destination, after all. Rather, when she occasionally asked Doug or Freddy to do the chores that she usually did with her abilities, she passed it off as not wanting them to get too soft or lazy—she covered her apprehension by mock-shouting at them to move faster or work harder.

Meera didn't even tell Kennick about her struggles. At night, she climbed into her top bunk and pretended to sleep to be left alone. Other than mealtimes, she barely saw her companions: Linus got over his sea sickness after a few days and spent his time drinking and playing cards with the crew, Kennick and Shael took turns keeping watch day and night and occasionally helped out on deck, and no one knew what Emmaline spent her time doing, but she rarely left her room. Overall, the days passed in an exhausting, monotonous blur much like the endless view of blue water stretching out around them.

Occasionally, Meera altered the wind to avoid nearby ships, but it wasn't until they were two weeks into their journey that they seemed to reach the boundary Terratelle's navy enforced. She and her helpers were getting dinner ready; they were making a stew—another one. Every morning they made grain mush, sometimes with eggs or potatoes, every afternoon they made sandwiches with cold meat and cheese, and every evening they made stew. Meera was doing her best with what she had in the ship's larder, but there wasn't much to work with. Captain Mel had warmed to her substantially since she had started cooking, so she supposed she was doing an okay job by ship's standards. Still, she knew Cook wouldn't be impressed.

Doug was busy cutting a large hunk of beef into cubes, and she and Freddy were chopping vegetables. Doug and Freddy had spent most of their childhoods on ships and had taken to teaching Meera the words to their favorite sailing songs—most of which were appallingly inappropriate in one way or another. Freddy was teaching her a new one and recited the line: "So Lady Jane did hoist her sail and back her stern up to the whale." Meera laughed heartily, wiping tears from her eyes and repeating the line several times to learn it.

"She's cryin' with mirth!" Doug shouted, pointing at her.

"I'm crying from the onions!" Meera objected, still chuckling.

"Here, switch with me, missus," Freddy said, taking the onion from her hand and pushing his stack of peeled carrots toward her.

Meera smiled at him and let him make the switch. Despite the guilt they churned up within her, she was really starting to enjoy her time with the boys; she liked teaching them about cooking and listening to their ridiculous, long-winded stories. Vaguely, she wondered if that was what motherhood would have felt like, then she froze, feeling the flaming wound in her soul threaten to burst open. That was not something she usually let herself wonder about. Just then, she heard running footsteps down the corridor, and Kennick burst in. "Navy," he said simply.

Meera dropped her knife and followed him onto the deck where the crew were all standing around looking extremely nervous. Their attention wasn't focused in any one direction, so she turned to Kennick. "Where?" she asked.

"They're closing in on us!" Captain Mel shouted, walking toward her and gesturing in several directions.

Spinning in a slow circle, she counted the ships on the horizon. Three. There were three warships, and they were definitely heading toward them. Meera might have felt calm and confident except that her abilities had been so spotty lately. Still, she held her head up high and tried to look like she had everything under control. The last thing she needed was the entire crew panicking. "Just keep going, and I'll handle the ships," she told Captain Mel.

At random, she picked a ship on the horizon and walked toward the railing to focus on it. She wanted to swirl the water beneath the vessel to spin it around then blow wind into its sails. She didn't need to permanently disable the ships, after all; she just needed to hold them off indefinitely. She seriously doubted the navy would follow them all the way to Kallanthea. The trouble was, Meera was scared; she was scared she wouldn't be able to shape at all, and she was scared that if she did, she might lose control. What if she broke the ship? What would happen to the men? She didn't want any more lives on her conscience ...

Inhaling a deep, shaky breath, she continued to stare at the ship approaching them without acting. She was stuck—frozen. She couldn't bring herself to even try to shape the water. Kennick stepped up behind her and put his hands on her shoulders. "What is it?" he asked. He knew what she was capable of. He knew she should have dealt with all three ships already.

"I'm losing control," Meera told him quietly, knowing she should have told him weeks ago. And rather than turn around and risk seeing disappointment in his eyes, she continued to stare at the warship growing larger and larger on the horizon. She had kept something from Kennick again and couldn't bear to see how badly she had hurt him. She didn't want to see the scared crew standing around waiting for her to do something either. Suddenly, Meera's eyes filled with tears and not from the onions she'd been cutting.

Kennick didn't try to turn her around. Wrapping his arms around her shoulders and chest, he leaned down to whisper in her ear: "You once told me your water shaping was linked to your feelings for me. I am right here, Meera. You can do it."

She leaned back into him. He was right; she could always shape water when he was with her. Taking another breath, she focused on the ship again. Then she shaped the ocean water around it, swirling it like a whirlpool. It was easy to catch the large vessel in her current. But it was harder for her to still the current suddenly in order to face the ship away from them without letting it continue to spin or tip over. She missed her opportunity the first time, sending the ship around in a full circle, but she got it the second time. Once the warship faced away from them, she shaped a strong wind into its sails with just a thought, not even stopping to consider whether she could.

Meera sighed in relief the second before the crew erupted in cheers all around her. She had done it—once, anyway. Grinning, she disengaged from Kennick's arms to find the other two ships on the horizon and repeat the process. Meera didn't usually feel an immediate drain in her strength when she shaped, but the magical energy required to redirect all three ships took an immediate toll on her body. When she was done, she slumped against the rail, fatigued.

"That was something!" Captain Mel shouted, slapping her on the back. "We'd have been a pair in my day!"

Meera laughed and wondered what it was Mel had done in his day, but she didn't ask. The captain and his crew went back to their stations, and Kennick came up behind her once more and wrapped his arms around her. Pressing a kiss to the scarred side of her neck, he sniffed her. "Have you been chopping onions or rolling in them?" he asked.

Meera groaned. "I have to go finish dinner," she told him. Still, she didn't move except to shut her eyes and rub them.

"The boys can't finish without you?" he asked.

"Not if I want dinner to be edible, and I do—I'm starving," she replied.

"You cannot put it off any longer, Meera," Kennick told her in a soft voice. She knew what he meant—her feelings. She couldn't ignore her feelings any longer; she had to let them in, to process them. Otherwise, her inconsistent shaping would only continue to get worse.

"When we get where we're going," she promised, disentangling herself from him. Now she really needed to get back to the galley. In the galley, no one talked about her feelings—the boys laughed and joked and sang, and that was what she wanted right now.

Kennick didn't say anything. He reluctantly let her go, and she could feel his eyes on her back as she walked to the stairs and descended below deck. What did he want from her? She had just rerouted three warships and was cooking for the whole crew almost single-handedly. She was tired! She knew she was losing control, but what was she supposed to do about that right then in the middle of the Cerun Sea?

Meera pushed open the galley door with a smile on her face, ready to suck up her exhaustion and resume cooking, but her smile flat-lined the second she entered and the acrid smell of burning filled her nose. Freddy and Doug were frantically trying to clean up what looked like a heap of sand on top of the fire hearth. "What happened?" she asked.

"We're sorry, Missus! We thought we'd get on without you. We knew you often flavored the stews with drink, and we knew you liked the meat browned before it simmered, so we stoked the fire real high, and we browned the beef, but when we added the rum there was a huge fire! We put it out with the sandbags, but we ruined the stew," Freddy confessed in a jumble.

"Rum? I add wine to the stews!" Meera cried. She was exhausted and didn't relish the thought of cleaning up their mess and starting dinner from scratch. "You two clean this up, and we'll have sandwiches for dinner," she said.

Both boys nodded fervently and got back to work scooping up sand. Meera was glad they had at least had the wits to use the sandbags that were left stacked in the corner of the galley in case of fire. The whole ship was wood and could have burned otherwise. The stove was metal and brick, but if even one ember had jumped, the room could have easily caught fire with the boys inside it. The thought sickened her; children shouldn't burn. Meera noticed that Doug had something wrapped around his arm. "Doug, what's that?" she asked.

"Nothin', Missus—just a small burn. I'll be fine," he said.

Meera grabbed his arm, tore off his makeshift bandage, and stared at the angry red burn on his arm. Suddenly, she couldn't breathe; the residual smoke in the room choked her, and her chest spasmed, needing air but not sucking it in. She hadn't even been there, she kept telling herself, but her conscience wouldn't listen to reason—she was a child burner. Everyone around her burned, burned, burned. The raek fire inside her burned—she felt it licking through the veins of her body, tickling under the surface of her skin.

"Missus, are you alright?" Freddy asked, reaching out and grabbing her arm.

Meera jerked away from him a split second before her arm ignited in pale flames. Both boys stared at her, wide-eyed and terrified. She couldn't stand it—she couldn't bear their fear and judgment. She already knew she was a monster! Meera threw herself violently toward the door and stumbled from the room, lurching down the hallway toward the stairs. She wasn't safe! She would burn them all! She had to get out of there. She tried to extinguish the fire on her arm but couldn't, and it ate away her sleeve where it danced and mocked her. She didn't have control.

She fell through the door onto the deck, landing hard on her hand and knees and holding her flaming arm away from the wood of the ship. She gasped in a breath of fresh, cool air and squeezed her eyes shut, willing the fire back inside her, but it was no use. Her magic was tearing free with her emotions, and she couldn't choke either back anymore. When she opened her eyes and saw the white fire still taunting her along her arm, she let out a strangled cry and rose to her feet, running for the railing. She was a monster, a child-burner, destructive, not safe! She needed to get away from the ship and save everyone from herself!

Shouts rang out around her, but she ignored them. Leaping onto the ship's rail, she crouched there, clinging with her unburning hand and staring down at the ocean far below. The ship's movement churned the otherwise calm water, and Meera had the oddly disjointed thought that the Cerun Sea in no way encompassed the steady nature of the raek she had named for it. Someone grabbed her flameless arm, and she whipped her head around to find Kennick holding her, fear and intensity in his dark eyes. "I've lost control," she gasped. Her whole body trembled with fatigue and emotion. She had just moved three ships with her abilities, but she had never felt so powerless—her fire hovered under the surface, bursting from her arm as her mind spiraled down into her darkest thoughts. It was all coming out now, and she couldn't stop it.

"What can I do?" Kennick asked desperately.

"Let go!" she shouted. She felt her fire surge and had to get away from the ship.

Kennick let go and so did Meera, allowing herself to drop from the rail a moment before her entire body burst into pale flames. She fell, plummeting toward the water below, incapable of slowing or stopping herself. Her fire blinded her to her surroundings and incinerated her clothes and boots. The initial slap of cold water was such a shock, the air was forced from her lungs, and her fire went out.

Her body plunged into the water and was tossed, disorienting her. She opened her eyes and was met with only blue. Blue-green stretched out all around her, and her panicked mind could only think that it wasn't the right color—Cerun's feathers were much brighter and bluer. Then she gasped involuntarily, and icy salt water rushed into her mouth and lungs. It felt like her chest was burning—like her insides really were on fire.

9

KENNICK

This time when Meera fell, Kennick did not hesitate; he stepped onto the railing and dove after her. He saw her hit the water and her fire go out a moment before he broke beneath the surface. Opening his eyes under the water, he searched, but the wake from the ship frothed his surroundings, obstructing his view. His lungs burned with the need to breathe, but he ignored them. He needed to find Meera. He had no idea what state she was in or whether she could get herself back to the ship. He needed to find her and get her out of the frigid ocean.

After an agonizing few seconds, the water settled, and Kennick spotted Meera's naked figure and swam for her. She was still—so still, except for the lazy drift the current propelled her into. Kennick's heart thudded with his rapidly moving limbs, fighting to reach her. He grabbed her waist and thrust her limp body upward. Meera's head broke the surface just before his, and he gasped in much-needed air, treading to keep them both afloat. His clothes and boots dragged at him, and the cold water seized his muscles, but he kept moving and gripped Meera's face. She was not breathing.

Kennick felt like his own heart and lungs were screaming and failing. Pinching her nose, he covered her mouth with his, forcing his breath into her body, once—then again, kicking frantically with his booted feet to keep them above the surface. After the second breath, Meera coughed, spraying water from her lungs. She tried to breathe in and choked, coughing again. Kennick allowed himself a moment of relief, clutching her to him and kissing her face while she breathed and spluttered. Her whole body shook. When her coughing subsided, she let her head hang forward and her forehead rest against his face, too drained to hold it upright. She was exhausted and cold, but she was alive.

Kennick's relief quickly dissipated; he had to get her back to the ship, which was moving swiftly away from them, shrinking into the distance. As he stared at the rapidly progressing vessel, he sensed the iron anchors being lowered from the deck. Desperately, he grasped the anchors in his mind, clinging to them and dragging the ship to a halt even before the iron reached the ocean's floor. The magic sapped Kennick's strength, and he could not pull the ship any closer. He panted from the exertion, and for several breaths, he could only keep treading and holding onto Meera, keeping their heads above the water.

Meera roused herself, lifting her face from his. "Sorry ... can't shape," she murmured.

He shushed her; he did not want her using any energy to speak. "I have you," he said. "I have to swim. Can you hold on?" he asked, repositioning her behind him and wrapping her arms around his neck.

She clutched her forearms and managed to hold on, so he struck out, heading for the ship. It was far, and his progress was slow. Meera lay draped across his shoulders and remained completely still except for her shaking—clinging to him with sheer force of will. Eventually, however, her grip broke, and she began to slip from his back. Kennick grabbed her arms and shaped one of his metal wrist cuffs around her wrists to bind them. It was crude, but it was all he could think to do. They still had a long way to go, and he needed his arms to get them there.

At some point, Meera stopped shivering; she went completely and utterly still, halting Kennick's frantic heart for a beat. His muscles were tiring and his strokes slowing down, but in a burst of desperation, he held out his other wrist cuff and used it to shape them through the water. The cuff bit into the flesh of his hand as it dragged him forward, but he gritted his teeth and ignored it. The pain was nothing compared to his fear. Meera was so still, so silent.

They glided steadily through the water, draining what was left of Kennick's magical energy. He wished he had metal on his ankles and belt to speed their progress, but he did not. Since leaving Endu behind, he had gotten out of the habit of wearing what he considered his fall metal, and now he regretted it; he should have been more prepared for this—he should have pressed Meera harder to deal with her feelings. He should have made her rest after redirecting the ships, but he could not think about that now.

Shutting his eyes in concentration, he dragged them toward the ship, focusing his entire being on their destination. He had to get Meera out of the water. Suddenly, a noise caught his attention, and he opened his eyes, searching. There was a small boat paddling toward them. It was much closer than the ship and moving quickly. Kennick exhaled in relief but did not slow his progress. Rather, he drained every last bit of his energy propelling them toward the boat. Meera was dead weight on his shoulders, limp and cold.

Shael rowed the small boat alone and paddled up next to them, anchoring the oars in the water with such force that it waved and splashed briefly over Kennick's head. Shael called to him and reached for him, and Kennick swam the last few strokes to his friend, quickly removing the cuff from Meera's wrists and fumbling to get her to the edge of the boat. Shael reached over and grabbed her, hauling her up and laying her gently down. Kennick gripped the lip of the small vessel but was too tired to pull himself up. Once Shael had removed his jacket and shirt and laid them both over Meera's prone body, he grabbed Kennick's wrists and hauled him aboard as well.

"—she breathing?" Kennick asked, gasping. He slumped against the side of the boat. He wanted to go to Meera but could not seem to move.

"She's breathing," Shael replied, picking up the oars and rowing them back toward the ship as fast as he could.

When Kennick could move again, he crawled over to Meera and lay with her, trying to give her what little warmth he could offer. Then he listened to his friend's steady rowing and waited. He wished he could help, but he could not. Eventually, Shael slowed the small boat alongside the ship and tied ropes to the hooks on its sides for them to be lifted onto the deck. Their upward progress was slow, but they were almost there. When the ship's crew pulled them over the rail and settled the lifeboat onto the deck, Kennick found the energy to rise and get out of the way. It was Shael who scooped Meera up and carried her from the boat.

"She alive?" Captain Mel asked. Shael must have nodded because the captain then shouted for someone to fill a basin with warm—not hot—water for her.

Kennick managed to clamor out of the boat, but then he just stood, swaying. Shael was already disappearing with Meera down the stairs. He wanted to follow but could not seem to get the message from his brain to his legs. Then Linus was beside him, putting Kennick's dripping arm over his narrow shoulders and supporting his weight. Linus was thin and weak, but he helped Kennick get down the stairs. Together, they hobbled to their shared room, where Shael and Emmaline had Meera in a tub of water covered by a blanket for modesty. She was unconscious but breathing.

Emmaline held a rag to her head, and Shael slowly added steaming water to the tub. "She's warming up," Emmaline announced, touching Meera's cheek with her slight hand.

Kennick sagged in relief, causing Linus to grunt and buckle under his weight. They both fell to the wood floor, and Shael walked over to help. Linus waved away his proffered hand and stood, brushing himself off and looking annoyed. Kennick just sat and shivered, staring at Meera's face. "You need to get warm too," Shael told him, starting to remove his clothes like he was a child. Kennick let him, helping only when he absolutely had to. Emmaline turned away, looking scandalized, but he was too tired to care. They did not have much in the way of spare clothes, so when he was naked, Shael deposited him on his lower bunk and covered him in all of their blankets.

"Don't worry about me. I'll sleep without blankets," Linus remarked testily. Everyone ignored him.

Eventually, Shael pulled Meera from the tub and tucked her under the blankets with Kennick. Emmaline looked like she wanted to object but did not. She merely threw up her hands and left the room in exasperation, disgust, or both. Linus followed her.

With Meera pressed up next to him, Kennick felt like he could finally let his exhaustion drag him into a deep sleep. Her even breathing was the sweetest lullaby. "Thank you," he rasped to Shael before closing his eyes, once more grateful that he was not the only one who cared for Meera.

"I will bring you food and water," Shael replied, but Kennick was asleep before he even reached the door.

10

LINUS

L inus left the room, relieved that Meera would be okay but not wanting to be alone with her and her knell men. The three of them together always weirded him out. Not sure what to do with himself now that the drama had passed, he trailed after Emmaline, curious to know where the lady spent all of her time. He hadn't even seen her since the day they had boarded the ship. She had only appeared on deck when Meera had stumbled out of the door on fire and chaos had erupted. Linus still wasn't sure what had happened exactly, but Meera had clearly lost control of her extraordinary powers. It had made him glad to be human and only human.

Emmaline had watched from the deck with everyone else until Meera was returned safely, and she had accompanied Shael into their room for the sole reason that she was the only other woman aboard the ship and thought it indecent to leave Meera alone with a man. Linus had suspected that Meera wouldn't have cared, but he hadn't said anything. He left people to themselves— for the most part. In this case, he continued to follow Emmaline out of curiosity. The lady walked quickly down the corridor and up the stairs, and Linus trailed behind her to an upper deck door, which presumably led to her room. Emmaline disappeared inside, and without knocking, Linus pushed the door open and followed her.

When he beheld the lady's room, he whistled in appreciation. Emmaline spun around, affronted. "This is some room you have —all to yourself too!" he remarked. The room was large with a big bed and high windows that let in an abundance of sunlight while still allowing for privacy.

"What are you doing in here?" Emmaline asked, clutching her hands in front of her. She straightened to her full diminutive height and raised her chin proudly. Despite spending all of her time alone, she was fully dressed in a stuffy purple gown with frills and had her wavy hair pinned away from her face and hanging long down her back. Through narrowed eyes, she appraised Linus and awaited his explanation.

Studying the lady in return, Linus suddenly realized that he had barged into the private room of a very pretty young woman, and he didn't know what to say or what to do with his hands. Attempting to look half as regal as Emmaline, he stood up straighter and tucked his stump close to his side, out of sight. "Well, seeing as my room is pretty full, and you have all this space ... I thought you might let me sleep on your floor tonight," he said with false bravado.

The lady gaped at him. "Absolutely not! Sleep with the crew," she replied.

"Alright, I will," he said, but instead of leaving, he sat at the edge of her pristinely made bed. Emmaline was standing near a desk against one of the walls. "So, Emma—"

"Lady Emmaline," she corrected him.

He knew; it was the name of the damned ship they were on,

after all. He continued his train of thought, unperturbed: "... as nice as this room is, how come you spend all your time in here? Why don't you go on deck or eat with us?" he asked. Peering at her, he supposed she was too high and mighty to eat with the likes of them. Linus had shared plenty of meals with princes and kings, lords and ladies, but Emmaline had a certain self-righteousness that only some of them possessed.

Emmaline shifted and looked toward the door, then back at him. "Ships are breeding grounds for illnesses," she replied.

Linus nodded and hummed in understanding. He had forgotten about her supposed sickness. She looked healthy enough to him. Glancing past her, he noticed that the desk she stood in front of had some drawings scattered atop it, and he rose and walked toward them. The lady jumped back, slamming her thin frame into the wall, and Linus held up his hand and stump and tried to look non-threatening; he hadn't meant to frighten her. Emmaline stared at his stump, so he tucked it self-consciously behind his back. He supposed he shouldn't have cornered the lady, and he stepped back and gestured for her to pass in front of him toward the door. She did so, looking extremely nervous.

Linus continued to the desk and picked up one of the drawings. "Is this how you spend your time?" he asked. He considered the picture, which depicted running horses and was done in colored pencils. "Do you like horses?" he asked when Emmaline didn't answer his first question.

"I don't dislike horses," she replied tersely.

"Then why did you draw these?" he asked.

"My father always compared me to wild horses, and I never quite understood why," she admitted, looking down at the floorboards.

Linus studied her instead of the drawing. She was small but proud—and she was very pretty. Swallowing, he put the drawing down and averted his gaze to the floor as well. He wanted to say the right thing, but he wasn't sure what the right thing to say might be ... "Sometimes a horse can take down a wolf," he said, remembering when a trampled wolf was found in back of the palace, apparently killed by one of the royal's mares.

Emmaline regarded him quizzically, then smiled ever so slightly, and Linus exhaled in relief; he hadn't said the wrong thing, at least. When he relaxed, he let his stump return to his side, and the lady looked at it again. "Did you lose your hand to infection?" she asked.

"A burn," he replied vaguely.

Her thick eyebrows rose up on her forehead. "That must have been a very bad burn," she replied.

He shrugged. "It couldn't be saved—not by human healing, anyway," he added. They were on a journey to find the lady healing magic, and he didn't want to quash her hopes. He was sure the world would do that all on its own.

"Does it make you angry that the king kept magic from you that might have saved it?" she asked.

Linus stared at her for a moment, wondering what she knew of his relationship with the former and current king, but Emmaline seemed to be referring to the Crown's rejection of magic in general. He shrugged again. "I don't think about it," he said. He didn't see any point in thinking about it; his hand was long gone.

"What *do* you think about?" she asked.

Linus thought that was a strange question, but he figured the lady had been cooped up alone for a long time and was bored. "Not much," he replied. "Thinking has never gotten me anywhere."

"Then what brought you here—to the middle of the Cerun Sea?" she asked. "Following a woman who is clearly in love with someone else?"

Linus crossed his arms over his chest defensively. "Meera is my friend," he explained. In truth, he still didn't understand his motivations enough to relay them to another person. At least, he was too embarrassed to admit to Emmaline or himself that he was on some sort of misguided mission to become a better person and do something worthwhile with his life.

"What's that like?" the lady asked.

"What?" Linus shot back, not understanding the question.

"Having friends," she clarified, looking up at him with big, vulnerable eyes. Her eyes were greenish-brown and stood out in contrast to her copper skin.

"Oh ... you don't have any?" he asked. The ladies that visited the palace were always talking and giggling in gaggles together.

"None my own age," she replied.

"What age is that?" Linus asked. He really thought the lady was quite attractive and suddenly hoped he wasn't having indecent thoughts about a young girl. She was slight, but he didn't think she was that young.

"Old enough," Emmaline said defensively, crossing her arms over her chest.

"Old enough for what?" Linus teased, taking a step toward her, grinning. Flustered, Emmaline opened her mouth to speak but didn't say anything. "Anyway, Meera is a good friend if you're looking for one," Linus said, changing the subject to spare her.

"She got my father killed!" the lady replied indignantly.

Linus shrugged. "She lost me my hand, and I'm still friends with her."

"Sounds like she makes a lot of poor decisions," Emmaline remarked dismissively, not asking him what he meant.

"At least she ... makes her own decisions," Linus said absently. Meera wasn't perfect, but she tried, at least. Most of the people he knew didn't even try.

"What do you mean?" Emmaline asked.

He sighed, exasperated with himself for sharing so much. "I mean, at least Meera acts on her beliefs—she tries to be a good person," he explained.

"Do you act on your beliefs?" she asked.

How had this become about him? "I don't have beliefs," he replied. "What about you?"

Emmaline twiddled one of the ruffles on the side of her dress. Then, very quietly, she said, "My parents always made me believe that real love existed. I hope to find that before I die."

Linus laughed but not unkindly. "I'm no expert, but you're not going to find love sitting in a room by yourself," he told her. Then he walked past her toward the door, unwilling to answer any more personal questions. He would rather find a bottle and a card game.

"But if I leave, I risk dying ..." Emmaline said, spinning toward him.

They were standing close together now, and Linus couldn't help but notice how fresh and clean the lady smelled compared to the rest of the ship. What kind of idiot had he been barging into her room and asking to sleep on her floor? He looked at her— really looked at her—and she seemed so small and scared. He wanted to say something reassuring, but in his experience, life sucked and kept sucking. Who was he to promise her she'd be okay?

Finally, he said, "Emma, we all die—most of us horribly. None of us know when it'll happen, so there's no point being afraid of death. Living is much harder and scarier—that's what you risk if you leave your room." And he left. He needed a drink after that speech.

11

MEERA

Meera awoke suddenly to a beam of light hitting her face. Disoriented, she blinked and jerked under a mound of heavy bedding. Kennick quickly moved next to her and blocked the sun from her eyes, shushing her. She calmed when she saw him, but she still couldn't piece together where she was or what she was doing there. "Wha—" she started to say, but her throat burned, raw and thirsty.

"Here," Kennick said, reaching over her to get a glass of water.

The sunbeam from the small circular window in their shared room immediately blinded Meera again, and she shifted and tried to sit up. She wondered briefly why she was in Kennick's bunk and where her clothes were, then she remembered; it all flooded back to her, and she wished she hadn't woken up—she wished she were still blissfully ignorant. She had lost control; she had completely lost control of her emotions and her shaping and had nearly incinerated the entire ship.

Kennick handed her water. She took it automatically, but then she grabbed his forearm, staring at his wrist. The base of his hand was raw and bloody all the way around. "It doesn't hurt," he said.

Meera drank her water so that she could speak, but when she put down her cup and turned to Kennick, she didn't know what to say. Gazing into his dark eyes, she brushed her fingertips along his angular cheek. He looked about as tired and sad as she felt, and she hated it. She wanted him to be grinning and laughing, eyes glinting at her. She hated that she caused him so much pain and sadness. She ruined everything. She wanted to tell him he'd be better-off without her, but then she thought of Shael—that was what he had said to her, and he had been wrong.

Instead of saying anything, Meera pressed her face into Kennick's shoulder and let her tears spill onto his skin. He held her tightly against him, and she felt his own tears trickle down the side of her face. "You have to let it all out, Meera. You cannot keep running from your feelings. I—I cannot lose you again," he said, his voice cracking. He put his hands on her face and pressed her away to look into her eyes. "You stopped breathing, Meera! You stopped breathing ..." he told her.

Meera felt like her heart stilled a moment, seeing the terror in his eyes. She hadn't realized it had been that close. All she could think was that her last words to him would have been *Let go.* "I—I had to jump," she said. "I would have killed everyone. They all would have burned like—" She broke off.

"Like the boys," Kennick finished for her. Meera shut her eyes and tried to pull her face from his hands, but he wouldn't let her. "You have to face it, Meera. You have to feel it."

She shook her head feebly, and her face crumpled. She couldn't do it; she was too tired, too hungry, too weak. She didn't think she could handle it, and she didn't want to break—to lose her mind. "I can't," she breathed.

"You can. Do it, Meera. Do it now while you are too weak to

shape. Let it all out. Tell me everything," he said.

She shook her head again, but then she told him—haltingly at first until it all poured out of her: she told him about the duke, about Linus getting burned, and about the boys she had killed. She told him even though he already knew. She told him her worst thoughts about herself and her deepest fears. And when she finally cried for their baby, he cried with her. Then he told her over and over again that it wasn't her fault until she even started to believe him.

Meera let herself feel everything she had been holding back since leaving her dungeon cell, and afterward, she lay spent with a throbbing head and puffy eyes. She was exhausted and hungry, but she was not broken. She felt torn down, reduced to rubble, leveled out ... but ready to rebuild herself. Kennick held her against his naked body, stroking her face and neck. Pressing a kiss to her temple, he said, "I love you, Meera."

His love was like a balm to her soul. He had seen and heard the worst parts of her and still loved her. She was not alone in her grief or her obligations, and that knowledge gave her strength and hope. When would she finally learn to run toward Kennick and not away from him? Turning her face, she kissed his lips rather than answer, and when she did, their mental connection clicked into place. She smiled at the feel of Kennick's consciousness joined with hers, and his dark eyes smiled back at her.

Eventually, they fell asleep face-to-face, and when Meera awoke again, she couldn't ignore her hunger anymore. She kissed Kennick lightly before dragging herself out from under their mountain of blankets. The sun was still shining, but the sunbeam had moved substantially across the room, and someone had left them a covered tray of food on a small folding table. Pulling off the cover gratefully, she started eating bread and cheese.

"This is how I like you best—naked and eating," Kennick said from the bed.

Meera laughed and pulled the table over to where he could reach it, sitting down next to him. There was some sort of soup on the tray, and she tasted it and grimaced. "Doug and Freddy are sweet boys, but neither one of them has a promising future as a cook," she said, pushing the soup away.

"Do you think you will be able to go back to working in the kitchen?" Kennick asked.

Meera sighed; now that they had talked about everything, she knew that they had to keep talking about everything, but her instinct was still to deflect and distract herself. With considerable effort, she overcame that instinct. "The boys might be afraid of me now, but I think I could handle it. I haven't tried shaping, but I feel steady," she replied.

Her hair was slowly falling from its braid, and she reached up and pushed one of her short curls behind her ear. When she did, she felt the smushed remains of the pins that had been holding her braid tucked under. Trying to tug them out, she winced, and Kennick moved her hand and shaped the metal out of her braid, releasing her newly short hair from its confines. Meera still wasn't used to her impromptu haircut and patted at her head disconcertedly. Kennick pulled a springy little curl and grinned at her when it bounced back into place. She smiled in return, but then she realized if her hair pins had melted ...

Meera grabbed at her left hand, panicked. She released an exhale when she found her ring still on her finger. However, when she looked closer, she saw that it was deformed. Her raek fire may not have been hot enough to melt the platinum off entirely, but it had been hot enough to reshape it. "No!" she cried, showing Kennick.

He took her hand and kissed it. "I will fix it," he assured her.

She gave him a small smile, then she took inventory: her only set of clothes was gone, her boots were gone, and the bracelet Linus had given her was gone—every last bead lost at sea. She rubbed her wrist, feeling naked from the bracelet's absence, but she thought maybe it was for the best; the bracelet had reminded her of Linus but also of her mistakes, and she wanted to move forward and not linger so much in the past. "I suppose everyone on board has seen me naked," she said absently.

"Yes, but only I got to sleep next to you naked—finally," Kennick replied, pulling her toward him and kissing her.

Meera kissed him back briefly then leaned away. As long as they were talking, there was something else she needed to say. "Kennick, I really did want our baby," she prefaced self-consciously.

"I know you did," he said quietly, giving her a searching look.

"I did—but I'm not ready for the possibility of getting pregnant again," she told him, tensing in anticipation of his disappointment.

"I understand," he said. "Neither am I."

Meera felt a huge weight lift from her. She had been keeping Kennick at arm's length, fearing their true-mate fertility for no reason. He was in the same place that she was—they were united in wanting each other and not wanting another pregnancy yet. She exhaled and kissed him again. She could no longer remember why she had been so afraid to face Kennick after her miscarriage —after the boys. He made everything better. "I should have gone home to you right away," she said against his lips.

"But then I would have never gotten to meet Linus, and what a pleasure it has been," he replied. The humorous glint had returned to his eyes, and his pointy canine showed on his lower lip.

Meera laughed. She actually was glad that she had gotten to see Linus again, but she didn't say so. She kissed Kennick's pointy tooth and pushed him down on the bed. They proceeded to kiss and touch one another with a lot of fumbling and laughing because the lower bunk was hardly big enough for Kennick let alone both of them. But neither of them cared; their laughter helped to strengthen their bond and heal their wounds.

Eventually, Meera climbed from the bed and stared dolefully at their near-empty food tray. She was not going to eat the cold soup. "I need clothes," she said.

Kennick turned over and appraised her, his face telling her clearly that he didn't think so, and she rolled her eyes at him. "You can have mine," he offered.

She laughed. "Then what will you wear?" she asked.

"I can wear raek fire—oh wait, that's you," he replied, grinning.

"I should just walk around covered in raek fire? On a wooden ship? After my meltdown?" Meera asked skeptically. Now that she had rested and eaten, she could once more feel her flames lingering within her, ready to be called. They lay settled and dormant, however. Working through some of her emotions had helped to clear her energy channels, and her fire no longer pressed threateningly toward the surface of her skin.

Looking around the room, she spotted Shael's bag hanging off his top bunk. Since they'd been aboard the ship, he had been wearing his knell clothes again. Hoping the human clothes he'd bought were in the bag, Meera pulled it down to look in it. "Should you really rifle through Shael's things?" Kennick asked, watching her. He didn't seem in any hurry to get out of bed or find food. Sometimes Meera wondered if he even needed to eat. This incident, however, had proved his infallibility; she had never seen him so completely drained before.

"I don't think the three of us have any secrets at this point," she replied unconcernedly. With any luck, she would also find some of Shael's lip balm. She pulled out his human-style pants and shirt. They were simple men's clothes—brown trousers and a white, cotton tunic with sleeves—and she donned her new outfit, tucking the long shirt into the pants and holding the pants up so they wouldn't fall down. "How do I look?" she asked Kennick.

"I like it. I can see your nipples," he replied with a grin.

Rolling her eyes at him again, she bent to fold up her pant legs, wondering whether Emmaline would have a breast wrap for her or if the stuffy lady only wore corsets. Meera would rather let her nipples show than wear a corset. Then she supposed she would have to go barefoot and didn't relish the idea on the splintery wooden ship. "Can you make me a belt?" she asked Kennick.

"You can shape metal, you know," he said teasingly, finally dragging himself out of bed.

"Not nearly as well as you can," she replied, fingering her ring, which was still smushed.

Kennick noticed the gesture and held out his hand for it. He proceeded to fix her ring and make her a chain link belt to hold up her pants with some of his spare metal. Then he got dressed, and Meera noticed that he put his ankle cuffs on and his metal belt. She felt a pang of guilt knowing it was because of her and what she'd put him through. When he straightened up, she grabbed his injured hand and kissed it. "Thank you," she said— for saving her, for loving her, for helping her through her issues.

Together, they left the cabin to find food. Kennick offered to carry her to spare her feet, but while Meera was tempted by the idea, she didn't want to be dramatic. Walking to where they normally ate with the captain and the rest of their group—since it seemed to be about dinnertime—they found them already seated and eating what looked like cheese and pickle sandwiches. Meera laughed at the sight; she knew Doug and Freddy were doing their best.

She and Kennick sat down in the empty chairs next to Shael, and to Meera's surprise, Emmaline was sitting across from her next to Linus, looking sheepish. "How are you feeling?" she asked Meera politely.

"Much better, thank you," Meera replied. She caught Emmaline glance down at her outfit, but the lady didn't comment on her strange attire or visible nipples. She also had the decency not to pester Meera about what had happened the day before.

"I see you went through my bag," Shael said, eyeing her.

Meera shrugged. "They look better on me anyway," she said, smiling. She was in a good mood; she felt light and free and new.

Shael seemed to sense it. Leaning toward her, he whispered, "I would offer you my spare socks, but I would not want you to carry on and blubber about how you never brought me any."

Meera laughed heartily and proceeded to eat her cheese and pickle sandwich and challenge everyone in the room to various contests in order to win their boots from them. She didn't actually want to take anyone's shoes and doubted they would fit anyway, but she had fun proposing increasingly ridiculous contests until everyone joined in, making their own suggestions for the best challenges. Somehow, the conversation resulted in Captain Mel and Linus arguing and arm wrestling. Everyone laughed when the burly old captain beat Linus in a matter of seconds, and Linus glowered, looking rather embarrassed.

The next day, Meera went back to working in the galley. Doug and Freddy welcomed her with relief and resumed her education in ship's songs. Meera continued to wear Shael's spare clothes and wrapped some cloth around her feet to protect them from splinters. She also borrowed a breast wrap from Emmaline and used her raek fire when necessary to keep herself warm. She felt in control of her shaping again, and the rest of their days on the ship passed relatively uneventfully.

12

SHAEL

S hael kept a close eye on Meera after her incident, but she seemed to be doing better. He, however, was not doing quite so well. Being aboard the ship had intrigued and entertained him for a time, but now their journey was beginning to wear on him; he missed Cerun and felt lost without their constant connection, and he missed being able to run and train. Tugging ropes and pacing the length of the deck was not enough exertion for him, and it was all he could do some days not to pull a Meera and dive overboard for an impromptu swim.

Shael knew he was not the only antsy person aboard the ship, and he knew they would get to land as soon as they could. Meera shaped wind into the sails almost constantly, and they had not seen Terratellen ships in so long that he thought they must be getting close. Captain Mel seemed to be the only person who was not in a rush to reach their destination. He grew jollier and jollier the longer they were at sea and the further they roamed from Terratelle. He had even gone so far as to trim his unruly beard, and Shael began to feel anxious that the captain would never return them to Harringbay. He did not mention his anxiety to anyone, however; they still had to reach Kallanthea before they could worry about returning to Terratelle.

Strangely, despite the time of year, the weather was getting warmer rather than cooler as they sailed. Shael wondered whether Kallanthea might be hot like Cesor, and he dreaded staying any amount of time in a desert-like climate. He wanted to run in a forest, not on sand. Even so, the warm air felt good, and he was standing on deck enjoying the sun beating down on him and the gentle breeze when Captain Mel finally shouted, "Land Ahoy!"

Shael jumped and ran to the front of the ship with everyone else to squint into the distance. Mel was grinning and peering through his spyglass. Shael could not see anything yet, but when Kennick appeared next to him, his friend nodded in affirmation of the captain's claim. "It will not be long now," he assured Shael, patting him affectionately on the back.

Shael sidled out of his reach. He knew Kennick meant well and was glad his friend had been so happy lately, but he and Meera had been a little insufferable since her meltdown. Shael was sick to death of sharing a room with them and could use a little more space in general. He stared and stared into the distance until he, too, could see land. Then he stood and watched the shore grow closer and ships materialize in the distance. As relieved as he was to see their destination, he was also nervous; they had no idea what to expect from this land or whatever magic its people might possess.

He was clearly not the only nervous one; the whole crew started acting jumpy and clumsy. Captain Mel's previous good mood quickly soured as he had to continually correct small mistakes and order messes cleaned up. Shael would normally help, but he just stayed out of the way; the deck was more crowded than usual with everyone anticipating their arrival, so he climbed into one of the lookout towers to keep an eye out for trouble.

Eventually, ships descended upon the *Lady Emmaline*. Meera stood on deck, but she did not reroute the ships or otherwise hold them at bay. They were not warships; they looked more like trawlers for fishing. When the Kallanthean vessels neared, their inhabitants waved and smiled in universal gestures of friendly welcome. Some of the tension in Shael's muscles released at the sight, and the *Lady Emmaline's* crew all waved back and cheered in excitement.

The fishing ships led them to a port to dock, and when Shael filed off the ship with everyone else, many of the Kallantheans slapped his back and welcomed him along with the ship's human crew. They did not seem to think his knell clothes were any stranger than the Terratellen's attire, nor did they appear to see anything in his face that they found suspicious. The Kallantheans spoke the common tongue, though with a different inflection. Their skin varied greatly, but many of them had curly hair, and they all wore colorful clothing. Kallanthea was hot, but it was not a desert—the air was humid, and there were large fruit-bearing trees everywhere and white, sandy beaches.

Shael stayed close to Kennick, who followed Meera, who stood protectively next to Lady Emmaline. Linus already appeared to have made some native friends and was drinking and laughing with a group of them off to the side. Shael shook his head at the sight and wondered if they could maybe just leave Linus there when they departed. Their group was quickly herded into what seemed to be a town center. Kallantheans watched them pass with shocked expressions—their subsequent wide smiles flashing in the sunlight.

Shael wondered at the Kallanthean's clothes; they all wore the same type of skirt, and he could not distinguish between men's and women's attire. For that matter, he could hardly distinguish between men and women at all—the Kallantheans were a well-fed people with full, indistinct figures under loose clothing, and their hair was worn in all manner of styles. Their genders were unclear, but their joy and enthusiasm were pervasive. Shael found himself smiling in return to their looks and waving at the small children that followed them through the brightly-colored town.

After being led to a large white building with columns, they were beckoned inside. It was a relief to step out of the sun, and the enormous hallway they entered had spinning fans on the ceilings to cool them. Shael wiped his sweaty brow and looked around in curiosity. All of the doors were open to the outside air, so he did not feel enclosed or have any reason to suspect a trap. He turned his attention to the walls, which were painted with large, intricate murals. He was staring at one of the paintings, silently waiting for something to happen with the rest of the crew, when a person hurried out of a far door and positively beamed at the sight of them.

"Visitors!" they exclaimed. "In my lifetime! Visitors! Can't believe it!" They were grinning broadly and straightening their clothes as they approached. Like the other people Shael had seen, they wore a loose, tunic-style shirt over a wrapped skirt. Their outfit was bright orange, their skin was pale, and their sandy hair was short and stuck out in springy little curls. "Welcome! Welcome, visitors!" they cried. "Name is Adari. Am in charge of foreign relations. Welcome to Kallanthea, land of love!"

Shael gaped at Adari, and Meera chuckled next to him. "Thank you, Adari," she responded. She and their little group stood with the captain, and his crew stood behind them, looking curious and a little frightened.

"You are?" Adari asked. Meera proceeded to introduce

everyone in their group and gestured to the ship's crew behind them at large. "Welcome all!" Adari cried. "Welcome you," they added, gazing directly at Shael with unmistakable attraction that made Shael flush.

Meera stifled a laugh and nudged Shael with her elbow when he did not immediately respond. "Uh—thank you," he said awkwardly.

Adari continued to make eyes at Shael for a second, then they gestured to a room where refreshments were being laid out and suggested the crew sit and relax. The rest of them, Adari invited for a tour. Captain Mel decided to go with his crew, leaving Shael, Kennick, Meera, Linus, and Lady Emmaline to follow their guide. Adari did not actually take them far, leading their group to the end of the hall before gesturing at a mural on the wall. Shael stared at the mural which depicted a man and woman on a raek together. "Know the story of Kallanthea?" Adari asked.

"Kallan, the rider, rescued Queen Thea of Terratelle from pirates, didn't he?" Meera asked.

Adari laughed, and their belly jiggled with their mirth. "No!" they cried. "Kallan and Queen Thea loved each other. They ran away to be together but had nowhere to go! Our people were always here on this island, but not one people—many different groups of people from different places. Some of us welcomed them to the land. They came and made their home here. We were inspired by their love, and the groups met and decided to join together. We call our land Kallanthea in their honor."

"Were they like—the king and queen?" Meera asked.

Adari laughed again. "No! They were visitors! We have our own way of life in Kallanthea."

Shael thought that certainly seemed to be the case, but he did not say so. "It seems like a great place!" Meera said enthusiastically. "Emmaline and I have ancestors from Kallanthea," she added, smiling at their guide.

"Oh! That what brings you to our land?" Adari asked. "Visitors never come! Sent out ships to Terratelle a little over seventy years ago, and ships were attacked. Keep to ourselves since then, but good to have friendly visitors!"

"Really?" Meera asked. "That's when Terratelle started the war with Aegorn ..." Shael suddenly wondered what she seemed to be wondering—whether the events were related. From what he knew of Terratelle, he would not be surprised if the ruler at the time had felt threatened by the unknown and had lashed out at their closest, magical neighbor for no good reason.

"War?" Adari asked. "How terrible! Don't have war in Kallanthea. Kallanthea is a land of love." They nodded their head so seriously that Shael had to respect Kallanthea's commitment to their ideology. "You flee the war?" they asked.

"We came in search of magical healing," Lady Emmaline replied, stepping forward hopefully. "My grandfather believed there were healers on Kallanthea who might be able to help me."

"Healers? Yes, we have healers—some with magic," Adari said, smiling at her. Lady Emmaline looked excited, and Shael hoped she would get the help she needed.

"Do you have raeken here?" Meera asked. Shael started at that; he had not considered that Kallanthea might have raeken and riders, though he supposed Kallan's raek had resided here, so they might.

"Yes! Raeken we have," Adari cried enthusiastically, then they turned and ushered the group to follow. They followed their guide around the corner and into a little garden courtyard. Adari whistled, and a bright orange blur fell from a tree, landing at their feet. Shael gaped; it was a raek, only very small—dog-sized. Adari fed the creature something from a pouch and patted its head affectionately. "Orange is my favorite color," they announced unnecessarily.

Shael stored a mental picture of the tiny raek to show Cerun when he returned. Meera crouched down to look at the creature and laughed. "It's so small! My raek could eat your raek in one bite!" she exclaimed.

Adari laughed again, causing their stomach to jiggle. "Yes, raeken here are much changed since Kallan came. We keep them as pets—they eat the vermin," they explained.

"I could get on board with these," Linus said, reaching his hand out tentatively to pet the friendly little raek. Shael thought that was a brave thing to do considering he only had one hand left —the raek's little teeth looked extremely sharp—but the creature merely rubbed its scaly head against Linus's palm and snuffed his pants for food.

"Adari, how long do people in Kallanthea live?" Kennick asked, speaking up for the first time. Shael was also curious to know the answer if some of Kallanthea's inhabitants had magic.

"Some live a long, long time—some don't," Adari answered. "All mixed with old magic here—some a little, some a lot. In Kallanthea, don't count age by years, and don't name genders. All are equal in love!" they exclaimed, throwing out their arms.

Shael stared at Adari and swallowed. Kallantheans were all different mixtures of knell and human, and they were all equal. They did not even account for gender in any way. After living with the shame of being a half-breed and having had a physical relationship with a man, Shael felt as if he had stumbled into a dream world. He sensed Kennick's attention on him, but he could not meet his friend's eyes in that moment; he was processing and a little overcome. A place actually existed where no one would care what he was or who he might love. When Adari caught Shael's eye and grinned at him, Shael smiled tentatively back.

"Ah!" Adari said, gesturing to someone who had just entered the garden, "This person is Inglesha. Inglesha will show you to your rooms if you would like to stay on the island. They will get you whatever you need and answer all of your questions." Inglesha looked to Shael like a short, large-breasted woman, but he supposed while on Kallanthea, he would have to try to dispel his notions of gender.

The others began to follow Inglesha inside, but Shael hesitated and turned back to Adari. He liked their easy laugh and obvious enthusiasm. "Adari, will you show me the town?" he asked. He was curious to see what life was like when age and gender did not matter.

Adari smiled broadly at him and took his hand. "Come! Show you everything!" they said. Shael did not know what to make of the hand-holding, but he allowed it. Then he wondered what wearing a skirt might feel like and thought that in the heat and humidity of Kallanthea, it might actually be pleasant. Glancing back at his friends fleetingly as he walked away, he caught Meera grinning at him. He quickly averted his eyes but not before he saw her attempt what he thought was meant to be a wink.

13

MEERA

"That was the worst wink I have ever seen," Kennick whispered in Meera's ear as they followed their new guide back into the building.

Meera grinned; it was all she seemed to be able to do since they had reached this enchanting place. So far, she loved everything about Kallanthea: the people were so happy and friendly, the raeken were adorable, and the weather was warm and breezy. She couldn't wait to try the food; judging from the people's figures, it was probably pretty good. Even though she knew they were there for a reason, Meera felt like she was on a vacation for the first time since she was a girl at the beach. She felt relaxed and happy and let herself sink into those feelings.

"Just one room for us," Kennick told Inglesha, taking Meera's hand.

Meera removed her hand from his and wrapped her arm around his waist instead. Why not? Shael was on a date, and they were in the land of love, after all. Kennick squeezed her to him, and Inglesha smiled at them. Linus and Emmaline both looked vaguely uncomfortable and out of place trailing behind their guide, but neither of them complained. Inglesha showed them each to their rooms and explained that a party would be thrown in their honor that evening. Mention of a party seemed to perk Linus up, but Emmaline looked troubled.

Meera sighed; all she wanted to do was go into town, buy new clothes, and spend the day lounging on the beach with Kennick, but she supposed she was there for Emmaline and had a job to do. "Where can we go to see a healer?" she asked Inglesha.

Inglesha offered to have a healer brought to them, and Meera agreed, saying they would be in Emmaline's room. Emmaline looked both relieved and excited, and Meera smiled at her before giving Kennick an apologetic look. He shrugged his shoulders loosely, the picture of confidence like he already owned a large portion of the island. Then he shocked her, saying, "Linus, I think I owe you a drink."

Linus looked about as shocked as Meera felt, but he didn't object. Meera grinned at the sight of them walking down the hallway together before turning toward Emmaline's door to wait in her room. The waiting was tense and awkward, and she lingered by the window, wishing she was outside enjoying the weather. She wasn't opposed to being friends with the lady, but Emmaline never seemed to have anything to say to her. Meera couldn't think of anything to say either, so they waited in silence.

Finally, a knock sounded at the door, and Emmaline sprung from her bed and answered it. The person who entered was very short and relatively thin with either deeply tanned or naturally brown skin. They were old but spry and introduced themselves as Ashiri. "Problem?" Ashiri asked simply. Meera had noticed that the people of Kallanthea often seemed to cut out any unnecessary words—they certainly didn't use titles or many pleasantries. And yet, every interaction felt polite and congenial. It was like they expressed more with their smiles and their body language than people in Terratelle and Aegorn did.

Meera did her best to smile in return and waited while Emmaline explained her trouble with her lungs and how every small illness threatened to overburden them and kill her. Meera still didn't understand what magic was like in Kallanthea, and she watched Ashiri attentively while they examined Emmaline and listened to her lungs. Eventually, Ashiri sat down on the bed next to Emmaline and took her hand. Meera saw the lady flinch at the gesture. She didn't pull away, but the hope in her eyes faded. "Your illness can only be lived with, not cured," Ashiri said with certainty.

"Don't—don't you have magic?" Emmaline asked in a small voice. Meera could see the unshed tears in the young woman's eyes and felt her own stomach dropping in disappointment. Had the whole journey been for nothing?

"Have magic," Ashiri said, nodding. "Magic in Kallanthea is like love—you know it is there even if you cannot see it or measure it. Is a knowing—intuition. I sense your illness and know I cannot do anything for it."

Emmaline ripped her hand away from the healer and looked down at her lap. Meera nodded her thanks to Ashiri on their way out, but then, on a whim, she followed the healer into the hall. "Ashiri, do you have something I could take to prevent pregnancy?" she asked. She didn't know what Kallantheans thought of contraceptives, but it was the land of love ...

Ashiri laughed. "Naturally! Have sent to your room," they said and proceeded down the hallway.

Meera wanted to follow them and go into town to find Kennick, but she wouldn't leave Emmaline alone with her disappointment. She went back into the room and found the lady standing at the window, staring out of it. "Are you okay?" she asked. It was a stupid question—one that no one liked to be asked or to answer—but she didn't know what else to say.

"'Live with it' she had said, not 'die from it' like the healers in Terratelle," Emmaline mused absently.

Meera thought to correct her use of pronouns, but she didn't. "I'm sorry they couldn't help you," she replied lamely.

"I'm going to go to the party tonight!" Emmaline announced, determination in her voice. "I've never been to a party."

"Good!" Meera said. "I've never been to a Kallanthean party ... I'm going to go get something to wear. Do you want to come?"

"You're going to wear their clothes?" Emmaline asked, turning to her and looking repulsed.

Meera shrugged. "I like them, and anything is better than this," she said, fingering her grubby men's shirt.

"No, thank you. I'll wear my own clothes," Emmaline said.

"Okay ... Do you want to come along into town?" Meera asked.

"I don't think so. I should ... rest before the party," she replied.

Meera nodded and slowly backed toward the door. She wanted to be there for Emmaline but thought maybe the young woman wanted to grieve on her own. "I'll see you later," she said uncertainly. She hoped Emmaline really would go to the party; she hoped she would make the best of their trip even if she couldn't be magically healed. Emmaline turned away from her, so Meera left, hesitating on the other side of the door before walking away.

———

MEERA FOUND new clothes in town. She had money to pay for them—Aegornean money, anyway—but the friendly shopkeepers kept insisting she take things as gifts. She didn't want to be rude, so she took them and thanked everyone profusely, smiling everywhere she went. She supposed Kallantheans must generally have everything they need; they were all so well-fed and generous. Meera took two outfits, a green-blue one, and a pale pink one. They were bright and gaudy, and she loved them. She also got an outfit for Kennick to wear to the party and some sandals for them both. She wondered if she could find boots and pants anywhere before they left but didn't think it seemed likely.

Then, inadvertently, she found Linus and Kennick. They were at what looked like an outdoor tavern near the beach and were being continually plied with food and drink by the locals. Meera laughed to see Kennick eating so much and wondered if he was being polite or if the food was really that good. Linus looked positively giddy, and she could only hope he wouldn't drink too much. For a moment, she stood back and watched, enjoying seeing two people she loved talking and laughing together, but then Kennick caught sight of her and waved her over.

"You look like you belong here," he said, eyeing the new green-blue outfit she had already put on.

"I feel like I belong here, but there's one last test," Meera said.

"What's that?" Linus asked, so Meera reached over and took the fork from his hand, transferring the food on it into her mouth.

The tender meat on the fork was so sweet and delicious, she practically groaned. "I love Kallanthea!" she shouted loudly, and the Kallantheans pressing in around them all cheered. Meera had no sooner sat down than there was a heaping plate of food in front of her. She dug into her food and even drank some of the fruit juice and alcohol mixture Kennick was drinking.

"How did it go with the healer?" Linus asked, drawing Meera's focus from her food and sobering her good mood.

"Not well," she replied. "They couldn't help Emmaline."

Linus put down his fork and looked uncharacteristically serious. "How did she take it?" he asked. Meera studied him in surprise. Did he care for Emmaline? When did that happen? Meera had hardly seen the lady on the ship until the end of the journey. She supposed she had often sat next to Linus at meals ...

"She wasn't a fiery mess or anything like that," Meera replied self-deprecatingly. "I couldn't really tell how she was feeling. She said something about living with her illness instead of dying from it and didn't want to go into town with me."

Linus stood suddenly and mumbled about forgetting something in his room before walking away. Meera gaped after him; had he really just left an unfinished drink behind to check on Emmaline? She couldn't believe what she was seeing. Kennick clearly hadn't missed the exchange, either. "When did that happen?" he asked.

"No idea," she replied, "But we're on the land of love!" Smiling, she continued to enjoy her food. Kennick was slowing next to her and looked like he might be sick or fall asleep on his plate. "You don't have to eat it all!" she told him, laughing and wiping sauce from his cheek.

"I don't wish to be rude," he groaned.

Meera had a feeling the Kallantheans were an easy-going people who would be hard to offend. Standing, she tugged Kennick to his feet. "The food was amazing!" she called, smiling broadly at everyone. "Best food ever!"

The crowd around them cheered again, and she led Kennick through them toward the beach for a walk. After they traipsed across the sand for a long while, they stopped and reclined for a rest in the sun. Meera enjoyed the airiness of her new clothes and the warm breeze coming off the ocean. She didn't even shape it—it was perfect as is. "We'll have to come back here one day," she told Kennick.

"After we end the war, we can take a long vacation here," he replied.

Meera appreciated his confidence but didn't feel quite as certain of their success as he did. How exactly would they end the war that seemed to have started for absolutely no reason and waged for over seventy years regardless? "Do you think Terratelle really just freaked out and started attacking Aegorn because some ships full of friendly Kallantheans attempted to land on their shores?" she asked.

"I think when people are afraid of something, their fear can supplant all reason," he replied.

Meera knew he was right, but it didn't help her understand how she was supposed to stop Terratelle from turning fear into violence. There was nothing she could do about the war from Kallanthea, however, so she tried to put it from her mind. Even if Kallanthea had an army, she wouldn't ask them to leave their peaceful home to fight and die for her cause; that would just add to the violence and death. Meera shut her eyes and cleared her mind, focusing on the breeze and Kennick's even breathing. Then she dozed off for a bit.

14

MEERA

That night, they all gathered in the hall and waited for Inglesha to show them to the party. Meera and Kennick both wore Kallanthean clothes, Linus was dressed in the same black outfit as always, and Emmaline was dressed like she was ready for a ball. She looked very pretty by Terratellen standards but very out of place. They all stood around rather awkwardly as they waited. "How do I look in a skirt?" Kennick asked, trying to break the uncomfortable silence.

Meera was about to tell him he looked strange without his hands in his pockets when Shael approached from behind him and caught her eye. "Not as good as Shael looks in a skirt!" she cried in surprise. Shael was also dressed in Kallanthean garb and appeared rather embarrassed by it.

The shocked look on Kennick's face before he turned to look made Meera choke in a laugh; she didn't want Shael to think she was laughing at him. "Look good!" Inglesha said, appraising Shael as they approached the group down the hall.

Shael blushed, and Meera couldn't hold in her laughter anymore; Kallanthea may have been a wasted trip for Emmaline, but it was doing wonders for her spirit. As they all followed Inglesha out of the building and around back to another courtyard, she nudged Shael and said, "The Kallantheans just love you, huh?"

He shrugged. "It is the land of love," he replied.

The Kallanthean motto coming out of Shael's mouth was too much for Meera, and she hung back until Kennick caught up to her. "I bet you Shael dances at the party," she said to him in a low voice.

He smirked, making his pointy tooth show. "What are the stakes?" he asked conspiratorially.

"If I win, the first thing we'll do when we get back to Levisade is egg your parent's house, and if you win, you can have me tonight in any place of your choosing," Meera whispered. Leaning in closer, she added, "I'm not wearing anything under this skirt."

Kennick grinned and whispered back, "Neither am I, but I suspect I could have you anywhere I want tonight regardless of whether Shael dances or not."

Meera shrugged and laughed. He was right. She was ready, too; she had taken the herbs the healer had sent for her. "Fine, what do you want if you win?" she asked.

"How about, we do both of those things, and if Shael dances, we feel gratified to see our friend happy," Kennick replied.

"You're no fun!" she told him, shoving his arm. Still, she grinned, feeling like she had already won a bet.

The party consisted of several long tables covered in heaping platters of food and a musical group. Several Kallantheans played instruments Meera had never seen before while a person with a beautiful, low voice sang. The fruit trees all around the tables were full of candles in glass containers, and the ambiance was relaxing and romantic. Inglesha had already told them they would be eating with the heads of the Kallanthean government. Meera hadn't fully understood how Kallanthea's government worked when Inglesha had explained it, but she had been shocked that they didn't have a king or queen and seemed to let the people as a whole make decisions.

As they approached their table, she smiled to see Adari clearly waiting for Shael, and she nudged Kennick when Shael greeted them with a hug. Then they all took their seats at the end of the table, and she and Kennick sat across from Emmaline and Linus. Emmaline looked distinctly uncomfortable, and Meera, as always, couldn't seem to lure her into conversation. Linus, on the other hand, appeared surprisingly sober and had even combed his hair which was loose on his shoulders. Meera watched the two of them and wondered what was going on there, but they both seemed to be resolutely ignoring one another.

Captain Mel and the rest of the crew arrived after them, looking well-rested and in good spirits. The captain appeared to have already met some of the present Kallantheans and greeted them warmly. Meera waved to Doug and Freddy, who waved back and grinned at her, clearly enjoying their adventure. When everyone was seated, several officials welcomed them to Kallanthea and gave speeches about love and peace. Then they were encouraged to eat and drink and enjoy themselves, and they did.

A lot of the food on the table was—unsurprisingly—fish, so Meera reached for a platter of shredded meat. "What kind of meat is this?" she asked Adari as she gripped the serving fork.

"Oh! Raek meat!" Adari replied. Meera dropped the fork in shock and gave them a look of obvious revulsion, but Adari merely laughed, their white teeth flashing in the dim light. "Don't have any predators here, so if we didn't eat them, they would overrun us," they explained. "Very well treated beforehand," they assured her.

Meera nodded at them, but she steered clear of all meat after that. She was a raek rider even if her raek was not currently speaking to her, and she would not eat raeken. Linus, however, had no such qualms. He loaded his plate with raek meat with a devilish gleam in his eyes. "When I meet your beast again, I'll tell him that I have tasted the flesh of his kind!" he told Shael excitedly.

"Do that, and you might lose more than your other hand," Shael replied.

Meera watched in disgust as Linus dug into the food on his plate. Between her large meal earlier and this conversation, she didn't have much appetite. She talked to Inglesha for a while, and when the music became livelier, she rose to start the dancing. Kennick was—to her amazement—still eating, so she looked around for someone else to dance with. One of the Kallanthean officials saw her and stood, smiling and offering her their hand. She took it and followed them to the center of the garden, curious to see how Kallantheans danced. Others immediately rose and joined them.

Meera's partner showed her some basic stomping and clapping movements, and she mimicked them, enjoying herself immensely. Eventually, most of the Kallantheans were dancing while the ship's crew sat in their seats, watching. Meera danced over to Freddy and Doug and took their hands, yanking them from their seats. Bashful at first, they eventually copied her movements with relative ease, and she shouted, "Your dancing is better than your cooking!" They both laughed, and some of the other crew joined in, Captain Mel at their helm.

After a couple of songs, Kennick stole Meera away from her boys and danced with her. Neither of them really knew what they were doing, but they were laughing and enjoying themselves. When dessert was brought out, however, Meera found her appetite again and wanted to sit and try everything. A lot of the dishes included coconut, which she had never had before but found that she really liked. She was polishing off some sort of coconut pudding when Adari rose from the table and offered Shael a hand. Meera held her breath, eyes widening in anticipation. Would he do it? She grabbed Kennick's hand and clutched it under the table, smacking their conjoined hands against his thigh in excitement.

He did it! Shael took Adari's hand and followed them to the other dancers. Meera smiled so wide as she watched them dance that her cheeks started to ache. Finally, she tore her eyes away to see if Kennick was watching and found him gazing at her instead. "This place is magic," she said to him.

He smiled at her, but she read the desire in his eyes and was immediately reminded of their earlier agreement. Oblivious to the party around them, Meera rose from her seat and sat on Kennick's lap to kiss him. As usual, his lips melted her insides. She would have kept kissing him right there except that she could feel Linus and Emmaline's eyes on her back and didn't want to scandalize either of them. "Let's go," she told Kennick.

"If I am going to stand up, I either need a minute, or I will need to use you as a shield," he replied.

Meera laughed; she could feel the reason why under her butt and supposed skirts didn't leave much to the imagination. Subtly, she shifted on his lap just to torture them both. "Use me," she told him. She wanted to get out of there.

Kennick stood, cradling her in his arms, and walked into the night with her. "Where are we going?" he asked.

"It was your choice, remember?" she said.

"Then we're not going far," he replied.

Meera kissed his neck and could feel his racing pulse under her lips. She didn't know where they were or where they were going, but she was ready to hike up her skirt anywhere. When they could barely hear the party anymore, she said, "Here is good." They were still in a garden or park of sorts.

"Here? Are you sure?" Kennick asked, sounding skeptical. There wasn't much in the way of coverage.

"We'll keep our skirts on," Meera said, laughing. She wondered vaguely if there was something in the Kallanthean water; she felt positively giddy.

Kennick put her down, and she walked to a nearby fountain with a relatively high stone rim. Sitting on the rim, she opened her legs in invitation, and Kennick followed and leaned over her, putting his hands on her thighs and his mouth to her ear. "You are going to get us kicked off of this island," he told her. Then he pushed her skirt up even higher and knelt between her legs, taking her in his mouth and teasing her with his tongue.

Meera gasped and put her hands in his hair, clutching him to her. He looked up at her, dark eyes glinting in the moonlight. When she was more than wet enough, he pulled away and lifted his own skirt in the shadow of the fountain wall, raising his eyebrows in question as to how she wanted to proceed. Meera looked down at his erection and grinned at him. Then she stood, turned around, and bent herself over the fountain. She had liked sitting in his lap earlier and wanted him from behind.

She had no sooner pulled up her skirt and bared herself to the world, than Kennick pressed slowly inside of her, relishing their reunion. When he was seated fully within her, he paused, giving her body a moment to stretch and expand for him. He pulled out just as slowly before reaching around her and pressing two fingers into her sensitive bead and simultaneously thrusting back into her, hard. Meera cried out rather loudly, then put a hand over her mouth and laughed, gripping the fountain with her other hand to keep herself steady.

Kennick chuckled low behind her, but when he started to move again, they were both lost in their own heavy breathing and sensation. He was hitting just the right spot, and Meera went over the edge quickly, gasping and pulsing. He paused, waiting for her to ride her pleasure, then he pulled out, sat on the fountain's edge, and pulled her onto his lap. Meera kissed him and grasped his still rock-hard shaft, guiding him back into her. She rose up and down, letting his hold on her hips guide her speed. When he was close, he moved his hands to grip her butt cheeks like she liked, making her climax again when he spilled into her.

For several long moments, they kissed and held one another, forgetting they were in a public place. Then Meera climbed off of Kennick, pulling her skirt down hastily and burning their refuse. Looking around surreptitiously to see if anyone had seen them, she laughed in relief, feeling a little embarrassed now that her lust was satiated. Kennick stood, straightened his own Kallanthean outfit and pulled her back into his arms. Meera was so happy, she felt like she could stand there forever.

"I want to see you dance again," he murmured, surprising her.

She looked up at him. "You want to go back to the party?" she asked.

He nodded and smiled, and they roamed back in the direction of the music and laughter to rejoin the party. When they got there, almost everyone was dancing, but Linus and Emmaline still sat at the long table. Meera thought maybe they should ask them to dance, but Linus gave her a look like he knew what she had just been doing and said, "I'm surprised you two came back—what did you duck into a bush or something?"

Meera suppressed a guilty smile and bit her lip, unsure of how to respond. "What else are gardens for?" Kennick asked smoothly before putting a hand on her back and directing her to the dancing.

15

LINUS

Linus instantly regretted teasing Meera because it made Emmaline stiffen uncomfortably next to him. They had already been sitting in relatively awkward silence for some time watching the party around them. Linus knew Emmaline was trying to have new experiences—trying to make the most of her life—but he could also tell she didn't know how to relax and enjoy a party. He wanted to help her, but he wasn't sure how to go about doing that ... So far, he had settled for not leaving her alone at the table.

Earlier that day, he had gone to her room to make sure she was okay after seeing the healer, but she hadn't opened the door or talked to him. She had merely called that she was resting and asked him to leave. Then, like now, he had loitered outside for a time, not wanting to leave her but not knowing what else to do. He needed to do something this time, he told himself—anything. Clearing his throat, he asked, "Do you want to dance?"

Emmaline looked startled and wrinkled her nose at the idea. Linus wasn't sure if it was at the thought of dancing in the

Kallanthean style or at the thought of dancing with him. "No," she replied simply.

Okay ... he thought, now what? "Do you want me to walk you back to your room?" he offered. She didn't seem to be enjoying herself.

Emmaline hesitated a moment, in which Linus wondered if he should just leave the lady alone. "Yes, alright," she said after a breath.

Standing, he pulled her chair out for her. Emmaline was wearing a very pretty dress in a soft blue color. She looked like she belonged at the palace in Altus rather than this strange foreign party. Linus offered her his right arm uncertainly, and she took it, clutching his nonexistent bicep with her dainty hand. Then he led her away from the noise of the party and back into the building. When it quieted, he said, "I'm sorry the healer couldn't help you."

She didn't look up at him. "I've seen many healers in my life, and none of them could help me," she replied tonelessly. She didn't seem to want to talk, so they walked in silence for a time.

Linus supposed if he had received bad news, he wouldn't want to talk either—he would be passed out drunk somewhere. "What do you usually do to make yourself feel better?" he asked, looking down at Emmaline's pretty, sullen face.

She did look at him, then, her thick eyebrows drawing together in confusion. "What do you mean?" she asked.

Linus shrugged. "When I feel lousy, I drink or play cards. What do you usually do when the healers disappoint you?"

"Nothing ..." Emmaline replied. "I don't do anything—I never do anything." There was a slight sheen in her eyes, but no tears fell.

"Do you cry?" he asked. Meera always cried. Linus wouldn't mind holding Emmaline while she had a good cry if it would help her feel better.

"No," she replied. "I never cry."

He nodded and compressed his lips briefly. "Well, is there something you want to do?" he persisted. He would do whatever she wanted, he realized—dance, drink, walk through the night. He had left a perfectly good party with extraordinarily good alcohol to walk a sad girl to her room. Was he besotted? He hoped not. Emmaline was a lady, after all, and he was ... a one-handed former general who drank too much. Linus tried to tell himself he just hoped to prey on a sad, pretty girl who was away from home, but he knew it wasn't true.

"I don't know how to do anything," Emmaline responded very quietly, and all too soon, they were standing at her door.

"Well, okay," Linus said. When she released his arm, he turned to face her. The tears that had been in her eyes were gone, and she stood straight with her chin lifted proudly. He thought to tell her how strong she was, but the words seemed to escape him. He really wanted to kiss her, but he didn't want to frighten or offend her.

"Goodnight," she said, turning her doorknob and pushing the door inward.

"Goodnight, Emma," Linus said, hoping she would correct him indignantly.

To his surprise, she didn't. She opened her mouth like she might, but she quickly shut it and smiled at him of all things before walking into her room and shutting the door behind her. Linus stood there a minute, kicking himself for not at least trying to kiss her, then he went to his own room. He could return to the party—he could drink—but he didn't feel the need. Emmaline smiling at him had raised his spirits, and he thought he might be able to fall asleep without any alcohol for once.

THE NEXT DAY, the ship's crew took a long time to rise from their comfortable beds and gather where the Kallantheans had been providing them their meals. Linus went looking for food and found Meera, Kennick, and Shael sitting with Captain Mel discussing next steps. "As much as I'd love to stay forever, this crew was told they'd be home before winter," the captain was saying.

Linus sat down with a plate of food and started eating. "I would also love to stay, but there's a war waiting for me across the sea," Meera said gloomily.

"Is Lady Emmaline ready to go?" Shael asked. He was still wearing his clothes from the night before, and Linus studied him, wondering if he had spent the night with the odd Kallanthean, Adari. Adari looked like a man to Linus, and he found the thought unsettling. Knell clearly did things their own way, but such things were taboo in Terratelle. Still, he had to admit that Shael looked more cheerful than he had on the ship.

"I don't know," Meera replied. "Linus, do you know if Emmaline is ready to leave?" she asked, yanking him from his thoughts.

"No. Why would I?" he asked defensively.

Meera shrugged and looked aside, and Linus regretted his tone. He had obviously been spending more time with Emmaline than everyone else, though that time hadn't gotten him anywhere with her. She had barely even talked to him. After he finished eating, he offered to ask the lady if she was ready to leave, and he grabbed her some food in case she hadn't eaten. When he reached her room, he hesitated, then knocked softly with his stump since his hand was full. Emmaline answered the door, fully dressed, with her hair perfectly done as always. "I brought you breakfast," Linus said.

"Oh. Thank you," she replied, taking the plate. Then she just stood there looking at him.

He cleared his throat awkwardly. "Can I come in? I ... need to talk to you about something," he said. He knew he could just ask her right there whether she was ready to sail home or not, but he really wanted to spend some time with her.

Emmaline looked uncertain, but she moved aside and let him in. She put the plate of food down and didn't touch it. Instead, she stood in the middle of the bright little room and gazed at Linus expectantly. "What is it?" she asked.

"Well, I—we were all wondering whether you had completed your business here and were ready to set sail ..." he said lamely.

"Oh. I guess so," she replied, looking down at the floor.

"You don't have any plans?" he asked.

"No," she said simply.

"Is there anything else you want to do while you're here?" he asked. He knew this was the land of her ancestors and thought she might want to see or do more before they left.

"No," she responded once more.

"Well, I'm sure we won't leave until morning, so you still have all day ... I mean, are you sure there's nothing you want to do?" Linus asked again, thinking he wouldn't mind walking through town with Emmaline or visiting the beach.

"Why do you keep asking me that?" she cried in a voice higher than usual, sounding exasperated. Then she quickly clutched her gloved hands in front of her dress and composed herself again. "No. There is nothing else I want to do here," she amended in a low, quiet voice.

Linus regarded her for a long moment. He had finally cracked her poised exterior a little bit and wondered whether he should leave her alone or pick at that crack. He was never one for being polite, however, so he asked her again: "What do you want to do, Emma?"

Emmaline turned abruptly and went to the window, gazing

out of it, so he couldn't see her face. "I want to live," she said quietly. "I want to really live and not just sit alone all day every day, but I don't know how! I want to laugh and dance and fall in love, but I can't seem to do any of it! I'm going to die. I'm going to die, and I've never even been kissed!" She broke off and put one of her gloved hands up to her face.

Linus stared at the back of her head and the sparkly clip placed into her perfectly neat little bun. This was his moment; the lady had just said she wanted to be kissed. His heart was suddenly beating double-time in his chest, and his palm was sweating. He knew how to kiss, he reassured himself—it had been a while, but he had kissed plenty of girls in his youth. He walked forward slowly, not wanting to alarm the lady. When he got close, she turned around and looked at him, once more composed—her eyes completely dry—and the sight of her serious face gave Linus pause. "Can I kiss you?" he asked stupidly.

Emmaline's eyes widened, and she nodded ever so slightly. "Yes," she breathed, swallowing visibly.

Linus licked his lips and bent forward hesitantly to bring them to hers, shutting his eyes. The lady didn't move; her lips were firm and compressed beneath his, and when he pulled away, she was staring at him like a startled deer. Linus smiled and scratched his head sheepishly. "You know, you could kiss me back—if you wanted to," he said.

Emmaline bit her lip. "Okay," she said.

Linus bent forward again and pressed his lips to hers, bringing his hand up to cup her face. Emmaline was slow to respond with pressure of her own, but when she did, he dared to slip the tip of his tongue between her lips. Her tongue flicked against his, and blood suddenly rushed to his groin. Dropping his hand from her face, he tucked his erection under the waist of his pants, hoping she wouldn't notice. When he returned his hand to her cheek, she reached out and gripped his neck, holding him to her.

The rasp of Linus's beard against Emmaline's smooth skin was a little disconcerting for him since he hadn't kissed anyone since he had grown his beard. He broke away and asked, "Is this okay? Is my beard uncomfortable for you?"

"It tickles a little, but it's okay," Emmaline replied, not stepping away from him.

Linus couldn't quite believe that the lady seemed to want to keep kissing him, but when he bent back down to her, she met him halfway and held him there, kissing him as fervently as he kissed her. Suddenly, there was a knock at the door, and it sprung open. Linus and Emmaline jumped apart, both breathing hard from what they'd been doing and from the shock of being interrupted.

Meera stood in the doorway, looking about as surprised as Linus felt. "Oh! Sorry, I—" she started to say, looking between Linus and Emmaline. Then in a slow, painfully awkward voice, she continued, "I just ... came to tell Emmaline about my first time sleeping with Kennick and, uh—how I accidentally got pregnant because I was not prepared. That—that's what I came to say. Okay ... see you later!" She backed out of the room and closed the door behind her.

Linus stared at the door for several seconds, feeling the blood drain from his groin and flush his face. Reluctantly, he looked at Emmaline and found her standing once more with her hands clasped, staring down at the floor. "I—I didn't think—" he started to say.

"Meera left her child to bring me here?" Emmaline asked.

"Oh—no. She lost the baby," Linus said. He was not pleased with Meera at the moment. Scratching his beard, he studied Emmaline, wondering how she was feeling about kissing him now that someone had seen. She had seemed to be enjoying herself before then ... When Linus couldn't decipher anything from her poised stance, he said, "You've been kissed. What did you think?"

"I liked it. Thank you," she replied stiffly.

Linus laughed. "I liked it too," he said. "I could ... keep kissing you. I could ... touch you—if you think you would like it." He gazed at the lady with his heart in his throat. She was acting like he'd done her a service, and if that was the case, he was happy to keep serving.

Emmaline looked vaguely startled, but she didn't immediately refuse him. Linus could see her heart beating rapidly above her neckline and wondered what she would look like naked—not for the first time. Then she glanced toward the door where Meera had been. "I'm a lady ..." she said uncertainly like she was trying to dissuade herself.

Could it be that she wanted to? Linus suddenly felt clammy all over and wondered if he should make his excuses and leave, but the possibility of kissing and touching Emmaline rooted him to the spot. "I promise, I won't get you pregnant or take your virtue," he rasped, his mouth drying up.

Emmaline stood very still, staring at him like she was inspecting his worth, so Linus stood just as still, his stump tucked into his side. He felt like his whole body quivered from the force of his thumping heart. "Okay," she said finally.

16

EMMALINE

Emmaline couldn't believe what she had just agreed to. Was she a whore? Then again, what *had* she just agreed to? She wished Meera hadn't burst in and interrupted their kissing. For once, she had been enjoying herself—she had forgotten her impending death and had just been living. Then again, considering what Meera had said, maybe it was for the best that she had burst in ... Would she have let herself get that carried away?

Emmaline was used to being a lady—she had always been a lady. And yet, until now, she had still felt like a girl. She was a woman, she reminded herself; she had lived to be a woman. She had a woman's body and a woman's desires, she thought. Then she cringed inwardly—she hadn't actually realized she'd had a woman's desires until Linus had kissed her. Now what? Rather than make a fool of herself, she remained very still and left whatever came next up to Linus, watching him to see what he would do.

He fidgeted with his hand a little, keeping his other arm

pinned to his side like she wouldn't notice it—like it didn't draw even more attention to his deformity. Emmaline didn't mind his stump, and she thought Linus had a handsome—if shaggy—face and kind eyes. After a moment, he turned and went to the door, bolting it. The action made her slightly nervous, but she thought it was probably a good idea, considering.

When he faced her again, she took a tentative step in his direction. Linus saw it and closed the distance between them, kissing her with even more enthusiasm than before. Emmaline matched his kiss and tugged off her gloves, reaching a tentative hand to touch his bearded jaw. Sliding that hand from his face down his neck to his chest, she could feel his heart thudding as rapidly as hers, and it brought her some comfort; she was not alone in her excitement and nerves—she was not alone in her room, for once.

For a long time, they kissed, and Linus kept his hand to himself. Then he reached up and lightly brushed his fingertips across her collarbones to the edge of her dress. Breaking their kiss, he asked, "Can I undress you?"

"Yes," Emmaline replied, hardly believing what she was saying. Her dress was laced up the back—something she had been struggling with since leaving her maids behind in Harringbay. She had been having considerable difficulty getting in and out of her dresses on her own, but she had been managing. It was one of the many things she had learned to do by herself on this trip.

Linus reached his hand behind her and tugged at her laces, but he frowned and couldn't seem to get them. "Here—" Emmaline said, twisting her arms to reach back.

"No. Let me," he insisted, stepping behind her. So far, it was the only thing he had insisted upon—everything else had been a polite question—so she let him. He fumbled with the silky ribbon for a moment, but it must have knotted because he couldn't get it.

Suddenly, Emmaline felt his warm breath between her shoulder blades as he bent to work the knot out with his teeth. Her flesh pebbled, and she felt a shiver run up her neck in response.

Once Linus had worked the knot free, he loosened her laces and pushed her sleeves from her shoulders, letting her dress drop to the floor. Emmaline stood in her corset and petticoat, breathing quickly and waiting for him to remove those. He didn't, though—not at first. Instead, he kissed the side of her neck from behind and ran his fingertips down her arm, making her shiver again. Her heart was beating so fast, she thought it might break out of her chest and fall on the floor. She wondered briefly whether her weak lungs could handle all of this, then she dismissed the thought—she didn't care.

Reaching back, she undid the laces of her corset, pulled it off, and let it drop to the floor. She felt Linus's breath on her back again, then his lips and beard as he trailed kisses down her spine. Emmaline trembled. She had rarely even been hugged, and now *this*? It was almost too much—the knowledge that someone else's mouth was on her body. Almost. Shutting her eyes, she let herself feel it—let herself live.

When Linus reached her petticoat, he tugged it down, and that, too, fell to the floor. Emmaline almost laughed; she was naked with a man! Then he rose and reached his hand around to her front, trailing it up her stomach and between her breasts to where her heart was hammering so loudly, she thought he must hear it. As he held her there and kissed her neck, she felt the unfamiliar wetness between her legs grow, and she tilted her head to the side, baring her neck to him.

His hand dropped to her right breast, and he kneaded it, making a low sound against her neck. He swiped his thumb across her nipple, and she gasped. Embarrassed, she quickly shut her mouth and straightened up, automatically regaining her composure. Linus pulled away and dropped his hand before walking around to face her. Emmaline tensed as his eyes roved down the length of her naked body. "You're beautiful," he told her, looking into her eyes and touching her face lightly. "Do you want me to stop?" he asked.

"No," she replied almost inaudibly.

Linus smiled, took her hand, and led her over to the bed. "Lay down," he told her gently. She did, propping her head on her pillow and lying in the middle of the made bed, but then she stared at him anxiously. "Try to relax," he said, sitting on the bed next to her.

Emmaline shut her eyes and took a deep, shuddering breath. A moment later, Linus's mouth was on hers and his hand was on her body, rubbing up and down her side and settling on her left breast. When he swiped her nipple again, she reached out her own hands to touch him and realized that she was completely naked, and he was still fully dressed. Opening her eyes, she tried to tug his shirt up, but he stilled her hands with his own. "You don't want to see that," he said.

She did, but if he wasn't comfortable taking off his shirt, she wouldn't press him. Instead, she let her hands fall to the bed and lay prone while he kissed and touched her body. He hovered over her, supporting his weight with his left arm, and as he kissed her neck, his hand traveled down through the springy curls of her mound and cupped her, fingering her wetness. He paused and made a choked sound against her neck.

"What?" she asked, eyes flying open and heart racing.

"God, Emma, you're so wet," he said thickly near her ear.

Emmaline thought to jump up and grab her clothes, but Linus was slipping one of his fingers inside her, his thumb pressing into her particularly sensitive bundle of nerves. Losing all sense of embarrassment, she drew in her feet, spread her legs wide, and arched her back to press into his hand. Kissing her, he inched further down her body and took one of her nipples in his mouth, flicking it with his tongue. She gasped and writhed. Linus removed his finger from her and added a second one to it, thrusting them into her. Then he removed them both and rubbed his fingers, slick with her wetness, rapidly over her sensitive bead.

Lifting his mouth from her breast, he watched her face as she gasped and trembled, throbbing with pleasure. She opened her eyes to find him gazing down at her, then suddenly, he pulled his hand from her and lurched off the bed. Startled, Emmaline pushed herself up and watched him, feeling vaguely loose and boneless. Linus snatched a small towel from beside her washbasin and plunged it down the front of his pants, turning away from her. Breathing hard, he then tucked the towel in his pocket and continued to face the other direction, rubbing his hand over his face.

Emmaline couldn't help but think where that hand had just been and looked away in embarrassment, grabbing her robe to pull over her nakedness. She suddenly felt foolish and confused, unsure of how she had ended up in this situation. And yet, she felt happy. A man had kissed and touched her! This would've never happened if she'd stayed at home, so the trip no longer felt like a complete waste of time.

"Linus?" she asked tentatively when he continued to face away from her. She didn't know much about men, but she understood that he had just taken his own pleasure. What she didn't understand was why he now seemed so uncomfortable. She was the one who had squirmed under him making all manner of noises and leaving her juices on his hand; she was the one who should be mortified, and yet, she felt vaguely gratified that he had clearly enjoyed touching her so much.

Linus turned around but couldn't seem to meet her eyes. The

used towel poked out of his pocket, and his one hand was clenched at his side. Emmaline wished now that she had insisted he remove his shirt—assured him that his scars didn't bother her. She also wished she had the nerve to go to him and kiss him, but a lifetime of remaining poised and keeping away from people prevented her. She raised her chin but couldn't seem to move her feet. He had never professed any feelings for her, after all. Linus had been a gentleman, but he had not proclaimed to care for her. Emmaline thought maybe he did, but she wasn't sure. "Are you okay?" she asked.

"Yes, I—I should go," he replied, still not looking at her. He didn't immediately move to leave, however.

"Oh," she said. "Okay." She wanted him to stay, but that seemed too forward a thing to say. She wondered if she should thank him or something.

Linus stepped forward and kissed her stiffly on the cheek before turning away, unbolting the door, and leaving. Emmaline was left staring after him, wondering what had just happened. She felt like she might laugh or cry, but she rarely did either. Instead, she cleaned herself thoroughly, dressed, and ate the cold food that Linus had brought her earlier. Then she donned her shoes and went to inform Meera that she was ready to leave Kallanthea. She hadn't gotten what she had wanted from the land —she had hoped for magical healing and some deep connection to her ancestral heritage and had found neither—but she would be leaving with something, even if she wasn't sure exactly what it was she and Linus had.

17

MEERA

Meera shut Emmaline's door behind her and returned to her and Kennick's room, grinning. "What is it?" Kennick asked when she entered.

"I may have just barged in on Linus and Emmaline kissing," she replied.

"And why does that make you so happy?" he asked, walking up to her and wrapping his arms around her waist.

"Because!" she exclaimed. "It's Linus! I want to see him happy."

"I still struggle to understand what it is you like about him," Kennick admitted with a smirk.

Meera shrugged. Linus had been her first real friend, and she would always love him. She wanted him to be happy, although she wondered whether falling in love with a terminally ill future duchess was really going to make him happy in the long run. She hadn't seen Emmaline sick, but she had seen the fear in the young woman's eyes and believed that she could fall sick and die at any time like she claimed. She wondered whether Soleille might be able to help her, but she doubted it; Soleille always said that hereditary illnesses and mental illnesses were almost impossible to shape away.

"So ... did you find out if we're leaving?" Kennick asked, interrupting her thoughts.

"No idea," Meera replied, and she plopped down on the bed, tired from their long night of dancing. With the warm breeze and sunshine coming in through the window, she felt like she could nap. Then she marveled at how far she had come from when she had first left the dungeon and couldn't stand to be still or left with her thoughts. Kallanthea had been exactly what she had needed, and now that she was refreshed, she felt ready to face her life again.

Kennick sat down with a book Adari had given him, and Meera shut her eyes and dozed until there was a knock on their door. She sat up, but Kennick got there before she could. Emmaline was standing at their door, looking small and uncomfortable. "Come in!" Meera called from the bed.

Emmaline stepped in past Kennick, shooting him a wary look. Meera met Kennick's eyes briefly, and he took her hint. "I am going to go find Shael," he announced before promptly leaving.

Emmaline took two more steps into the room. Meera gestured at the chair Kennick had vacated, but the lady ignored her and remained standing. "I came to tell you that I am ready to leave," she declared.

"Okay. I'll let Captain Mel know," Meera said. Lately she felt less like a raek rider and warrior and more like a trip coordinator, but she didn't entirely hate the change. She waited a moment, but Emmaline didn't say anything else. "Did you maybe want to talk about something?" Meera asked.

"No, that was all," Emmaline replied.

Meera sat up straighter and leaned toward her. "I'm sorry I

barged into your room earlier. I hope you know you can talk to me about these things if you want to," she said gently.

"No, that won't be necessary," Emmaline replied tersely, clasping her hands in front of her dress.

Meera sighed and leaned back, taking in the uptight young lady. She had been trying so hard to break through to Emmaline but just couldn't seem to do it. "I'm the only woman on this trip if you do need to talk to someone. I know I needed to talk to another woman about sex," she tried again.

At the word *sex*, Emmaline seemed to pull herself up even straighter and lift her chin higher in indignation. "I'm ready to depart when the crew is," she repeated, and she left the room.

Meera lay back on the bed and rubbed her eyes. She might need to give up on trying to connect with the lady. It didn't seem like it was going to happen. She wondered whether she should talk to Linus, but she had once offered him a sex talk in jest and figured that he knew where to find her if he had any questions. Besides, maybe a man should talk to him. Kennick walked back into the room at that moment. "Did you find Shael?" she asked.

"I did not even look for him," he admitted. "Are we leaving soon?"

Meera nodded. "Any chance you'll talk to Linus about sex for me?" she asked.

Kennick laughed. "What about? Meera, he's young, but he was a general in a war. I'm sure he has heard all there is to know," he replied.

"Really? Is that what men talk about when they hang around without women?" she asked.

He just gave her a mischievous smile and a shrug.

MEERA HAD to wander the whole town before she finally found Captain Mel inside a cheerful little tavern, eating and drinking with a group of Kallantheans. She almost missed him when she poked her head into the establishment, but his white beard stood out among the crowd and gave him away. He had traded his Terratellen clothes for a Kallanthean tunic and skirt and was entertaining his new friends with a story from his adventures when she sidled up to the table.

She heard Mel explain how an angry crab had once blown his hiding spot when he was running from authorities, and he had escaped by throwing the crab into the face of his pursuer. Meera laughed with everyone else at the story and waited patiently for the captain to notice her. Eventually, he took a long drink from his cup and met her eyes, rising from the table to speak to her. "I take it you spoke to Lady Emmaline," he said, following her into the street.

"She's ready to go when the crew is," Meera relayed.

Captain Mel scratched his newly trimmed beard and looked down at his sandaled feet, giving Meera a sinking feeling in her stomach. "I've been givin' it a lot of thought n' I've decided to stay here," he said, looking into her face. "My whole life I've been sailin' n' didn't know where I was tryin' to go, but I've found it! I've come home at last!" he added, gesturing around them and grinning.

Meera couldn't blame Mel for wanting to stay in Kallanthea, but still, who would captain the ship? She hadn't gotten the impression that any of the crew members were especially experienced, and Captain Mel didn't even have a second in command. "Okay ..." she replied. "Who do you suppose gets us back to Terratelle?"

"I was thinkin' your Shael could do it," Mel said.

"That was Shael's first time sailing!" Meera objected. She knew he had an interest in ships and navigation, but she wasn't sure that was enough to make him captain.

"He can do it!" Mel assured her. Then he slapped her unceremoniously on the back and said, "You take care of Lady Emmaline —get her home safe," before he turned and reentered the tavern without a backward glance.

Meera stared after him, open-mouthed. He was tasking her with getting the lady home safe when he was supposed to be their captain? Irritation rose within her but was quickly replaced by nerves because—captain or no captain—she did have to get everyone back to Terratelle. She supposed the next step was to talk to Shael, and she had no idea whatsoever how that conversation was going to go. He had been spending so much time with Adari, she almost wondered if they would be leaving without him too.

When Meera didn't find Shael in his room, she asked for directions to Adari's room and knocked on the door, feeling distinctly uncomfortable doing so. The last thing she wanted was interrupt another romantic tryst, but this conversation was important and couldn't wait. "Coming!" Adari called, and Meera heard two people laughing and some rustling, telling her she probably had interrupted something.

Stepping back from the door, she contemplated running away just before it swung open, and a robed Adari poked their head out and grinned at her, looking flushed. "Sorry, Adari," she said. "I'm looking for Shael. Is he here?"

"Of course!" Adari said, laughing. "Shael hasn't even been to his own room."

Meera laughed with them, knowing Shael was likely cowering with embarrassment somewhere behind Adari's substantial figure. "I need to talk to you, Shael!" she called. She would have apologized, but she and Shael tried not to apologize to one another anymore.

Shael materialized next to Adari dressed in his Kallanthean clothes and gave her a bashful look before stepping into the hall with her. "What is it?" he asked.

Meera wandered away from Adari's door before broaching the conversation, and Shael followed, giving her a look of mild annoyance. "Meera, I am kind of in the middle of something ..." he said unnecessarily, growing exasperated with her.

"I know—I know. Everyone seems to be today," she muttered. He didn't ask what she meant by that; he simply waited for her to spit out what she had to say, arms crossed in front of his chest. She took a deep breath. "Captain Mel isn't sailing back with us," she said, watching Shael's distracted face focus on her words and his eyes widen in alarm. "He says you should be the captain."

Shael choked out a laugh in disbelief. "What?" he asked, running a hand through his loose hair.

"Do you think you can captain the ship back to Terratelle?" Meera asked. If he couldn't, she didn't know what they would do.

"I ... guess," he replied, his eyes clouding with thought.

"You are going back with us, aren't you?" she asked anxiously. She didn't think she could handle saying goodbye to Shael. She liked seeing him with Adari and wanted him to be happy, but she also selfishly wanted to keep him with her.

Shael glanced back toward Adari's door but replied, "Of course, I'm going back."

Meera exhaled in relief. "I'm sorry you have to leave them," she said.

He shrugged. "I am glad to have known Adari, but Aegorn is my home," he assured her. "Most of my family is across the sea— the other riders, my parents, my godchildren, and Cerun. I guess if I have to navigate us back, then I will."

Meera smiled at him, understanding the implication that she was counted among his family. "You know, I was considering getting you a puppy, but you're doing so well, I might just keep it for myself," she told him.

Shael laughed. "Is there some reason we can't both have puppies?" he asked, apparently forgetting his rush to return to Adari. Meera noticed he wasn't trying so hard to repress his human way of speaking anymore. Kallanthea seemed to have been as good for Shael as it had been for her.

"That would be fun! They could play at the peninsula together, and you could train yours to ride Cerun," she said, hoping they would make it back to the Riders' Peninsula safely and still be welcome there when they did.

"And Shaya?" Shael asked, giving her a penetrating look.

"Isn't Adari waiting for you?" she asked in return, avoiding his question. Meera had no idea what would happen between her and Shaya. First, she would have to get back to Aegorn.

Shael hung his head uncomfortably before turning to return to his lover. "Don't forget to tell your crew we're leaving tomorrow, Captain!" she called after him. She could see his shoulders tense at her words and laughed, thinking Adari was going to have their work cut out for them getting Shael back in the mood. Then she went to look for Kennick. Everyone else seemed to be embracing their last day on Kallanthea, and she would too.

18

SHAEL

Shael barely slept after breaking the news to the astonished crew that he would be captaining their journey home. Many of the men had never even spoken to him and had spent the journey there giving him wary looks and making hand signs he didn't quite understand when he passed them, clearly uncomfortable with him being knell. Shael suspected the crew may have even refused to go except that the alternative was staying on Kallanthea for the rest of their lives. While the land of love was a tempting lure for many—himself included—they all had family waiting for them across the sea.

After a night of tossing in their bed, Shael lay staring at the ceiling next to a gently snoring Adari, waiting for the sun to rise. The crew was to gather and depart immediately after breakfast. Shael knew how to navigate, and he knew how the ship worked— he wasn't worried about that. What he didn't know was how to lead. He especially didn't know how to lead men who were inherently afraid of him. He had only just started to respect himself; how could he make others respect him?

Feeling like his thoughts were beginning to spiral unproductively, he rolled to admire his sleeping companion. He liked Adari for the way they never let anything bother them and moved boldly through life, embracing who they were. Shael felt like he'd been trying to absorb some of Adari's joy and confidence during their time together. He thought he had been at least minimally successful, but mostly, he had just enjoyed his time with the big, bold, beautiful person next to him.

Feeling grateful for Adari, Shael put a hand on their stomach and slid it under the covers to gently grasp their penis and wake them up the fun way. Adari stopped snoring and smiled with their eyes still shut. "Making the most of our last morning?" they asked.

"Giving you a Kallanthean goodbye," Shael replied, slipping the covers over his head and shimmying further down on the bed.

Adari laughed, making their whole body shake with mirth. "First thing in the morning, Shael—let a person pee first!" they cried, getting up from the bed and walking over to a chamber pot in the corner. Shael watched and waited, smiling. Adari was always happy and always straight-forward. "Still want to be on top?" they asked, returning to the bed.

Shael nodded. "Up for entrance?" he asked.

"Use the oil," Adari replied, grinning.

Shael grabbed the oil from the bedside table and kissed Adari deeply before ducking back down under the covers. By the time he got there, Adari was already fully aroused, and he licked up their length before taking them in his mouth. As he sucked, he doused one of his fingers in oil and gently prodded Adari's opening, slicking and stretching them. Adari moaned appreciatively—as loud in bed as they always were.

Shael was hard, but he wanted to take his time and make sure Adari enjoyed the penetration. When they were both ready, he coated himself in oil and brought his sensitive tip to Adari's opening, pressing in slowly. Then he thrust a steady rhythm, aiming upward toward Adari's pleasure spot while also taking their erection in his oily hand and rubbing it. Shael groaned, but his low noises were drowned out by Adari's ecstatic cries. Adari put his hands on Shael's head as they finished—they liked his straight hair and always insisted he wear it loose. Shael finished soon after and rested on top of Adari's soft form while they stroked his head.

SOMETIME LATER, clean and dressed in his knell clothes, Shael left Adari's room for the last time. They kissed and smiled at one another but didn't say anything; they had both always known their time together would be fleeting, though Shael hoped Adari's carefree spirit would stay with him for some time. Clenching his fists at his sides, he walked to breakfast to face his new crew. He was a captain now, he reminded himself, trying to stand taller.

With purpose, he strode to where Meera and Kennick sat eating with Linus and Lady Emmaline and ignored the stares of the human crew appraising him. He might have worn his human clothes to make them more comfortable, but Meera had never given them back to him. Still, he couldn't be mad at her; she had been in such a good mood since landing on the island. "Good morning, Captain Shael!" she called as he approached.

"Morning," he replied with half a smile.

Kennick nodded at him, but Linus and Lady Emmaline both stared fixedly at their food. Shael loaded his own plate, but he didn't have much appetite—even considering his exertions that morning and the night before. His stomach was all nerves. "Don't worry," Meera said, studying his face and leaning toward him, "If the crew acts up, I'll put them in line with a little raek fire."

Shael smiled for real, at that—he was glad Meera could joke

about her abilities after her meltdown. Then he noticed she was still wearing her Kallanthean clothes and sandals while everyone else was dressed for the return trip, and he wondered if he would ever see his human clothes again. He didn't ask; he had bigger things to worry about.

"He doesn't look like he's ready to be captain," Lady Emmaline remarked like Shael wasn't there. Linus chuckled but didn't add anything, and Shael glared at him; he had not warmed up to Meera's old friend.

Kennick clapped him on the shoulder and gave him a reassuring look.

"I trust Shael," Meera said rather loudly and dramatically. "He can do it!"

Shael resisted the urge to rest his face in his hands and instead focused on putting food mechanically into his mouth, chewing, and swallowing. He wished he could enjoy it; the food on Kallanthea was far better than the food on the ship. He didn't say so to Meera, however, knowing she did the best she could to feed the entire crew with what they had in the larder.

Not long after breakfast, they were all standing aboard the *Lady Emmaline*, and Shael was surveying his new crew while most of the town gathered on the dock to wave them off. He was a little sad to depart, but he was eager to sense Cerun in his mind again; he'd been feeling oddly vacant and disconnected without his raek. After waving briefly to those gathered on the dock, he turned his attention to his work. He shouted loudly so that the crew could hear him, but unlike the crew, Shael had half-knell hearing and caught most of their whispered remarks about him.

That first day, he tried his best to act like a leader and emulate Captain Mel, but it didn't seem to get him anywhere. So, in the coming days, Shael quieted down and often did the work himself to avoid the task of delegating altogether. To his surprise, when he stopped trying to earn the men's respect, he started to hear them praise him more and more—often commenting that they'd never had a captain who worked as hard as he did or yelled as little. He also found that they were more likely to obey the commands that he did give as well as apply themselves to tasks that needed to be done without being asked at all.

Shael felt extremely gratified by the progress he was making with the men until he caught on to his nickname: Captain Pretty. He tried to be courteous to his human crew and pretend he couldn't hear them when they referred to him as such, but Meera found the nickname extremely funny and often used it when no one else was around. Shael supposed it could be worse; the crew at least liked him even if they thought he was *prettier than the most lady-like Kallanthean with smoother cheeks than their wives and mothers back home.*

Shael found himself occasionally wishing he could grow a beard—something he hadn't wished since living with his parents in Sangea—but Linus's constant scratching dissuaded him from the notion. Besides, he needed to stop altering himself for the benefit of others; he would never be full-human or full-knell, and that was okay. For once in his life, he shrugged off what was being said about him. He thought Adari would be proud.

19

LINUS

Linus spent most of his time on the return journey thinking about Emmaline. Really, he alternated between picturing her perfect little purple nipples and reliving the humiliation of ejaculating into his pants and running away. At first, he had felt ashamed for losing control of himself in front of the lady, but now he mostly felt ashamed for leaving her room and never racking up the nerve to talk to her again. Because he hadn't—he hadn't managed to say anything to Emmaline since that day, not a single word.

While Linus stood or sat near her whenever possible, he couldn't seem to broach a conversation. He didn't drink with the crew on the off-chance that the lady approached him—but she didn't approach him. And as much as he wanted to, he didn't approach her either. Linus had enjoyed his time with Emmaline and liked her very much—too much, even—and he thought she had enjoyed herself with him too ... Still, neither of them made any attempt to repeat the experiment. Neither of them so much as attempted to be friendly acquaintances again.

After a while, Linus supposed Emmaline had gotten the experience she had wanted and didn't require anything else from him. She was a beautiful, high-born lady, after all, and he was a presumed-dead nobody. In his mind, he knew he should keep his distance from the lady and get used to not seeing her every day—he'd probably never see her again once they reached Harringbay. However, his body and heart acted of their own accord, gazing at Emmaline longingly and placing him near her whenever possible.

One day he was on deck, watching her look out over the far rail. She was clutching her jacket to herself, and he hoped she was warm enough—it was getting colder as they left Kallanthea's climate behind and sailed into Terratelle's late fall. Then Kennick surprised him, walking up beside him and saying his name: "Linus?"

Linus jumped and turned, vaguely embarrassed to be caught mooning over Emmaline—though he suspected his feelings were obvious to everyone aboard the ship by then. Kennick had the decency not to mention it. Linus liked that about Meera's pseudo-husband; he didn't pry or even speak to him unnecessarily. That was also why Linus raised his eyebrows at the man now, wondering what he wanted. "I had some free time, so I made something for you. I thought you might want to come to the room to look at it," Kennick said vaguely.

"Okay ..." Linus replied, pushing off from the side of the ship and walking hesitantly toward their—reluctantly—shared room. Kennick and Meera had at least been sleeping in their own bunks at night. Even so, Linus knocked on the door when he went in during the day, suspecting they used the room for more than sleeping when no one else was around.

When they reached the room, Kennick pulled something out from under his bottom bunk and handed it to Linus, a strangely hopeful glint in his dark eyes. Linus held out his hand automatically and gaped at what the other man put into it: it was a hand, a perfectly sculpted metal hand with hinged finger joints. For a long moment, he just stared at it uncomprehendingly, then he grinned. "Can you attach it to me?" he asked, too excited to act nonchalant.

"Let me see," Kennick said, and Linus pulled up the sleeves of his jacket and shirt, revealing his stump. The hand was attached to a metal tube. Right before his eyes, the metal tube became liquidy and moved out of his right hand, positioning itself seemingly of its own accord over his stump. Slowly, the metal tightened around his forearm. "Is that too tight?" Kennick asked.

Linus shook his head, a little overcome at the sight of his left arm ending in a hand—albeit a functionless metal one. The prosthetic hands he had been offered in Terratelle had always been clunky and ridiculous looking, drawing more attention to his deformity than his stump. This one was sleek and matched his right hand almost perfectly. Being made of metal made it even cooler looking than a regular hand. "Can you take it off and put it back on?" Kennick asked.

Linus pulled at the hand, reluctant to remove it. With some pressure, it slid free from his forearm, then he pushed it back on. It fit perfectly. "Thank you ..." he said, at a loss for the right words to express his gratitude. He continued to stare at his new hand, seemingly incapable of looking away from it.

In his peripheral vision, he saw Kennick shrug and put his hands in his pockets. "You had mentioned wanting a hook, but I thought this would be better."

"It is," Linus replied, eyes still fixed to his new hand. It was better than he ever could have imagined. He expected Kennick to move away, but the knell man lingered. Looking up at him, Linus wondered if he wanted to be thanked again or something.

Finally, Kennick said, "Meera wanted me to tell you that you can talk to me about sex if you want to ... and you can."

Linus gaped at the other man in horror. "No, thank you!" he replied, and he turned with his new hand and left the room, shaking his head about Meera. He was going to have to get back at her for that somehow.

Linus spent the rest of the day fiddling with his new hand and admiring it, and he walked to dinner with a new swagger and a smile on his face. He always ate in the small private dining room with Meera and her knell men because that was where Emmaline ate. Otherwise, he would've eaten with the crew. He hadn't been enjoying the awkward meals they'd been having lately, but he also couldn't resist the opportunity to sit next to Emmaline three times each day either. That evening, however, Linus was genuinely excited for dinner, and he walked in with his head held high and his new hand shining at his side.

"What do you think?" he asked Meera, sitting down across from her and forgetting to be mad about Kennick's comment earlier; he was in too good a mood.

"Looks great!" she replied, beaming at him.

"What is *that*?" Emmaline asked from his left. They were possibly the first words she had spoken to Linus since he had left her bedroom, and his heart immediately started beating out of control.

"Kennick made me a hand ..." he replied, holding it out for her to see and chancing a glance at her pretty face. Emmaline's nose wrinkled at his new metal hand, making his stomach drop. Swallowing, he averted his eyes.

"Why?' she asked.

"So that I don't look so lopsided and deformed," Linus replied defensively. He knew it wasn't as good as a real hand, but it was better than his disgusting stump.

"But it doesn't do anything," she protested, still glaring at the metal hand like it offended her.

The others at the table were listening to the exchange and looking distinctly uncomfortable. "I think it looks good, and Linus likes it, which is what really matters," Meera said pointedly to Emmaline like she was talking to an insensitive child. Her comment only embarrassed Linus more, and he suddenly wished he had eaten with the crew and not made such a show of his new hand.

"Yes ... but Linus looked fine without it. It doesn't do anything, so I don't see the point in him wearing it," Emmaline insisted.

Linus's eyes shot back up to her face. Her girlish lips were pressed together obstinately, and her thick eyebrows knitted in indignation. Linus gaped foolishly at her while she stared with intensity at his hand. Had she really thought he'd looked fine without it? Suddenly, he felt like his chest might burst open, and he completely forgot that he was there to eat dinner; he didn't even get a plate.

"He looked fine without it, but if it makes him happy, we should support him," Meera responded, sounding annoyed. Linus looked at her in bewilderment. Why were they fighting about this? What was happening?

"*Or*, maybe we should let him know that he doesn't need a useless metal hand to be happy," Emmaline replied tersely. Linus's gaze whipped back to her.

"Emmaline, why don't you just try to be nice?" Meera retorted, and Linus's mouth fell open.

"Nice?" Emmaline snapped. "How is making Linus think he isn't good enough without a prosthetic hand *nice*?"

Linus glanced back at Emmaline in confusion then looked to Kennick and Shael for assistance. Kennick gave him a loose shoulder shrug, and Shael stared at his plate, avoiding the conflict completely. "Stop, okay?" Linus said finally. "Not everyone likes my new hand, and that's fine." He tucked his metal hand under the table like he would have with his stump and reached for a plate, hoping the conversation was over.

An uncomfortable silence descended over the table for several tense moments as they all focused on the food on in front of them. Then Emmaline turned to Linus and said, "See? It's pointless. I've been holding your hand, and you didn't even know it."

Linus's eyes shot down to his lap, and he found that Emmaline really was holding his metal hand. He about dropped his fork in shock. What was she trying to prove? "Yeah ... but it's not like you would have held my stump," he mumbled. Even if he couldn't feel her hand on his metal one, the sight of them both in his lap brought him joy.

Emmaline raised his metal hand onto the table, pushed back his sleeve rather forcefully, and proceeded to yank his new prosthetic off of him. Linus had only worn it for a day, but the sight of his stunted forearm on the table made him feel oddly naked and exposed. Emmaline wrapped her small hand around his stump and held it. Linus stared at her perfect little hand around his scarred nub. His arm was desensitized from the burns he had received, but he could still feel it; he could feel the tender pressure of her fingers and glanced up to see that her face was not wrinkled in disgust.

Linus didn't know what to make of this new development. He didn't know what to make of it, and he didn't think he could handle it. He knew it was stupid to fall in love with a future duchess; he knew whatever was happening here would only hurt him. Suddenly, his chest clenched, and he stood and walked out of the room, tearing his arm free from Emmaline's grip and leaving his metal hand on the table. He strode to the crew's quarters, got roaring drunk, and stayed that way for most of the remaining journey.

20

EMMALINE

The return trip to Harringbay went relatively smoothly, overall, in that there weren't any major dramas or mishaps. Meera redirected any ship that approached them, and Shael seemed to know what he was doing as captain. Emmaline, however, was in agony the entire journey. She felt her doom approaching more than ever—except it was the fate of sitting alone in her room at home that hung over her more so than her impending death. Now that she had experienced a taste of living, she wasn't sure she could go back to her old existence—to long days sitting and reading and painting and resting by herself. Then again, she wasn't sure what else to do.

Emmaline wished Linus would speak to her again, but he didn't. After the incident in the dining room, she barely saw him at all. She was as patient as a person could be—she had spent eighteen years patiently sitting in her room, waiting for something to happen, after all—but as the shore of Harringbay came into view on the horizon, her patience ran out. Was that it? Was it all over? Was she about to go back to her old life and never leave her house again—never see Linus again?

In agitation, she paced the deck, unsure of what to do. She knew where she could find Linus, but she never went into the crew's quarters for fear of illness. She had been lucky on this trip to have avoided any serious sickness, and she wasn't about to risk her life on their very last day. Taking a deep breath, she stopped pacing and stood at the bow of the ship, gazing toward Harringbay. As the town grew nearer and nearer, she felt uncannily like she was staring toward her past, not her future.

Meera sauntered up next to her and leaned against the rail. "Are you ready to be home?" she asked. She was always trying to get Emmaline to talk to her.

Emmaline knew Meera was just trying to be nice and even wanted to talk to her sometimes, but she didn't know how. Linus seemed to be the only person capable of wearing down her defenses. "I'm sure it will be good to be home," she lied politely. It would be terrible to be home. Her mother would probably lock her in her room without even her dull maids for company. No one would ever hug her or touch her again—especially not like Linus had. Tears pricked her eyes, but she forced them back.

"Do you want me to still the wind?" Meera asked, studying her face.

"No, thank you," she replied. She had grown to like the wind; it was *something*, at least. It was nothingness and stillness that Emmaline feared now more than anything. Feeling Meera's eyes still on her, she turned to face the woman. Meera had large, kind eyes, and the more time Emmaline spent with her, the more she could see that Linus was right; she was a good person even if she had spied for the king. "Thank you, Meera," she said with some effort. "Thank you for taking me to Kallanthea."

"I'm sorry it wasn't everything you wanted it to be," she replied.

Emmaline turned away and faced the shore once more. Kallanthea hadn't been what she had been hoping for, but it had definitely been *something*. Eventually, Meera drifted away, and all too soon, they were docking. Emmaline had already packed, and one of the crew members retrieved her possessions from her room and unloaded her trunk from the ship. Dolefully, she crossed the gangplank herself and stood beside it, waiting patiently for whatever would happen next.

Meera stood near her with Kennick and Shael, and Emmaline appraised the little group; she'd gotten used to their strange appearances and didn't find them frightening or intimidating anymore. While she hadn't spoken much to the knell men, they had always been cordial and well-behaved. "You're all welcome to stay with me while you remain in Harringbay," she told them, surprising herself.

Meera looked surprised as well, but she smiled and said, "Thank you. I doubt we will stay long, but I would rather sleep in a bed than on the forest floor."

Emmaline nodded and looked down at the worn wood beneath her shoes. Slowly, all of the crewmembers departed the ship with their sparse belongings. Emmaline wasn't sure what she was going to do with her father's ship now that Captain Mel wasn't around to commandeer it. She supposed it would sit in warehouse storage much like herself—collecting dust and waiting for another adventure that would likely never happen.

Most of the crew nodded to her appreciatively on their way past; she had paid them well for their work. When two young boys exited the ship together, she watched Meera hug them and get teary-eyed over their goodbyes. Emmaline suppressed a smile as a few of the bolder crew members called, "Goodbye,

Captain Pretty!" on their way past Shael. But the knell man merely smiled and waved, not appearing too upset about the nickname.

Eventually, the trickle from the ship ended, and only their group was left standing on the dock. "Where is Linus?" Kennick asked. Emmaline had been wondering the same thing. Had he snuck past already? Had she missed her chance to see him one last time—to say goodbye to him? Her stomach flipped at the thought. She didn't want to say goodbye to Linus, but she wanted to say something to him—she wanted to see him again.

"I can sense him in our room," Meera replied with a far-off look on her face.

Emmaline stared at her for a moment, wondering if there was anything she couldn't do. Then she pulled herself up to her full height, announced, "I'll get him," and before she could change her mind, she walked back up the gangplank onboard the ship. It felt very strange being on the now-empty deck, but she didn't pause to marvel at the feeling; she walked briskly and purposely to the stairs and descended below deck. When she reached the room Linus had shared with his friends, she didn't stop to knock—she barged right in.

Linus was lying on his bottom bunk, seemingly unconcerned that the ship was empty, and they were waiting for him. Suddenly, Emmaline's confusion and exasperation with the man turned to anger and threatened to burst out of her. "You know, you're officially squatting on my property!" she said harshly.

Linus's eyes flew open, and he sat up quickly, nearly banging his head on the upper bunk. "Emma, what are you—" he started to say.

"What am I doing? What are *you* doing? We're all waiting for you on the dock!" she cried, cutting him off.

He stood and took a step toward her, appearing sober and serious. "I guess I—I just wasn't ready to say goodbye yet. I'm going to miss you," he said earnestly, gazing into her eyes.

Emmaline took a step back and spluttered, "Miss me? How could you miss me when you haven't been spending any time with me? You haven't talked to me at all!" Her heart was raging in her chest, and she took a deep breath, afraid of getting herself too worked-up. Quickly, she composed herself and clasped her gloved hands before her, squeezing her fingers hard. Then she studied Linus.

He was wearing the same dark clothes as always, but he was clean. He wasn't wearing the ridiculous metal hand Kennick had made for him, and his beard was freshly trimmed. At her words, he hung his head. "I'm sorry. I ... guess I just knew we were going to go our separate ways and didn't see any point in dragging out our goodbyes," he said quietly.

"What will you do next?" she asked, swallowing her emotion about the possibility of never seeing him again.

"I don't know ... I'll either follow Meera wherever she's going or live in the gutters of Harringbay, I guess," he replied.

Emmaline felt a small swell of hope. "Well, if you might stay in Harringbay, then why wouldn't we see each other?" she asked.

Linus huffed a short laugh. "Why would we? You'd be a lady living in a grand house, and I'd be ... a drunk nobody. I wouldn't be able to visit you where you live, and you wouldn't visit me," he replied with a shrug.

Emmaline stared at him. "How do you know what I would or wouldn't do?" she asked indignantly. Her mother might lock her in her room, but if Linus was in town, she would certainly try to see him. She couldn't think of anything she'd rather do.

"Oh yeah? You'd come visit me in my dingy little room over a tavern? Why?" he asked, sounding incredulous.

With as much determination as she could muster, Emmaline

walked forward and grabbed his scruffy face, pulling him down to where she could reach him. She kissed him and clutched his shoulders. Linus wrapped his right arm around her waist and kissed her in return, holding his left arm back and away from her. Emmaline gripped his left elbow and put his stunted forearm on her waist; she wanted to be held in both of his arms. Then she wound her own arms around his neck and clung to him, unwilling to say goodbye.

The others were waiting for them on the dock, but knowing she might be having her last moments alone with Linus, she couldn't bear to waste them. She pulled her body far enough away from him to start tugging up his shirt. "What are you doing?" he asked, breaking their kiss.

"Taking off your shirt," she replied.

"Why?" he choked.

"Why not?" she asked in frustration, pushing his shirt up to his chest until he lifted his arms and let it slip off over his head. He looked distinctly uncomfortable to be standing in front of her shirtless, but Emmaline pulled off her gloves and reached out to touch the many scars covering his left arm and side. Then she ran her hand over the smooth skin of his bony chest. She was nervous, breathing hard, and didn't know quite what to do, but she wanted to make him feel as good as he had made her feel.

She thought to tell Linus he was beautiful as he had told her, but the words stuck in her throat. Instead, she reached up and kissed him again, trailing her hands down his body until they reached his pants. Linus, again, tried to prevent her from undressing him, but Emmaline pushed his hand away, unfastened his pants, and let them fall to the floor. Now he was the naked one, and she led him to his bed, taking him all in as he lay down.

Linus watched her intently as she sat on the bed next to him and wrapped a tentative hand around his manhood. He put his hand over hers and showed her the movement he liked. Then he kissed her and pulled her down on top of him, holding him to her with his left forearm while his right hand traveled over her clothed body. Emmaline kissed him and stroked him, and he was the one to moan and writhe under her. When he was about to finish, he widened the gap between them to avoid making a mess on her dress, and she watched as his face scrunched and then smoothed in release.

For a minute, Linus lay panting and spent. Emmaline kissed his scarred and bearded cheek and looked around the room for something to clean him with. She picked one of her white gloves up off the floor and used that. He watched her, his face unreadable, then he rose and put his clothes back on, tugging on his boots as well. "Okay, you've made your point. You're a lady, but you can do whatever you want," he said quietly as he positioned his pant legs over his boots.

That was not the point Emmaline had been trying to make at all. She had wanted to make him feel as beautiful and alive as he had made her feel—she had wanted to show him how much she cared for him. "Did you not like it?" she asked, stiffening.

Linus stood and scratched his beard. "Of course, I liked it," he replied. "But I don't think I can sit in Harringbay and wait to see if and when you will deign to visit me in my hovel. I—I think I'll just go with Meera ... See if I can make myself useful somehow."

"Oh," Emmaline breathed. She stood straight and tall with her chin raised, but her heart melted and pooled in her gut. She was disappointed—devastated—but she usually was. She was good at not letting it show. "Okay."

Linus stepped toward her, touched her cheek gently, and planted a soft kiss on her rigid lips. "Goodbye, Emma," he said. Then he left, and she was forced to follow him or be the last person on the ship, holding up the group.

21

LINUS

Linus shook with emotion and tried not to let Emmaline see. He walked ahead of her to the gangplank and onto the dock, so she wouldn't notice the grief in his face. She had made her point: she was willing to touch his gnarled body, willing to lie with him on occasion even though he was beneath her. But Linus loved her—really loved her—and he didn't think she loved him like that; he didn't think she would leave her comfortable life as a lady to be with him.

Keeping his face down, he stared at the warped wood of the dock as he approached Meera, Shael, and Kennick. "Sorry," he said vaguely for making them wait.

They didn't ask why he had taken so long; they simply picked up their bags—and Emmaline's enormous trunk—and began the walk to the Harringtons' house. Linus trailed behind, and Meera slowly worked her way back to him, taking his hand in hers as they walked. She didn't say anything; she just held his hand and remained at his side. It was comforting. Linus wondered how Kennick might feel about it, but if the knell man noticed, he didn't react. Emmaline strode at the front of the group with her head held high like she owned the entire town. Linus figured she probably did. "I'm coming with you," he told Meera.

She squeezed his hand. "I'll be glad to have you with me," she replied. He knew that; it was why he would go even though he didn't really want to travel to Levisade or fly on a raek again. "We're staying at Emmaline's house tonight and leaving tomorrow," she told him.

He nodded. He didn't really want to stay in Emmaline's grand house either, but he supposed he could sneak out and get drunk somewhere. He had won a decent amount of money off the ship's crew playing cards.

When they reached the Harringtons' house, Emmaline picked up her pace, and Linus assumed she was glad to be home. Horses always walked faster and taller when they neared their stables. Linus's heart, however, sank as he approached his future without Emmaline. The group's presence in the front courtyard was quickly noticed from inside; a whole slew of servants came running out of the front door, the duchess among them.

Emmaline's slim mother was sobbing and running for her daughter, but Linus noticed sadly that she did not embrace Emmaline in welcome; rather, she stopped five feet from her daughter and put her hands to her tear-streaked face. He supposed the duchess's raw emotion was at least preferable to the aloof, medicated state they had last seen her in. However, her joy and relief at seeing Emmaline quickly turned to anger. "Where have you been?" the duchess cried, face pinched. "I thought you were dead in a ditch somewhere! How could you do that to me? What are you doing with these people?"

Emmaline stood as straight and still as ever, and Linus considered whether her poise could be a defense mechanism. She gestured behind her to the rest of them and said, "Mother, these

people took me to the land of my ancestors and have returned me
home safely. I told them they could stay with us until they leave
Harringbay." Linus heard her voice quaver slightly, but he could
see that her eyes were dry and her chin held high.

He wondered, then, if he might have been wrong—if he might
have falsely read her stiff composure as a lack of affection for him
—but before he could give it much thought, servants were
herding them inside. Emmaline directed them while her mother
continued to cry and shout. On his way past, he reached out and
touched her back reassuringly where her mother wouldn't see. He
didn't look forward to his own mother's wrath when he eventually
returned home after being presumed dead. Emmaline started at
his touch and turned toward him, her face fracturing slightly.

Linus almost stopped—almost pulled her to him for a hug—
but he didn't; he followed everyone else inside and was led to a
nice guestroom to *bathe and change before dinner*. He didn't have
anything to change into, but he bathed and washed his clothes.
Then, clean with a wad of wet clothes under his arm, he
wandered the halls in his towel, looking for Meera to dry them for
him. But when he walked past a closed door and heard Emmaline's voice, he paused to listen.

"—told you in my note, Mother. I went across the sea to finish
what Father had started. I went to Kallanthea to find a healer. I'm
sorry I scared you, but really, I had to do something! I couldn't sit
here for the rest of my life while you treated me like I was already
dead!" she cried, her voice rising and trembling.

"Emmaline, that was an incredibly foolish thing to do running
off with those strange people! You are lucky to be alive, and you
are lucky to have made it back here!" her mother replied.

"Am I?" Emmaline asked quietly.

"Of course, you are—don't be absurd! Now, these people can
stay here tonight, but then I want them out! I'm going to have the

entire house cleaned, we will get you all new clothes, and you will stay indoors and rest until we are sure you did not pick up any foul illness on that ship—a ship of all things! What were you thinking?" her mother asked, sounding deeply exasperated.

Emmaline didn't answer, and Linus moved away from the door before he could be discovered lurking in nothing but a towel. Walking back toward his room, he resorted to whisper-calling Meera's name, knowing she had remarkable hearing. Eventually she popped her head out of a door and grinned, seeing him meandering the fine house half-naked. "Making yourself at home?" she asked.

"Can you dry my clothes?" he asked in return, thrusting them at her.

"Sure, come in," she said. "It'll go faster if you put them on. Here, let me fix your hair."

Linus followed her into the room and let her comb his hair back and retie it. He averted his eyes from Kennick, who had also just bathed and was getting dressed. Then he made Meera turn around and put his wet clothes on for her to magic dry. "All good," she said when she was done.

Linus took a step toward the door but hesitated. Facing Meera and the room once more, he fidgeted with his newly dry pants and asked, "Do you think it's possible Emmaline cares for me?"

Meera didn't appear shocked by his question, and he avoided looking at Kennick altogether. "I can't get Emmaline to talk to me about anything, but I think she cares for you," she replied, giving him something between a smile and a grimace.

"In my experience, human women can be very hard to seduce and excruciatingly slow to admit their feelings," Kennick added, smirking at Meera.

Meera laughed, and Linus nodded dumbly and turned to leave, both embarrassed and unsure of what to do with that information. The next thing he knew, he found himself at a very awkward dinner with Meera, Kennick, Shael, Emmaline, and her mother. Duchess Harrington could barely bring herself to look at any of them and merely moved her food around on her plate, whereas Emmaline kept shooting them all apologetic glances, and Meera did her best to keep a conversation going. "Kallanthea was an amazing place. Are your ancestors also from across the Cerun Sea, Duchess Harrington?" she asked politely.

"No," the duchess replied tersely.

"Only my father's," Emmaline clarified.

Linus was relatively light skinned for a Terratellen and assumed he had ancestors from Arborea, but he didn't say so—nobody asked. He didn't say anything at dinner at all; he just picked at his food and stared longingly at Emmaline. He wished they could be alone again—he had the burning urge to tell her how he felt about her—but he didn't think he'd get her alone that night and knew the duchess wouldn't appreciate him professing his love for her daughter at the dinner table. If Emmaline noticed his eyes on her, she didn't let on.

Finally, dessert ended, and Meera announced: "We will be leaving early in the morning to return to Aegorn. Thank you for letting us stay here, and please don't feel like you need to get up to see us off." Linus assumed she was trying to avoid another awkward meal like this one by having them all skip out before breakfast.

The duchess didn't look like she felt the need to see them ever again. She didn't even reply to Meera; she simply turned to her daughter and said, "Bed, Emmaline. I want you in bed resting until we know you are not sick. Say goodbye to ... these people."

Emmaline swallowed visibly and moved the napkin in her lap to the tabletop. "Thank you all for accompanying me on my journey," she said quietly.

"We wish you the best, Emmaline," Meera said, and the rest of them nodded their agreement like hand puppets with tired puppeteers.

Linus longed for Emmaline to at least look at him, but she was staring at her empty dessert plate. He glanced at Meera, who shrugged and looked like she was about to stand up to leave when Emmaline took a deep breath. "I ... would also like to thank you, Linus. I—I thought the trip was a waste when the healer couldn't help me, but you made it worthwhile. Thank you," she said, looking at him with the same stiff poise as ever.

Linus gaped at her, at a complete loss for what to say. His eyes roved inadvertently to her mother, who was glaring at him—clearly suspicious—and he suddenly wished the duchess was still on whatever drugs had made her so agreeable on their first visit. "My pleasure?" he replied awkwardly. If Emmaline was thanking him for what he thought she was thanking him for, it really had been his pleasure. He saw Meera stifle a laugh and had to hold back his own grin.

"Emmaline, what are you talking about?" her mother asked, sounding weary. "The trip was a waste—a foolish decision and a waste. I need you to recognize that. I need to know you won't run off again to do god-knows-what with the likes of these people." She leaned toward her daughter, peering at her beseechingly. Her words were harsh, but she was clearly just afraid for Emmaline.

Emmaline seemed to grow taller in her seat with her indignation. "It was not a waste, Mother! How was I supposed to ever really live sitting in this house alone? If I hadn't left, I would have never done anything!" she cried.

"And what did you do that was worth possibly ending your life and never coming home again? You slept in a small room on a ship? You saw a strange place with strange people? None of that matters, Emmaline! You should have been at home with me!

Family matters above all else—I thought your Father had taught you that!" the duchess shouted before quickly pressing her lips together, tears in her eyes.

"Father taught me that love matters above all else, and if I had never left home, I would have never fallen in love! I would have sat here with you while you cried and acted like I was already dead!" Emmaline shouted back, finally losing her composure.

Linus's heart leapt in his chest. Was she talking about him? Did she love him?

"Love? Are you talking about this pathetic excuse for a man?" her mother asked incredulously, gesturing to Linus and asking his own question for him—though somewhat differently than he would have phrased it.

"Don't call him that!" Emmaline shouted, smacking her palms against the table in agitation. The gesture and noise were both so unexpected, Linus jumped in his seat, unable to take his disbelieving eyes off of her.

"No? Why not? I don't see him offering you any sort of life, let alone one that's better than what you already have ..." her mother replied, shooting him a nasty look.

Linus just gaped at them both. He wasn't offended, exactly—just shocked by it all. He could vaguely sense Meera and Kennick whispering next to him but didn't pay them any attention until Kennick nudged him with his knee and held something out to him under the table. Linus took it absently and stared at it: it was a ring. It was a little gold ring with flowers all around and small diamonds sparkling in their centers. Everyone at the table had gone still and silent and seemed to be waiting for him to say something. He could feel his heart beating wildly in his chest but couldn't seem to make his mind work as quickly.

As the silence stretched on, the duchess appeared smug. "Go

to bed, Emmaline. We will discuss this in the morning," she told her daughter.

This time, Emmaline listened to her mother and rose from her seat.

"No, wait!" Linus cried, standing and stumbling around the table to her. He heard the panic in his voice and wished he could have sounded more confident—more poised and manly.

Emmaline froze and gazed into his eyes, waiting. She looked as composed and intimidating as ever, but Linus was no longer fooled by the façade; he was no longer confused about her actions toward him—she loved him just as he loved her. Fingering the ring in his hand, he smiled. He finally felt certain—certain of where he belonged and what he wanted to do with his life.

Linus knelt down somewhat unsteadily on his shaking legs and propped the ring Kennick had given him on his knee so that he could take Emmaline's hand. She smiled before he even said anything and squeezed his hand in answer before he could ask the question, bolstering his resolve. "Emma, your mother's right— I don't have much to offer you—but I love you, and I want to spend my life making you happy. Will you marry me?" he asked, his voice only slightly tremulous. He knew it wasn't the best speech ever, but he hoped it was enough.

"Mother, call an officiator. I'm getting married tonight!" Emmaline announced, taking the ring from Linus's knee and slipping it onto her finger.

"Tonight?" her mother asked in alarm. "Emmaline—"

"I'm not waiting to live anymore," Emmaline declared, cutting her mother off. Then she tugged Linus up from the floor and kissed him right there in front of everyone. Linus wrapped both of his arms around her and kissed her back, smiling into her mouth.

22

MEERA

Meera was overjoyed to watch Linus and Emmaline get married. It was an unexpectedly gratifying end to their adventure, and she was glad her friend had found his person and his purpose. While she hadn't been entirely sure about Emmaline at first, she had admired the way the young woman had stood up to her mother and fought for Linus. Meera didn't even begrudge Emmaline the missing diamonds from the side of her engagement ring. Kennick hadn't wanted to use them, but she had insisted, telling him they could replace them when they reached Levisade—because they were flying home at last.

Linus and Emmaline had dragged themselves from their marriage bed early that morning to say goodbye, and Meera had cried, hugging them both and snotting on Linus's shirt. She hated goodbyes. As Kennick had led her out of the Harringtons' house, she had called back a promise to send Linus a carrier bird so that he could write to her in Levisade. Then she had reassured herself repeatedly that she could travel by raek to visit. While she was eager to return to her home, she knew that at some point she would miss her friend enough to fly back to Harringbay. She might even return to Kallanthea one day.

However, for now, Meera had to return to her life in Levisade. She didn't know what to expect when she got there, but she felt prepared for whatever might face her; she felt strong and steady after their trip, ready to return to her home, resume her training, and recommence trying to end the war. Still, strong as she may be, she leaned into Kennick where he sat behind her and rested her head against his chest, glad she wasn't facing the future alone.

Endu flew smoothly beneath them—much more smoothly than Shaya would have—and Meera wondered what her raek had been doing without her all that time. Shael and Cerun soared up ahead, and she watched the methodical movements of Cerun's wings as she contemplated what her reunion with Shaya might be like. She had watched Kennick and Shael reunite with their raeken early that morning with a mix of joy and jealousy, and she could only hope that Shaya would be amenable to speaking with her and not just attack her outright.

For the rest of that day, they flew high over Aegorn, and that evening, they stopped to eat and rest before continuing their journey the next day. When they finally arrived at the Riders' Holt, it was midday and much warmer in Levisade than it had been elsewhere. Meera was still wearing her Kallanthean clothes and sandals and had been warming herself almost continually with her raek fire. She felt a little ridiculous in her bright blue-green skirt sitting on Endu, but she agreed to go straight to Hadjal's house rather than stop home to change, feeling anxious to see the other riders.

Their arrival at the peninsula was met with a lot of raek screeching and shouts from below. Cerun landed first, then Endu. Kennick jumped from Endu's back and reached up for Meera—not because she needed help, just because he wanted to. She fell smiling into his arms, and he put her gently down in the grass. The riders had already run out to hug Shael, and they turned toward Kennick and Meera with wide smiles on their faces. Their smiles faded at the sight of Meera, however.

Meera had been so excited to return home, she had forgotten for a moment that she should be pregnant. Her growing child should be visible at this point, she realized, patting her flat stomach self-consciously. Kennick stood at her side and squeezed her shoulder in support. Soleille was the first to reach her and looked close to tears. "I am so sorry, Meera. I should have been there! I should have gone to you!" she cried, hugging her tightly.

Meera hugged her back and swallowed her emotion. "It's okay —I'm okay," she said, getting a mouthful of Soleille's blonde hair.

When Soleille finally released her, Meera saw that Hadjal was repeatedly kissing Kennick's face, and both he and his mentor were crying. She wiped tears from her own eyes. She had been expecting a joyful reunion with the riders and hadn't really considered this ... Still, it felt good to be greeted and hugged by her family one at a time. Even Florean embraced her and kissed her cheek. "What ridiculous human attire are you wearing?" he asked, peering at her through narrowed eyes.

Meera laughed. "It's a long story," she told him.

When Hadjal pulled Meera into her arms, she all but sobbed and apologized over and over again for not sending everyone after her. "I was scared, and I was wrong," she said, sniffing and shaping the tears from her face when she finally released Meera.

Everyone was clearly upset about her miscarriage and about remaining at the peninsula instead of going to find her. Even Katrea looked teary-eyed. Meera was doing her best to hold herself together, and she had to look down at the grass for a moment to collect herself. Kennick wrapped an arm around her and held her to his side. "It's okay everyone, really," she said at last, her voice thin from her constricted throat. "There was nothing any of you could have done."

"There was nothing you could have done, either," Kennick reminded her quietly.

Meera nodded and swallowed.

"So, what happened? I mean, I waited at the border for days then came back here thinking maybe you had returned already. Where have you all been?" Soleille asked.

"Kallanthea," Meera replied, grinning, and they all gaped at her.

"Do you think a couple of oath-breakers can eat at your table, Hadjal?" Shael asked. Their welcome had been so warm, it was obviously a rhetorical question.

Hadjal laughed and led them all toward her house. Sodhu ran ahead to bring out food, and Meera sighed and leaned her head against Kennick's shoulder; it was good to be home. Together they all sat and ate a meal, and she, Shael, and Kennick took turns explaining everything that had happened. Meera started with the horrendous negotiation meeting and her miscarriage, and there was more crying—herself included. Then they alternated, telling how they had gone to Harringbay and taken the duke's daughter to Kallanthea.

"Kallanthea! I cannot believe it!" Florean exclaimed for the fifth time. "I have never gone so far in my long life!"

"Perhaps you should change that," Meera suggested. The trip had been good for her.

"Do you feel you made up for your past, considering the duke's daughter could not be healed?" Hadjal asked her.

Meera shrugged. "I did my best to make things right, and I have forgiven myself," she replied. It was all she could do. She couldn't live with her pressing guilt anymore, and she wanted to live—there was still so much she longed to do.

"I cannot believe you needed a healer and went to Kallanthea," Soleille said sulkily. She hadn't enjoyed any part of their story.

"Well, I'm going to send Linus and Emmaline a carrier bird, so if they ever need a healer, you can go to them," Meera told her. Then she addressed the table at large and asked, "What news is there here?"

Everyone quieted and stilled ominously. Finally, Isbaen said, "Darreal is mobilizing knell warriors to go to the border. Terratelle has convinced Arborea and Cesor to fight with them in the war, and their forces are moving toward Aegorn as we speak. Darreal has told us to be ready to fly to the front and join the battle."

Meera stared at him wide-eyed. Shael's face mirrored her shock from across the table, and Kennick tensed next to her. "No!" she cried. It was all she could think to say. Even if this great battle would end the war—at what cost? She wanted to stop the violence, not escalate it. Hadjal nodded her head seriously to confirm what Isbaen had said, and the other riders looked grim but determined—ready to go if called upon. "I need to talk to Darreal," Meera announced, standing abruptly.

Kennick took her hand. "Tomorrow," he replied. "Tonight, we will go home. Tomorrow, we will go to the estate."

Meera took a breath, ready to argue, then she exhaled and deflated. "I guess we won't have time to egg your parent's house," she said.

Kennick gave her a joyless smile and stood with her. It was time for them to finally go back to their house. "Meera, Shaya has been at the estate," Sodhu informed her before they could leave.

Meera nodded at her in acknowledgement. Shaya was still blocking her out, so she couldn't sense the raek's location. Meera supposed she would have a lot to deal with the next day, and she sighed. Before they left, however, she gave each of the riders another hug—including Shael. She also thanked him again for all he had done for her. Then she ruffled his hair and walked away with Kennick, calling, "Goodnight, Captain Pretty!" over her shoulder.

GETTING to their house was strange because Meera hadn't seen it since the addition. The main space was changed slightly, and a new door to what would have been their baby's room stood ajar. She and Kennick both stared at it for a moment, then she started to walk toward it. "Don't, Meera," Kennick implored her softly.

With a glance back at him, she kept going. She would have to walk into the room eventually; she couldn't just live in their house and pretend it didn't exist. Stepping inside, she found that the room faced the lake like theirs did. She also found that Kennick had already decorated. There was a wooden crib and bright forest tapestries on the walls that she suspected Follaria had made. There were also two rocking chairs—one for each of them—on top of a soft, multi-colored rug.

"Oh, Kennick," she breathed. It was perfect, and Meera couldn't help but feel like she had ruined it. Then she was crying —again; it had been a long couple of days.

Kennick came up behind her and wrapped his arms around her. "Gendryl made the crib," he said quietly.

"I love it. I'll have to thank him," she replied. She would like to get to know Gendryl better, but the impending fight at the border didn't leave her feeling hopeful that she would have the chance any time soon.

"Come on. Let's get some rest," Kennick said, tugging on her.

"Don't move any of this, okay?" she asked. She didn't know

when they would get around to adding a baby to the room, but she wanted it to look just like this when they did.

"Okay," he agreed, kissing the side of her neck. She felt his pointy tooth when he smiled, and she smiled too; they had a long future ahead of them.

Together, they went into their bedroom, and Kennick immediately pulled off the clothes he had been wearing for weeks. "Please burn these," he said, tossing them on the floor at her feet.

Meera laughed and did as she was bid. Then she pulled off her Kallanthean clothes—which she didn't burn—and they got into their big bathtub together. As anxious as she felt about the war and seeing Shaya the next day, she put those thoughts aside; her troubles, she knew, would still be there in the morning. Focusing instead on the man in front of her, Meera washed Kennick's hair for him, rubbing his scalp and shaping warm water over his head. She took her time combing through the length of his hair. He was so relaxed and tired, he fell asleep in the bath, and she held him there for a long time before eventually waking him to move him to the bed.

23

MEERA

The next morning, Meera awoke and pulled on her knell warrior clothes. She chose a cream outfit since she didn't plan on doing anything especially dirty that day, and she let Kennick braid and tuck her hair for her. It was time for her to face Shaya, Darreal, and—she realized—her father. She heaved a sigh; they would all expect her to still be pregnant, and she didn't relish watching more people cry over her miscarriage.

Thankfully, when Kennick had been home without her overseeing the addition to their house, he also seemed to have commissioned more clothes and shoes for her from Follaria. Normally, Meera would've found the additions to her wardrobe excessive, but seeing as she had burned her only pair of boots weeks ago, she was glad to find new ones sitting at the bottom of Kennick's enormous closet. She didn't relish the thought of breaking in new boots, but considering everything else she had on her mind, she was glad to at least not have to go shopping that day.

"Can I send Linus your carrier bird?" she asked Kennick as he dressed.

"To keep?" he asked indignantly. "Have we not given Linus enough?" He was still a little peeved about the small diamonds in Meera's ring—not because of their value but because they were sentimental to him.

"Yes, to keep. We can get another bird, can't we?" she replied.

"Yes, but I like my bird," Kennick said, dark eyes glinting.

"Oh yeah? What's its name?" Meera asked, smirking at him. She didn't think he was actually overly fond of the bird.

He laughed. "Fine, we can send Linus my bird," he agreed. Then he started rifling through his drawers.

"What are you looking for?" she asked.

"Diamonds! I need to fix your ring, remember? You made me give part of it away," he replied, giving her a mock-exasperated look.

"Oh, come on! You saw Linus's face! You're lucky I didn't give him my whole ring," Meera said, laughing at the mere fact that Kennick seemed to think he might have diamonds thrown into any one of his drawers.

"Linus is lucky to have you as a friend," he said, pulling a small velvet bag out of a drawer and taking her hand. He proceeded to dump a mound of diamonds into his palm and sort through them for the sizes he wanted.

"Seriously?" she asked, watching.

Kennick grinned at her and shrugged. "I keep them around just in case I feel the need to make you something," he replied.

Meera supposed she couldn't complain about that. "Admit it— Linus grew on you," she said as she waited for him to add his selected diamonds to her ring. "You were tearing up at their cere-mony." It had been a short, simple ceremony, but Linus and Emmaline had looked so happy and in love. Meera had cried, and

Emmaline had seemed to finally warm up to her, hugging her and thanking her for bringing Linus into her life.

"Maybe I was crying because they managed to get married after being engaged for half an hour, and I may never get my fiancé down the aisle," Kennick teased.

Meera laughed. "I'm just making sure you have time to bedeck my entire body in diamonds," she replied, pulling away her hand when he finished. "Now let me concentrate. I need to write to Linus." Picking up a pen and paper, she wrote a brief letter to Linus, telling him they had gotten home and that she missed him. Then, as an afterthought, she added the news about Otto gathering Arborea's and Cesor's forces in case he hadn't already heard. She was glad Linus was no longer a general and wouldn't be anywhere near the ensuing battle.

WHEN ENDU SWOOPED low over the Levisade Estate, the first thing Meera noticed was Shaya's enormous figure in the back wildflower fields. She felt a whole flurry of emotions seeing her raek; she had missed Shaya and was glad to see her healthy and still working toward their goal, but she was also hurt that her raek had chosen to block her out for so long and hadn't looked for her. Meera may have been the first to put up a mental barrier, but it had been many weeks since then, and Shaya had not tried to find her or check in with her—not that she could tell.

When Endu momentarily blocked her sun, Shaya looked up, extended her wings, and fluffed her feathers. For a moment, Meera worried she would fly away and refuse to speak to her, but Shaya stayed where she was. Then she watched through her eerie pale eyes as Endu landed and Meera leapt down from his back. Meera eyed her in return. Kennick jumped down next to her but kept back when she walked toward her raek, watching and waiting—not because he thought Shaya would hurt her, she knew, but because they were both done being apart from one another. It was going to be a long day, and they would face it together.

Meera stepped up close to Shaya's head, while she remained crouched and still. The raek didn't so much as blink in acknowledgement of her presence, but she never was one for unnecessary pleasantries. Meera tried to grasp Shaya's consciousness in her mind and press into it, but her raek wouldn't let her. Unperturbed, she settled for speaking aloud and said a simple, "Hello, Shaya" —*frivolous human nonsense* as her raek would call it.

Shaya didn't respond in any way, and her eyes were as strangely devoid of expression as ever.

"I've missed you," Meera relayed honestly. She waited again, but Shaya seemed disinclined to answer. "I'm sorry I pushed you away. I was ... very upset," she added vaguely.

Shaya shifted her bulk slightly and lashed her tail. Finally, she pressed an answer into Meera's mind: "Warriors do not collapse and snivel when they kill their enemies."

Meera shrugged. "This one does," she responded aloud. "I'm sorry if I'm a disappointment to you, Shaya, but I am who I am—I don't want to kill anyone, I cry all the time, and sometimes, I run away from my feelings and the people who care about me."

Shaya huffed a puff of smoke in her face, and Meera quickly shaped a wind to carry it away. "You said we were partners," the raek said tonelessly.

Meera wondered if Shaya was actually more hurt than disappointed. She had never thought that her raek cared for her particularly or valued their bond, but maybe she had underestimated Shaya's sentimentality. "I'm sorry if I hurt you. I—I was upset about the boys and because I lost my baby, and I pulled away from everyone and everything—not just you ... I shouldn't have, and I'm sorry," she said, stepping forward and putting a tentative hand on Shaya's jaw. Even as she patted her raek, she remained tense and alert, aware that Shaya may choose to attack her at any time. Unfortunately, that was always a possibility with Shaya.

"I would have torn down any enemy and flown like lightning to get you to a healer," the raek replied with a ferocious snarl.

Meera could sense that the snarl was not directed at her but at any possible threats to her, and she smiled. With an exhale, she rested her forehead against Shaya's smooth scales. "It wouldn't have helped," she told her raek with certainty; she had known it was too late to save the baby—nothing could have been done.

"We could have tried—together," Shaya replied, her consciousness creeping hesitantly back into Meera's mind with her words.

Meera let her in, embracing her mentally. "Do you forgive me?" she asked in their minds.

Shaya huffed again and slashed her tail, but Meera could sense that she did and wiped a tear from her cheek before it could fall onto Shaya's gleaming scales.

"Would it make you feel better if you attacked me?" she asked her raek in jest.

Shaya hummed in amusement.

Meera let herself fall into their connection for a few minutes, savoring the partnership and friendship she had been missing. She showed Shaya all that she had done without her and got lost for a time in Shaya's own swirling, sucking memories. Then she sighed and stepped away. "We have a war to end," she said, looking into Shaya's pale, fathomless eye.

"Keep me with you," Shaya replied, wanting to hear what Darreal would have to say to her when they spoke.

Meera nodded and walked toward Kennick, a broad smile on

her face. "I was expecting more of a show," Kennick said, smiling back at her. He waved to Shaya, and she smacked her tail into the ground in response.

Meera liked that they were becoming more comfortable with one another's raeken; they were a big, weird family. "One down," she said, taking Kennick's hand and leading him toward the estate.

MEERA WENT to find Darreal before seeking out her father. Darreal's shape and bearing were so familiar to her, she could sense through the busy estate to find her location. The queen was in her council room, where she had questioned Meera on her first morning in Levisade. Meera tugged on Kennick's hand and led him through the estate until they reached the stained-glass door with the intricate forest scene.

Lethian stood outside the door and appeared both shocked and wary at their appearance, but Meera ignored him and pushed into the room without hesitation. Darreal sat at the far end of the marble table with her council around her. Everyone gawked at Meera when she walked in, but she gazed only at her friend. Darreal's usually serene demeanor fell away as her eyes widened then lowered to Meera's flat stomach. The queen opened her mouth slightly, but no words came out. "Everyone out! The meeting is over!" Meera cried forcefully, shooing the council members from the room.

The gathered knell looked appalled—Odon outraged—but they stood and left regardless when the queen didn't argue with Meera's assertion. As Meera watched the progression file out the door, she saw that Lethian had followed her and Kennick inside. However, she continued to ignore the blonde warrior, and the second the room was free of council members, she went to Darreal. Her friend stood jerkily from her chair and hugged her tightly, her gold circlet pressing against the side of Meera's face. "The baby?" Darreal asked quietly.

"Gone," Meera replied simply.

When she pulled away, there were unshed tears in Darreal's eyes, but she quickly blinked and regained her composure. "I am so glad to see you," she said. Meera could sense the regret and apologies she wanted to confess, but Darreal didn't seem comfortable saying such things in front of Kennick and Lethian.

Meera nodded her understanding and briefly squeezed her friend's thin upper arms. "What's going on? You're gathering troops?" she asked.

Darreal cleared her throat softly, and her face changed; she was suddenly in full-queen mode again. "The armies of three lands are descending on our border, and we have no choice but to meet them with our own strength. Otherwise, we risk them tearing through Aegorn, possibly even Levisade," she replied like she was reciting a well-used speech.

"Did you try to negotiate again? Is there no way to stop the battle?" Meera asked.

"Of course I tried to negotiate again," Darreal replied, and Meera could sense her friend's irritation even though her even voice didn't betray her emotion. "I could not stop the battle, so now we must try to win it."

Meera stepped back from Darreal and looked at Kennick. She could see her sadness mirrored in his dark eyes, and she tried desperately to think of a solution but couldn't. What could sway Otto against fighting? She didn't know, and Linus hadn't seemed to know either.

"I will leave soon with as many knell warriors as I can muster, and I expect you both to stand with me," Darreal added.

Meera turned to her in shock. "I'm not going to slaughter Terratellens for you!" she replied in indignation. She wasn't prepared to kill anyone for any reason.

"You see, Darreal?" Lethian asked, stepping toward his queen. "I told you she is not one of us."

Meera glared at Lethian briefly before turning back to Darreal. Her friend looked suddenly weary and wouldn't meet her eyes. "Lethian, I reinstate you as Queen's Champion," she said quietly. "Meera, you do not have to fight with us as you have never sworn your allegiance to this land, but Kennick, all of Levisade's riders are called upon to join the battle."

Kennick had his hands in his pockets and shrugged loosely at her words. "I have already broken my oaths," he replied unconcernedly.

Darreal didn't look especially surprised, but Lethian appeared outraged. "You are a knell warrior—have you no honor?" he spat.

Kennick removed his hands from his pockets and stared Lethian down, his face more lethal than Meera had ever seen it. "You speak to me of honor?" he asked. "Where was your honor when you left Meera behind in that tent? Surely a group of unarmed humans was not so threatening to you that you could not spare a moment to collect one of your own."

"One of my own?" Lethian asked, voice rising. "She is not one of us! I knew it then, and she proves it now."

Kennick stepped toward the other man, hand twitching at his side, and Meera wondered if he might actually strike Lethian— she had never seen him this angry before. She might have been offended by Lethian's words if she was not so overcome by her shock. Kennick didn't strike Lethian, however. "You just wanted your title as champion back," he accused the other man in a low voice. "You were glad to leave Meera behind to regain your position."

Meera looked to Lethian, wondering if that was true. She had always liked the blonde warrior and had never wanted his title. Lethian crossed his muscled arms over his chest defensively. "I was protecting my queen as is my duty," he replied stiffly.

Kennick sneered—actually sneered at Lethian—and Meera thought her eyes might pop out of her head in surprise. Then he shocked her even further: "Lethian, I challenge you to a fight for your title in two days," Kennick said. Meera gaped at him.

"I accept your challenge," Lethian replied, attempting to peer down at him even though Kennick was slightly taller.

Meera looked to Darreal like her friend might have the answers to this puzzling display of male bravado, but Darreal was gazing out the window with a far-off expression on her face, clearly too engrossed in battle plans to spare much thought for the minor conflict in front of her. Meera sighed; she knew Darreal had done everything she could to prevent the upcoming battle and didn't relish sacrificing her people to save her land, but she still wouldn't join her; she wouldn't contribute to the violence even if she didn't know how to stop it.

When Kennick took her hand, she followed him out of the room without a word. "Do you mind?" he asked when they were far away from the stained-glass door.

"Mind?" Meera asked distractedly.

"That I challenged Lethian," Kennick clarified.

"No! Of course not. I had my Champion's Challenge, and you're welcome to have yours if that's what you want. I just ... have other things to worry about at the moment," she said apologetically.

"I know," he replied, squeezing her hand. "We will continue to try to stop this battle, then I will take a few minutes to put Lethian in his place."

Meera laughed. "Someone's feeling confident," she said, then she nudged Kennick. "Why are you doing this, anyway? You don't want to be Queen's Champion, do you?"

He shrugged. "No, but I suspect Lethian left you behind in that tent to reclaim his title. I want to teach him the lesson that titles and honor are not the same," he replied.

Meera stopped him in the middle of the hallway and kissed him, not caring who was around to see. "You can be the Queen's Champion as long as you keep being my champion," she told him.

"Do you think I can win?" Kennick asked, searching her face.

"You would win any battle of honor," she replied confidently. Meera had never seen Kennick fight with his shaping before, but she had never seen him that angry and determined before either. She knew he could beat Lethian if he really wanted to.

Kennick kissed her again until, begrudgingly, Meera pulled away and sighed. "One more stop today," she said, meaning her father.

24

MEERA

Meera and Kennick found Orson Hailship in the room dedicated to his research. They walked inside without knocking, and Meera observed her father at work for a moment before anyone noticed them. He looked frazzled but happy, and she was glad to see it. Then, selfishly, she wondered whether he had been worried about her or had even thought of her at all during her long absence. Kennick rubbed her back comfortingly, seeming to sense some of her thoughts.

Ned was the first to notice their arrival and dropped what he was doing to run over to them. "Meera! You're back!" he cried, giving her a big hug.

Meera hugged the boy in return, bolstered by his enthusiastic greeting. Seeing Ned made her miss Doug and Freddy, and she felt tears prick her eyes—again. With some difficulty, she swallowed them back. "It's good to see you, Ned," she replied, looking him over. He looked happy, healthy, and taller than when she had last seen him.

"We're going to be brother and sister!" he cried, practically bouncing up and down.

Meera stared at him uncomprehendingly. "What?" she asked.

Before Ned could explain, her father seemed to register their arrival and stumbled toward them, tripping on a stack of papers on his way. One of his knell assistants helped him off the floor and tidied the papers after Orson continued toward them. By the time he reached Meera, she could see tears in his eyes under his wire-framed glasses, and her own tears surged again. "Meera!" he cried, hugging her and kissing her face. "I was so worried!"

Meera laughed and hugged him back. "I'm sorry," she said for worrying him.

Then her father pulled back to look at her and put a hand to her flat stomach. "Oh, no," he said. "You know, your mother had several miscarriages."

"No ... I didn't know," Meera said quietly. The knowledge made her feel a little better—like maybe losing her baby really wasn't her fault.

She and her father continued to look at one another for several long moments, then Orson sniffed and straightened himself up. "Yes, well, as Ned let slip, I have some news: I am to marry his mother, Doreen," he announced.

Meera stared at him in disbelief, then she smiled a little wood-enly. She didn't know anything about Doreen, but she was glad her father was not alone in this land of knell. "I'm happy for you," she said. She felt vaguely replaced, seeing how familiar her father and Ned were, but she was an adult with her own family now—she could not begrudge sharing her father with a boy who needed one. "I've always wanted a brother," she told Ned, and he beamed back at her.

For once, Meera hoped her father would insist on returning to his work, so she could slip away and process his news somewhere else. Orson gripped her hand, however, and held her there, looking into her face excitedly. "I have something for you!" he said.

"Oh?" Meera asked. She wasn't sure she could handle another shock that day.

"Ned, where are they?" her father asked, dropping her hand to rifle through the stacks of loose papers everywhere, seemingly at random.

"Here!" Ned cried, scurrying adeptly through the room to hand her father something.

"Ah, yes!" Orson said, holding the papers out toward Meera, who took them automatically without looking at them. "These were written by Aegwren!" her father told her excitedly.

Meera did look down, then. "Really?" she asked, wondering what they were.

"Well, no. These are copies I made, of course. The originals are in a safe location for preservation," he replied.

Meera smiled at her father's misunderstanding—it was very like Orson to be extremely literal when he wasn't using one of his many sayings or weaving a metaphor. "What are they?" she asked. It had been some time since she had connected to Aegwren, and she was simultaneously trembling at the thought of reading something he had written and trying to temper her excitement, telling herself that they were probably boring, unimportant documents.

"Letters!" her father cried excitedly. "They are letters that he wrote to a woman. I thought you might like them."

"Thank you," Meera replied, wondering who the woman was that Aegwren had written to. She just kept staring at the papers in her hand and couldn't seem to look back up at her father.

"Go ahead! Get out of here!" he said conspiratorially, winking at her when she met his eyes.

Meera grinned; she supposed if anyone could understand her

obsession, it was her father. Kissing him briefly on the cheek, she turned with Kennick toward the door, waving a goodbye to Ned over her shoulder.

"Are you okay?" Kennick asked when they were alone in the hall again.

Meera puffed out her cheeks, then she laughed. "Are you? I bet they'll get married before we do too," she joked.

He smiled and shrugged, and they both looked down at the letters in her hand. She needed to read them, but ... "Do you need to be alone?" Kennick asked, giving her an understanding look.

"I ... I'd like to take them to the cave," she admitted, grimacing up at him. Meera knew that going to the cave might be a sore subject with Kennick, considering she had hidden there after her Champion Challenge, but she felt closer and more connected to Aegwren when she was there and hoped she might get to experience more of his life with him.

"Go," Kennick said.

"You sure? I promise I'll be back for your challenge," she said.

"I'm sure," he replied, bending to kiss her. "My challenge does not matter. Do what you need to do."

"Your challenge does matter," she corrected him. "And I will be back for it."

He kissed her again, his pointy tooth scraping against her lip.

"I could use a flight," Shaya announced in Meera's mind, startling her and making her jump. With everything else going on, she had forgotten about her raek. She sensed Shaya standing and stretching, already ready to go.

"Give me some time," Meera told her mentally. "I need to restore the food in the cave." She and Kennick spent several hours collecting and packing food and supplies for her to take with her to the cave. Then Meera left for the mountains on Shaya's back, and Kennick left for their house on Endu. They would meet back at the estate in two days for Kennick's challenge. Then, hopefully, they would figure out what to do about the ensuing battle.

AS SHE AND Shaya flew into the mountains, Meera was glad for the extra layers she had acquired at the estate. It was getting cold outside of Levisade, and while she could keep herself warm with her raek fire, it required a constant stream of attention and energy. Shaya landed in Aegwren's valley between the two peaks, and Meera looked up at the one that resembled an eagle's head, thinking of Aegwren's Uncle Fendwren. Then she unloaded the stores of food and lamp oil Shaya was carrying and deposited them into the cave. She wasn't sure if she would ever be the one to use the abundant supplies, but they would be there—magically preserved—for whoever might need them in the future.

By the time she unloaded and ate something for dinner, it was dark out. Sitting on Aegwren's bed under the light of the oil lamps, she held his letters in her lap, a feeling of tingling anticipation in her stomach. She missed Aegwren; she hadn't been with him since she'd lain in the dungeon, and he had been about to take his first flight on Isabael's back. With no idea what he would do next or where his life would take him, Meera could only hope that he had recovered from his grief and loss as she was recovering from hers. Curious to know who the woman was who he had written to, she opened the top letter, knowing her father would have put them in order for her:

My Dear Leannon,

I do not know if I will ever be able to send you my letters, but I will bring them when next I visit. I want you to know that I

*thought of you the whole flight home. Meeting you was the high-
light of my travels, and I hope we will meet again soon. I had
heard of people from Cesor but had never imagined that a woman
could be as beautiful as you. I dream of your brown skin and silky
hair.*

At this point, Meera had to pause to laugh. She was surprised
but delighted to find that it was a love letter.

*I do not know when I will be able to travel so far north again.
The people I meet on my travels are always hesitant to accept
raeken among them as my people have, but your leader, in particular, abhorred the idea. I tried to reason with Sakhean but left
feeling unsuccessful. I can only hope that time will help to change
his mind and heart. Change has been slow this far south, but I find
that the young are open to new ideas, and the old remember the
violence and pain of the alternative.*

*There are now five raek riders, and we all do our best to hold
the tentative peace between our races. It is for that reason that I
cannot immediately return to you; there has been unrest in one of
the villages closest to the mountains, so I reside here with Isabael to
help deter the raek that seeks vengeance on these people for past
crimes inflicted on him. While I understand his pain and his anger,
I hope to prevent the continual chain of violence forged by revenge.*

*If you remember, I once told you of my Uncle Fendwren. It has
been ten years since his death, and I find myself endeavoring to
make him proud with my efforts. I wear his sword at my side—
you know the one, you admired the large opal in the hilt—and I
try to use it for peace. Oh Leannon, I yearn for our people to coexist
in this land peaceably so that we might form our own union.*

*While not all of my people have been welcoming, I welcome
the Cesoreans to this land, and I hope that one day we will be one*

people and live intermixed with one another. I believe it could
happen. I never thought to see raeken living among humans, after
all. I cannot help but wonder if perhaps you and I might join
together in love and lead a union of our people by example.

I will search for an opal worthy of you in my travels.

Yours,
Aegwren

Meera smiled at the sweet letter. Aegwren was quite a bit older than when she had last seen him, but he was still full of love and hope. She suspected his letters would never reach Leannon, considering her father had found them at the estate. Even so, she thought it was possible the two might have their happy ending. The next letter was short, and she read it quickly:

My Dear Leannon,

My people are uneasy as more and more Cesoreans arrive on
our shores. I remain hopeful that we can all learn to live in this
land together, but I am told by my fellow riders that fights are
breaking out. I am still needed near the mountains, but if the
conflicts persist, I may fly north. While I do not wish for our people
to continue to fight, in truth, I would not mind the excuse to be
near to you once more. The months pass, and still, I cannot get you
out of my mind. I wonder whether you think of me.

Yours,
Aegwren

Meera put the letter aside and pulled out the next one.

My Dear Leannon,

I am sorry to say that the conflicts between our people have progressed, and I find that I must fly north to address the issue. I do not proclaim to rule over the people of this land, but the riders have become a means for scattered villages to communicate with one another and for news to spread. We are symbols of hope, and the villages closest to where your people have settled ask for our assistance.

Isabael and I will fly tomorrow, and we will fly quickly. I will carry my letters with me in case we meet again. While I have not yet succeeded in acquiring an opal beautiful enough to do you justice, I find myself longing for a quick resolution to this conflict so that I might ask you to marry me. My mother tells me in my head that marriage lasts a long time, and we do not know each other well. However, my uncle bade me to remember love before he died, and Uncle Fendwren has yet to lead me astray.

Yours,
Aegwren

Meera flipped anxiously to the next letter.

My Dear Leannon,

You are so close yet so far away. For weeks, I have slept on the cusp between our people but can find no resolution that satisfies all. Men continue to gather and prepare on both sides, and I fear a war is coming. I have tried to meet with Sakhean but cannot entice him to speak to me. My people— the people who have lived for generations in this land—say that the land is theirs and only theirs; they do not wish to live with Cesoreans. Your people say that this is now their home as well, but they are not willing to coexist with raeken or those that do.

I say we are all the same—people who simply wish to eat and sleep and raise our families in peace—but no one listens to me. I often wonder what you would say, but close in distance as we may be, I fear I will never see you again. I have been wishing for a speedy resolution to this conflict, but I now fear that a resolution will entail a battle. One battle will likely lead to another, then another, and my people will, once more, be locked in a cascading torrent of violence. I do not know what to do, and I find that my mother and uncle are unusually silent within me.

Yours,

Aegwren

Meera rubbed her eyes and pulled out the next letter. She was getting tired after her long day, but she wanted to read at least one more.

My Dear Leannon,

Our people are to fight one another. There will be a battle, and I fear it will be soon. I have thought and thought on the matter and have sharpened my sword to join the fight. Since it does not seem possible to stop the fighting, I have decided to make sure that this battle will be the last. I will fight, and I will kill so that my children and my children's children can live in peace. I will fight so that the Cesoreans on our land will retreat farther north and keep to themselves. If I am successful, we will never meet again. My heart breaks for myself, but as a rider, I find I am not my own man——I am more—and resist as I may, I find I am the leader of my people.

Aegwren

Meera put the letters on her bedside table and lay down. Once more, Aegwren's life seemed to mirror her own in ways; he was on the precipice of a battle he did not want to join, and he was choosing to fight. Meera had told Darreal that she would not kill Terratellens, but was Aegwren right? Would it be better for her to join this battle and end the war once and for all in order to prevent future conflict? She had no idea, and her tired mind couldn't contemplate the question any longer that night. Extinguishing the lamps around her, she shut her eyes to sleep.

25

MEERA

Meera opened her eyes to a dim, moonlit night and looked around in confusion before realizing that she was in Aegwren's body. She felt a little thrill of joy to be reunited with her friend, but then she realized what he was doing and was downright embarrassed for them both. Aegwren was squatting over an open trench having a horrible case of diarrhea. Meera couldn't exactly step away to give him privacy, so she resorted to staring at the indistinct shapes in the distance through Aegwren's human eyes and trying to puzzle out where they were while she suffered through his cramps.

When Aegwren was finished, he walked through a small, forested area and entered a field of tents and other makeshift structures. It was a war camp, Meera realized. She had joined Aegwren where his letters had left off, and judging by his stomach discomfort, she guessed it was the eve of the impending battle. He stepped up to two large, lumpy shapes in the dark—one of which was a tent and the other of which turned out to be Isabael. "At least if I die in battle tomorrow, I will not mess my pants," he told Isabael.

The raek hummed sympathetically and pressed her scaley snout into Aegwren's arm. He patted and scratched her in return. "If we fight, we fight together, and if we die, we die together," she said in his mind, shocking Meera. Isabael must have joined their minds with her magic at some point.

For the rest of Aegwren's long night, Meera tossed with him and ventured back to the trench several more times. She was starting to fret that she would wake up before anything could happen when the sun finally rose, and Aegwren's people dressed and gathered their weapons. Aegwren strapped his sword to his hip and left his tent. Then he mounted Isabael, and they flew just a short distance away to where the men were gathering.

There were perhaps several hundred of them. They were no great army by any means; most of the men carried makeshift spears or clubs instead of real weapons—none of them looked like true warriors—and some didn't even wear shoes. Meera cringed to see the young boys standing among the men and suddenly wished that she would wake up before anything could happen; she didn't want to see the battle take place even if it had happened thousands of years ago.

"Today, we make a stand for our land!" Aegwren shouted from Isabael's back. Meera looked up and saw a few other raeken in the sky, presumably those that also had riders. She could feel Aegwren tremble, but his voice was steady and loud. "We will fight this one time to end all future conflicts with the Cesoreans! We will face them this one time and show them what we are made of, so they will never dare to cross the border again! We will fight, and we will die if we have to so that our children can prosper in peace!"

The men before him cheered and raised their weapons.

Isabael turned to face the other direction, and Meera could see through Aegwren's eyes a similarly sized group of men waiting across a large stretch of cleared land: the Cesorean army. Meera supposed the border with the Cesoreans would eventually be Aegorn's border with Terratelle. While these people did not call their land Aegorn yet or have organized leadership, this battle would be the beginning of two lands.

Aegwren's bowels clenched despite being thoroughly empty, and Meera could feel his heart thumping and sweat breaking out all over his body. He was full of bone-deep dread for what was about to take place. Meera didn't want to be there, and yet, she needed to know how this would end; she needed to know what she should do about the impending battle in her own life. Aegwren drew his sword, rolling his shoulder's back, and shouted, urging his men forward. He hoped attacking first would give them some advantage.

Isabael trundled forward on the land, heartening the men around her with her size and might, and the would-be soldiers ran in a ragged, poorly formed line toward their enemies. It was a longer distance to run than Aegwren had expected, however, and by the time they came close to the other army, many of the men were already slowing, making him regret his decision to attack first. Still, there was nothing to do but plunge ahead, which Isabael did; she lunged forward and burned a large swath of Cesorean men with her green flames, leaving nothing behind. Meera and Aegwren both squinted into the flames and winced at their destruction but neither turned away.

Then the two armies met, clashing in a cacophony of screams. Isabael could no longer use her fire without risking burning their own people, so she bit and slashed at the Cesoreans around her. When anyone got close enough, Aegwren swiped his sword at them, bloodying his blade for the first time. No one wore armor, and men fell quickly to their deaths. The other riders flew behind the Cesoreans, attacking from behind and forcing them to trample one another, desperate to escape the multi-colored flames. It was loud, chaotic, and horrible.

Most of the men were on foot, but Aegwren saw the Cesorean leader, Sakhean, atop a horse and urged Isabael toward him. The raek tried, but she could not move without crushing their own men underfoot and did not have the space to stretch her wings and leap into the air. Frustrated, Aegwren jumped from her back and inserted himself into the heaving, struggling crowd. Meera was scared for him—she didn't know how Aegwren had died and thought that this could possibly be it—but there was nothing she could do to stop him.

Indeed, nothing seemed capable of slowing Aegwren's progress toward his intended victim; he was a true warrior among farmers and tradesmen, and he ducked, dodged, and swung his blade, cutting through men with an ease that almost shamed him. He had fought and trained for the strength he had, but did that give him the right to kill? Even as he struggled with his actions, he pressed forward, stumbling over bodies and creating more. He forced his way toward Sakhean with a single-minded determination that he needed in order to keep moving at all. Otherwise, he might look around him—otherwise, he might see what he was doing and register the destruction he was wreaking.

Meera looked toward Sakhean with Aegwren, feeling her gorge rise in her distant throat. Each swing of his blade made her feel more sick, more certain that what he did was wrong. She knew why he fought, but she wished he would stop. For once, she didn't feel comfortable in Aegwren's body; she didn't agree with his actions, but there was nothing she could do. She was helpless ... She was helpless as Aegwren reached Sakhean's horse and stabbed the man through chest from below. She was helpless as Sakhean slid from his mount and twitched on the ground, gargling disturbingly when Aegwren wrenched his sword free. She was helpless as he continued to stab and to kill until only olive-toned men remained standing, and all of the Cesoreans lay dead or dying.

While his men cheered, Aegwren fell to his knees in a pool of mud and blood. The warm, fetid mess seeped quickly into his pants, and he stared uncomprehendingly as the moisture slowly crept up his knees, darkening his pant legs. "It is over," Isabael said, reassuring him. "We left not one man standing, and I doubt they will trouble your people ever again."

Aegwren did not respond. He had done what he had set out to do, but he felt more hopeless than ever; he had seen what humans were capable of, and it made him wonder how there could ever be lasting peace. Still gripping his sword in his hand—the sword his uncle had given him, the sword with the opal symbolizing hope and love—he stared at the gore clinging to its blade and dripping from its tip. With a jolt, he released its hilt, letting the weapon sink into the mud at his side. Then he began to shake, and all he could think over and over was that he hoped his uncle could not see him there.

MEERA AWOKE TREMBLING AND SWEATING. With a lurch, she pushed the covers off of her to lean out of the bed and vomit all over the floor. Light filtered in through the cave door, and she quickly burned the mess she had made before plopping back against her pillow and shaping herself some water to drink. After a minute or so of panting and clutching her stomach, she felt settled enough to sit up. For a long time, she sat and tried to clear her mind, but she couldn't seem to unsee what she had seen or forget the sounds and smells from the battlefield.

Eventually, she rose and made herself breakfast just for something to do—some way to distract herself. She ate what she had made so as not to waste it, but each bite felt wrong like she was indulging while men still lay bleeding and dying. Every swallow threatened to gag her, but she forced herself to eat regardless. She reminded herself over and over that the fight had taken place a long time ago—that the men had long since been buried and grieved for—but the thought didn't settle her.

After she had eaten, Meera stepped out of the cave just to look at the sky and breathe in the still, cold air of the valley. Shaya was there, lying in her usual spot and tracking her through one eye. The raek could surely sense how upset Meera was, but she didn't offer any words or feelings of comfort. Instead, she observed Meera's physical and mental state like she was determining whether she was worthy of carrying into battle. "We will have to join the fight as Aegwren and Isabael did in order to end the war," Shaya said finally, lifting her head.

"No," Meera replied bluntly, both aloud and in her mind. She wasn't doing that—she couldn't. Maybe Shaya had picked the wrong rider. Maybe she wasn't a warrior.

Shaya hummed in irritation and slashed her tail at the thought. "Being a warrior is a choice," she replied. "You must choose to fight even if it is not what you want to do."

"No," Meera said again, turning to reenter the cave. When Shaya could no longer see her, she covered her face in her hands and cried; she cried for what Aegwren had done, for the men on that field, and she cried for the choice she had to make. She wanted to end the war, but she didn't want to slaughter people; she knew she couldn't live with herself afterward. If she chose to fight, she would forfeit herself—forfeit the life she wanted to live with Kennick.

Aegwren had done that, she reminded herself; Aegwren had chosen to fight and lead rather than to find the woman he had loved and make a life with her. He had thought it was his duty. Was it her duty as well? Was she supposed to give up her life to be something bigger? Clutching her ring, she shuddered at the thought. What was she fighting for if she wasn't fighting to live in the Riders' Holt with the other riders? She had always said she wasn't more important than other people, but she was still important, wasn't she?

Meera sat down on the bed and reached for Aegwren's letters, hoping he had some wisdom for her. Surprised to find that there was only one letter left, she clutched it and read it in trembling hands:

My Dear Leannon,

The battle is over, and I am sure you know how it ended. We killed your people. I killed your people. I led men into that field to die and to annihilate, and I killed more than all of the rest. I killed Sakhean and countless others, and it was easy. My uncle once told me that a sword is a great responsibility because it is almost too easy to harm others with such a weapon, and he was right. I took men down like they were nothing, and to my shame, I did it with my uncle's gift.

I doubt this letter will ever reach you. I am sure you and I will never meet again, and for that, I am sorry. To be honest, I am sorry for all of it. The more time that passes, the more I wish I had stood between our warring people as I had once stood between my raek and my village. I think there would have been more honor in being crushed between the armies than in joining one group of men to kill another group just as human and worthy. I regret my actions.

So far, there have been no further attempts by your people to cross the border and attack my people. However, I do not see how this peace can last. I have always thought that violence only brings more violence, and yet, I enacted a bloodbath on the premise of establishing peace. There is quiet between our lands, for now, but it will not hold. This battle has solidified the uncertainty and mistrust between our people into hate and fear. This violence will eventually beget more violence, and it is my fault.

My people have named me the leader of this land. It is not a role that I want, but it is one I have earned for myself—not because I deserve praise but because I must now spend my life endeavoring to maintain the fragile peace between our lands. I will do my best, but I fear my actions on that battlefield will ripple long into the future.

I can no longer bear to carry my sword. The weapon that once reminded me of my uncle and my strength now only reminds me of my folly. The opal that you once admired is tainted by death. I wonder sometimes why my uncle gave me a sword at all and not some instrument of love and peace. If I have the privilege of seeing him again, I will ask him. And, if by some miracle I see you again, Leannon, I will bid you a long and happy life without me. I have doomed this land to live in wait of another conflict, and I have doomed myself to a life of fending off more war. I would not doom you to such a fate.

Aegwren

Meera read the letter several times over. Aegwren regretted it; he regretted fighting in the battle because it had only caused more hatred between the two peoples—hatred that had persisted and festered for thousands of years. Meera slapped the letter onto her side table and flopped back in the bed. How was she, one person, supposed to suddenly end thousands of years of violence?

"You are not alone," Shaya reminded her.

"You're right," Meera said, grateful for her raek. She had Shaya, and she had Kennick, Endu, Shael, and Cerun. She wondered, too, if the other riders might join her.

"Join you for what?" Shaya asked. "What is our plan?"

"We're going to do what Aegwren wished he had done," Meera replied. "We're going to get in the middle and prevent the battle from happening."

"How long could we possibly hold off five conjoining armies, and how will this help my kin reach our brethren?" Shaya asked tonelessly.

"I don't know," Meera replied honestly. "But it's the best plan I can think of."

Shaya hesitated a moment, then she hummed in agreement.

26

MEERA

Meera tidied the cave, leaving Aegwren's letters inside the trunk at the foot of the bed. Then she mounted Shaya to fly home. As tempted as she was to stay another night and learn what Aegwren had done next, there was a living man waiting for her who might need her support. Kennick's challenge was the next day, and Meera wanted to soothe his nerves and hold him through the night as he had done for her. She would not leave him waiting and wondering when she would return—not this time.

Shaya circled low over the peninsula around midday. Meera assumed Kennick would be training and eating with the other riders, preparing mentally and physically for his fight. When the sun glinted off his dark red hair, she noticed him by the lake and grinned down at him. The next time Shaya circled, Meera jumped from her back, slowing her fall and landing in a swirl of sand on the beach where Kennick and Isbaen had been sparring. Unapologetically, she inserted herself between them and hugged Kennick, leaning her face against his chest.

He was breathing hard and sweating from his exertions, but he held her back with his free arm. Meera knew she should pull away, but she didn't—the battle was still raging repeatedly in her mind. She needed the hug; she couldn't seem to shake the lingering horror of Aegwren's memory. "Are you okay?" Kennick asked, trying to look down at her.

Taking a deep breath, Meera pulled herself together. She wanted today to be about Kennick; she didn't want to distract him or sap his energy for herself. "Glad to be home," she replied, stepping back and smiling up at him.

Kennick didn't look entirely convinced. "Are you sure?" he asked.

"It was just a rough night with Aegwren," she said vaguely. Then she turned toward Isbaen. "How's he doing, Isbaen? Are you whipping him into shape?" she asked.

"I do not think Kennick's absence has dulled his abilities," Isbaen replied seriously.

Meera nodded and looked back at Kennick. "Don't train too hard. You don't want to be sore tomorrow," she warned.

"Soleille said she would heal my muscles at the end of the day," he told her, eyes glinting.

"What? She told me she doesn't do that!" Meera cried.

"She is making an exception for me," Kennick replied with a smug smile. "What was in those letters?" he asked, resisting Meera's best attempts at changing the subject.

"Wisdom from the past," she replied airily, doing her best impression of Darreal.

Kennick tilted his head forward and gave her a look, but she merely smiled and started backing up the slope. "Don't let me interrupt you!" she called, trying to slip away.

"It is time for lunch, anyway," Isbaen said, so they walked together to Hadjal's table. Isbaen and Kennick dropped their swords in the grass, and Meera sat at the end of the table across from Shael.

All of the riders gathered to eat as usual, and Meera wished she could enjoy it—she wished she could forget the night before and focus on being back with her little family. However, try as she might, she couldn't seem to distract herself from the gore she'd seen through Aegwren's eyes and the blood she'd felt splatter his skin. She could smell the food on her plate, but she could also smell the phantom stench of death. The other riders talked and laughed and discussed Kennick's upcoming challenge, but Meera could barely focus on their words.

She knew Kennick could tell she wasn't quite alright, but he wasn't pressing her to share. It was Shael who finally forced her to speak: "Meera, you aren't eating, and there's no fish on your plate. What's wrong?" he asked, eyeing her critically.

All eyes turned to Meera, so she smiled and shoved a large forkful of food into her mouth. "There, happy?" she asked around her mouthful. She chewed, grinding her teeth into the wad of chicken, but it felt wrong. Fixating on the fact that the food had once been flaccid, bloody flesh, she suddenly gagged and had to turn away awkwardly to spit it into her hand and burn it.

"That was convincing," Shael said sardonically.

Meera drank some water and avoided everyone's eyes. She really didn't want today to be about her. Kennick was tense next to her, and he abruptly stood from the bench and grabbed her arm with a firm grip, dragging her off with him and tugging her around the back of Hadjal's house. Meera stumbled after him, too shocked to object, and when they were out of sight and hearing range of the others, he whispered, "Are you pregnant?"

She just gaped at him for a second, registering the intensity in his dark eyes. "What? No!" she said. He squinted at her for a moment like he was trying to decide if she was being honest.

"I'm not!" she insisted. She supposed the last time she had returned from Aegwren's cave with changes in her appetite, she had been.

"Then what is it?" he asked with uncharacteristic agitation.

Meera sighed, exasperated with herself. "I'm just a little upset about something that happened thousands of years ago. I want you to focus on yourself," she replied. She knew Kennick would always be there for her, but she was tired of her burdens falling on his shoulders.

"Meera, I do not like when you keep things from me. Please, just tell me, or I will not be able to focus," he said softly, reaching out and taking her hand.

Reluctantly, she explained what she had read in Aegwren's letters and how she had experienced the battle with him. "It was disturbing and has also given me a lot to think about—that's all. It's nothing you need to worry about," she assured him.

Kennick held her to him and kissed her forehead. "Your concerns are my concerns," he murmured.

"And yours are mine, which is why I insist you focus on preparing for your challenge tomorrow. You've gotten soft from sitting on that ship for so long," Meera teased, pinching his sides even though they were solid muscle as usual. Then she coaxed Kennick back to the table.

Everyone tried to pretend they were interested in their food, but they kept shooting Meera concerned glances. Exasperated, she announced, "I'm not pregnant, and everything is fine." She forced herself to eat some of what was on her plate, avoiding the chicken.

"I want to spar a little longer, then will you shape rocks at me?" Kennick asked her, helping to break the tension around the table.

Meera grinned deviously. "Gladly," she told him.

"Are you even going to let Lethian swing his sword?" Shael asked.

Meera looked at Kennick curiously; it was a valid question. "I doubt he will bother bringing his sword," he replied.

"How much metal can you bring to the fight?" she asked.

"I can bring whatever I can wear," he said.

Meera supposed it would be more of a shaping fight than anything, and she looked forward to seeing what Kennick could do with his abilities in the stadium. "You're going to shred Lethian," she said, nudging him. Then she grimaced; she hoped Kennick wouldn't actually shred Lethian. She couldn't take anymore gore.

WHEN KENNICK ROSE from the table to continue training with Isbaen, Meera loitered, helping Hadjal and Sodhu clean up from lunch. Florean and Soleille also stayed to help, and Meera waited until they left before approaching Hadjal. "Is everything okay?" the older woman asked, noticing her strange behavior.

"I want to talk to you," Meera said, peering hopefully into her gold-hued eyes.

Hadjal looked a little nervous—she always looked nervous where Meera was concerned—but she nodded her head and sat down at the table. Sodhu brought her a cup of tea and sat down next to her, putting a supportive hand on her back. Meera was a little apprehensive to say what she wanted to say in front of Sodhu since she often reported to Darreal, but she trusted both knell women. "What is it?" Hadjal asked after Meera was silent and contemplative for a moment.

"Hadjal, I know Darreal has ordered the riders to fight in the upcoming battle, but ... I want to know what you think of another idea ..." she began hesitantly.

"What idea?" Hadjal asked warily.

"I will not fight—" Meera started to say.

"I know the Terratellens are your people, Meera, and I would not expect you to fight against them. But we must protect our land and our way of life. Darreal would not ask the riders to leave the peninsula unless it was necessary," Hadjal interjected.

"You are *all* my people!" Meera cried before taking a deep breath to calm herself. "Hadjal, what do you think about the riders standing between the armies to prevent the battle?"

Hadjal narrowed her eyes at her. "What would that accomplish? Even if we could hold the fighting at bay, we could not stay there forever," she replied.

"No ..." Meera said, "But maybe we could stay there long enough for Darreal and Otto to negotiate."

"I do not know how likely that is," Sodhu said sadly.

"I don't either, but what's the alternative? We kill as many of Terrattelle's, Cesor's, and Arborea's troops as we can just to wait for them to eventually attack again? If the riders go into battle, they would only be proving every notion the people of Terratelle have ever had about knell and raeken—that magic is evil and destructive and raeken are blood-thirsty monsters. What if we show them something else? What if we show them that we don't want to fight? Maybe they wouldn't want to fight either ..." Meera said. She knew she probably sounded naive and idealistic, but that was why she was asking Hadjal for her opinion; she respected the older woman's knowledge and experience.

Hadjal stared into her mug of tea, thinking. Then her eyes rose to Meera's, and she smiled. "It may not work, but I am willing to try," she said.

"Really?" Meera asked excitedly. She was going to stand

between the armies no matter what, but she would feel more confident and hopeful with the other riders to support her.

"I do not love the thought of putting all of the riders right in front of our enemies, but if we are to be there regardless, we might as well attempt to prevent the battle," she replied.

Meera beamed at her and felt Shaya's satisfaction in her mind. "You have done well," Shaya told her. "Now I will go to recruit wild raeken."

Meera started, but before she could ask questions or object, Shaya rose from where she was lying on the slope and launched into the air, flying away toward the mountains.

Then Hadjal spoke again, recapturing her attention: "Meera, I want to apologize again for not sending the riders to find you. When Kennick left, he said that the riders were meaningless if we could not even fight for our own, and I think he was right. I have been wondering ever since what our true purpose is, and it is not just to exist and perpetuate our traditions—it is to maintain peace and order. I realize now that I have been acting out of fear and that fear is not a noble motivation."

Meera reached out and took Hadjal's hand, squeezing it. "Don't be too hard on yourself, Hadjal. We're all just doing our best," she reminded her—something she had been reminding herself a lot lately.

"What next?" Sodhu asked, looking tired but determined.

"For now, we support Kennick in his challenge, then we prepare," Meera said, looking to Hadjal for agreement.

Hadjal nodded. Her lips were pressed together grimly, but a fierce light flared in her eyes.

MEERA DIDN'T MENTION her plans for the battle to Kennick yet. After a long afternoon of shaping dirt and rocks at him and opening holes under his feet, Soleille healed his sore muscles and many scrapes and bruises, and they ate dinner with the others and walked home arm-in-arm. "Do you feel ready?" Meera asked, enjoying the feeling of Kennick's strong arm around her shoulders.

"For the challenge or what comes after?" he asked.

"The challenge! Don't worry about anything else," she replied.

"What are you thinking, Meera? Do you think we should fight?" he asked.

She sighed. "What do you think?" she asked him. Kennick had told Darreal he wouldn't fight, but he had been supporting her at the time. She wanted to know what he wanted to do.

"I have seen a little of war and would rather not see any more of it, but if you think we should fight, I will," he replied.

Meera looked up at Kennick's face. He never talked about his time at the border. His eyes had a glassy, far-off look to them for a moment, but then he blinked and met her gaze. "Hadjal and I have agreed on a plan," she told him. His eyebrows rose in surprise. "We want to block the battle from happening—get in between the armies and hope that Darreal and Otto can negotiate while we prevent any fighting," she explained, studying him to see what he thought of the idea.

"You are not going to the border without me this time," he said simply.

"I don't want to go anywhere without you," Meera said, squeezing him tighter to her side. He smelled like he had been working hard all day, but she didn't care. "You need a bath," she added.

Kennick's eyes glinted mischievously, and he pulled her against him, tucking her under his armpit. She wrinkled her nose and squirmed but didn't actually try to get away. "Now you need a bath," he whispered in her ear before taking her earlobe in his mouth and sucking it. Meera grinned and turned in his arms to face him, getting all manner of ideas for what they could do in the water together.

27

KENNICK

K ennick woke early the next morning in anticipation of his challenge. Only a faint glow of sunshine illuminated the room. Meera lay facing away from him, still and serene. He contemplated getting up, but he didn't want to run that morning and tire himself out before his fight, nor did he want to make breakfast when they had told the others that they would eat at the peninsula. Unsure of what else he could do, he simply stared at the wood beams cutting across the ceiling, wondering how the day would go.

He wasn't nervous, exactly—more excited; his blood thrummed in anticipation of his fight with Lethian. They had sparred before but not with shaping, and Kennick was eager to test himself against one of the greatest warriors in Levisade— though he supposed the greatest warrior in Levisade was asleep next to him. Rolling onto his side, he looked at Meera's sleeping form. She was lying on her stomach with the covers pulled up to her neck and just one bare shoulder peeking into the air. His mind wandered to what they had done in the bath the night before, and his penis stiffened with the memory; Meera had shaped the bathwater in ways that had defied his imagination.

Suddenly, Kennick could not seem to stop himself from inching toward her under the covers and pressing his naked body against hers. He heard her breathing change slightly as she woke up, but she did not move from her comfortable position. Sweeping aside her short curls, he kissed the back of her neck and ran his hand down her spine to cup one of her butt cheeks, squeezing it gently. He saw her face twitch in a hint of a smile, but she still did not open her eyes or move.

Reaching a hand around Meera's front, he slid it between her and the bed. She lifted herself ever so slightly to give him space to move and touch her, and he caressed her breasts and stomach with his palm. The action made him think briefly of the day before when he had suspected she might be pregnant, and for a moment, he relived both his disappointment and relief at learning she was not; Kennick wanted a child with Meera but was not ready to face the fear of another pregnancy. He had been watching every night to see if she drank her tea.

When he trailed his hand lower and cupped her mound, she responded with a low hum that made his erection throb in response. Keeping them both under the covers, he inched himself further over until he lay partly on top of her, his hardness rubbing against her butt. Then he withdrew his hand from her burgeoning wetness and used it to grip under her thigh and bend her leg out to the side. Lifting onto his forearm, he brought the tip of his erection to her slick opening and paused in question.

Meera arched her back and pushed her butt into him in answer, so Kennick slid inside of her, meeting little resistance after their activities the night before. He went slowly, pressing himself all the way in and pulling almost all of the way out. Meera spread her leg out a little further to give him access but otherwise remained still and languid, letting him set the pace until eventually he thrust in one final time and collapsed over her, kissing her shoulder.

For a while they rested pressed together, unmoving. Kennick was warm and comfortable under their blankets, his spent penis tucked inside Meera's body. Slowly, the sun rose higher and brightened the room, and he began to wonder if she had fallen back asleep. "Are you awake?" he murmured.

She took a deep breath and shifted slightly. "I'm either awake, or I'm having a very convincing dream," she replied, her voice muffled by her pillow. Squinting in the light, she moved to rub her eyes, so Kennick lifted his weight off of her, sliding himself free as he did. "Oh!" she exclaimed, laughing. "I guess it wasn't a dream."

He chuckled and rolled her over to kiss her. He was ready to start the day, but he wouldn't leave the bed if she craved more. "Do you want to keep dreaming?" he asked against her mouth.

Meera sighed, which turned into a stifled yawn. "No. I think we should probably get up. Big day today!" she said.

Kennick kissed her again before climbing out of the bed and going into their washroom. He got ready quickly, having already decided what he would wear. Then he belted his sword to his waist and strapped on the harness of metal instruments he and Meera had devised the day before. He had made several flat, three-pronged tools for spinning in order to block rock projectiles and also carried some loose clumps of metal to shape during the fight. He did not know exactly what to expect from Lethian, having only sparred with him using swords, but he assumed the warrior would have a non-metal weapon for the occasion.

Meera dressed quickly as well, and they left for the peninsula to eat breakfast. "Are you nervous?" she asked as they walked hand-in-hand.

"I'm excited, but mostly, I feel content. We are finally at home together, and everything is as it should be," he replied, smiling down at her.

"For now," she amended with a frown.

"We will go to the border together, and we will return from the border together," he assured her.

At breakfast, the other riders offered him various tidbits of encouragement and advice for his fight. Kennick listened politely but really did not feel concerned about facing Lethian. He wanted to beat the current champion, but as he had just told Meera, he was happy with his life as it was. If he did not win, he would still mount his raek and return to his home with the woman he loved. All would be well either way.

When he was finished eating, Isbaen offered to do his hair for him and quickly added many small braids to his head, weaving them intricately together. "That's much better than I could have done," Meera said approvingly as she watched. Kennick smirked at her; Meera had a lot of skills, but braiding was not one of them.

"Isbaen, how's Gendryl? I haven't seen him since getting back," Meera asked, making Kennick cringe inwardly. Soleille had told him that Isbaen and Gendryl were not together anymore, but he had forgotten to relay the news to Meera with everything else they had going on.

Isbaen paused what he was doing momentarily, then continued his gentle ministrations to Kennick's hair, replying, "Gendryl and I are no longer spending our time together, but I am sure he is doing well on his farm."

Meera stiffened and made a face. "I'm sorry, Isbaen. I thought ... well, I hope you are both doing well," she said awkwardly.

"I have been better," Isbaen admitted. He had seemed his usual serene self to Kennick, but Kennick supposed he might just hide his emotions well.

When Isbaen finished with his hair, Kennick thanked him,

and they all stood to fly to the estate. Kennick was glad that Shaya was away, giving Meera an excuse to fly with him. He liked to hold her in front of him as they flew, and even though he was not nervous, he would rather have someone to talk to than obsess about the challenge the whole way to the estate.

They all flew directly to the stadium on the west side, and he could see that it was already teeming with people. Endu landed, then stretched and fluffed his wings proudly, making him laugh. The other raeken settled nearby, and when Kennick leapt from Endu's back, he turned and observed them all together, wondering if Meera's plan for the battle could really work. They were certainly a mighty group, especially with Shaya's bulk added in and Meera's shaping abilities. Kennick thought they could probably hold off the battle. The question was: for how long, and to what end?

The other riders walked into the stadium with him and gave him last pats of encouragement before they took their seats in the stands. Kennick was about to turn to Meera, but his eyes were caught by two people approaching––two people he had never wanted to see again: his parents. Andreena and Destin were striding toward him, looking grim but determined. Kennick glared at them as they neared, and Meera took his hand from beside him. Kennick suddenly wished he could face his parents in the challenge, not Lethian. Lethian had acted with a disregard for Meera's life, but his parents had actively attempted to harm her and their baby.

Clenching the hand Meera was not holding, he took a deep breath, trying to reign in his anger. It would not serve him, after all. He could have reported his parents officially for their crime, but he had not. Their punishment was living without their only child. Kennick turned away from his approaching parents and looked, instead, at Meera. She smiled up at him warmly. "I don't care if you win but don't get hurt," she told him.

He smiled back and kissed her. "I will do my best," he promised. "Why don't you go sit down?"

"Are you sure?" she asked, glancing toward his parents.

Kennick nodded. He did not think he could handle watching his mother simper at Meera and offer her condolences for her miscarriage. Meera looked reluctant to go, but she walked away, aiming for the other riders in the stands. When Andreena and Destin reached him, Kennick spoke before they could: "You should take your seats. I have nothing to say to you."

"Son, we know you are angry with us, but we just want to wish you the best for your fight. We were so proud to hear that you had challenged the champion and would be glad to see you earn some recognition," his mother said.

Kennick frowned, feeling less compelled to fight than ever. "Go," he told them again, turning away to look for his opponent.

Lethian and Darreal entered the stadium at the same time, and Darreal raised a hand for quiet. "I welcome the current champion, Lethian, and Rider Kennick for today's challenge!" she called.

The crowd cheered, clearly anxious for the fight. Kennick supposed with the upcoming battle, the challenge was a needed distraction for many. Lethian raised a hand at those gathered, enjoying the attention, and people yelled and clapped even louder. Kennick watched the blonde-haired warrior bask in the appreciation of their audience, and his desire to beat Lethian surged within him. He did not respect the man's values and did not think he deserved the title of champion after leaving Meera behind. Taking a deep, steadying breath, he found Meera in the crowd, blew her a kiss as she had for him, and faced his opponent. He was ready.

28

KENNICK

Lethian stood before him looking calm and confident, but that was fine with Kennick because he felt the same. He eyed the sheath on his opponent's waist, however, wondering what was inside; he could sense that Lethian was not wearing any metal. Before Darreal could call for them to begin, both men drew their weapons and tossed their sheaths to the side. Kennick left his metal instruments strapped to his torso and studied Lethian's sword, which seemed to be made of some sort of stone. Grinning, he wondered how well Lethian could swing his new blade; he was eager to find out.

Once they both stood ready, Darreal shouted, "Begin!"

Unlike Meera, Kennick did not wait for Lethian to make the first move; he shaped the three metal spinners he had made to fly behind him and on his sides to block any projectiles Lethian might shape at him, and he lunged for the warrior with his sword. Rather than blocking Kennick's attack with his blade, Lethian dodged and shaped a low wall between them. Kennick wondered at that; he wondered how durable the stone sword was. Was it only a last defense?

When a gaping hole suddenly opened beneath him, he was ready for it, shaping the metal cuffs on his wrists and ankles and the bars attached to his belt to prevent himself from falling. He and Meera had practiced the maneuver repeatedly the day before, and he did it without even losing control of his spinners. It was a good thing, too, because in the next second, Lethian shaped hard clods of dirt at him from all sides, and Kennick whipped his head around, using his spinners to block most of the projectiles. Several hit him and would leave bruises, but he was not incapacitated by any means.

Finding his footing once more, he continued to block hard dirt clods. For several minutes, Lethian's attacks were relentless, and he was forced to defend over and over again. He needed an opening to become the attacker, but the other warrior was barely leaving him any time or space to move. Finally, his moment came when Lethian shook the ground hoping to unbalance him and stumbled slightly. Even though Lethian only took a minute step to the side, his concentration broke long enough for Kennick to shape a hunk of metal at him. He aimed for the leg Lethian had stepped out, trying to wrap a cuff around his ankle.

Lethian moved fast enough that Kennick could not entrap his leg, but the partially formed metal strip clipped the side of his ankle, knocking him off-balance and gouging a line through his pants and flesh. Kennick immediately shaped two more hunks of metal toward Lethian and redirected the original one as well. Lethian quickly ducked down and formed a protective layer of rock over himself, completely disappearing into the ground.

Glancing in all directions, Kennick shaped himself into the air to hover, unsure of where his opponent would reappear. If Lethian had been wearing even a single metal button, Kennick would have known where he was, but his opponent had not been so foolish. Kennick hovered, waiting, and as time wore on, he wondered if Lethian was trying to wear him out. He could not hold himself in the air forever.

He threw a bit of metal to the ground, trying to bait his opponent, but nothing happened. All he could do was continue to hold himself aloft by his metal cuffs and remain alert. Gradually, the crowd became restless as everyone wondered where Lethian was. Kennick did his best to ignore their noise and concentrate. Slowly, he began to feel the strain of using so much magic. Then a bead of sweat dripped down his face, a stark reminder that time was passing, and his strength was not infinite.

After weighing his options, he decided to land; he would rather risk a trap than deplete all of his magical energy. Muscles tense and ready, he let himself fall to the ground. The second he landed, he took off running, sprinting in a nonsensical pattern through the arena, still waiting for Lethian to emerge. Kennick was growing both frustrated and tired and could not decide if Lethian was a coward or a genius for hiding in the ground beneath him and letting him deplete his own energy. Panting for air, he continued to run, looking wildly around for any sign of movement.

Eventually, Kennick slowed, and when he did, the dirt beneath him surged and encased one of his feet. Jerking forward, he only barely caught himself with his free foot before his forward momentum could snap his entrapped leg. Something tore painfully in his knee, however, and he gasped in a breath, wincing. He was caught, and he was hurt. Kennick shaped his spinners away from his body once more to protect his back and sides and looked all around for Lethian. The blonde warrior finally appeared, leaping from a new hole in the ground right in front of him and swiping at him with his stone blade.

Kennick blocked the attack with his sword and saw a small piece of stone chip away from Lethian's weapon when he did. Lethian did not pause to assess his blade, however; he continued to attack, attempting to make a final blow with his stone sword now that Kennick was trapped. Kennick wondered briefly if he should forfeit rather than force Meera to watch him get stabbed— it was likely to happen eventually, no matter how well he defended himself—but it was not in his nature to admit defeat. If anything, his predicament made the challenge that much more ... challenging.

Baring his teeth in half-grin, half-grimace, he continued to fend off Lethian's attack. Then, using his metal cuffs to hold him upright, he struck out at the other man with his free leg, surprising Lethian and clipping one of his knees. In Lethian's moment of distraction, Kennick shaped a mass of metal at him, managing this time to wrap a cuff around one of his ankles. Now they were both held by one leg. Kennick shaped the metal cuff to drag Lethian toward him as Lethian shaped the ground up Kennick's free leg, immobilizing him further.

Hoping to prevent his opponent from concentrating enough to encase his entire body in hard-packed dirt, Kennick lunged forward with his sword. Lethian blocked him, but Kennick kept attacking, slashing and stabbing over and over. They were trapped face-to-face, and Lethian was forced to defend with his blade— Kennick did not leave him time to shape a barrier between them. He swung and swung, and Lethian parried and deflected with the reflexes of a lifetime of sword training.

Each time their swords struck one another, however, the blonde warrior's stone blade chipped and weakened. Lethian knew his weapon would not last forever and made one last effort to shape the ground further up Kennick's body—attempting to debilitate him completely. The hard dirt reached Kennick's stomach, but the effort it took Lethian to shape caused his attention to waver. It was only the briefest millisecond of distraction, but it was just long enough for Kennick to have an opening.

He swung his sword—but not for Lethian—for his weapon. Kennick brought his blade down with all of his strength, aiming for a chip in the warrior's stone sword. He hit it precisely, and Lethian's blade snapped in half. Kennick's sword continued downward, lodging into Lethian's right shoulder—hacking through bone and muscle. Lethian cried out in agony the same second the crowd erupted in cheers so loud they startled Kennick. He had all but forgotten the gathered knell and looked toward the stadium blankly. The crowd clapped and smiled for his success even as Lethian bled out and collapsed to his knees at the end of his blade.

Kennick blinked and saw the healers running toward them, but then his eyes landed on his parents. His mother's dark red hair blazed like a beacon to him in the stadium, drawing his gaze to where she and his father sat. He stared at Andreena's smiling face and hated the joy and the pride he saw in it. She did not deserve to feel such things. Suddenly, Kennick wondered what he was doing. He did not wish to be champion. He had wanted to show Lethian that his title was meaningless—that titles and honor were not the same.

Before the healers could reach Lethian, Kennick raised both of his hands in the air and shouted, "I forfeit!" The crowd was so loud, they could not hear what he said at first, but they quieted when they saw him speak. "I forfeit!" he shouted again, just as the first healer reached Lethian and grasped his sword hilt to wrench from the warrior's shoulder. The other healers arrived right after, and together, they quickly shaped Lethian's wound away, leaving only a large tear in his shirt.

The healers were the only ones moving; everyone else was still with shock and confusion. Even Darreal looked uncertain. But Kennick made brief eye-contact with the queen, who then stood and shouted, "As Rider Kennick has forfeited, I name Lethian my champion!"

The crowd did not cheer. People were perplexed, processing what had just happened. Kennick glanced at his parents and saw the anger in his mother's eyes. He smiled, thinking that if there were candles in the stadium, they would all be flickering like mad with her emotion. His father seemed to shrink in his seat with embarrassment. Good, Kennick thought; he hoped they were disappointed and humiliated. He did not care what the knell in the stadium thought of him—what most of them thought, anyway.

His eyes sought Meera and the other riders—his true family. Most of them looked confused, but Meera was laughing and clapping. She was the only person clapping, but she was the only person whose opinion really mattered. When they locked eyes, she started to move through the stadium down toward him, and Kennick felt the dirt around him loosen and crumble apart, releasing him from its hold. He took one shaky, exhausted step out of the rubble, but when he attempted another, his injured knee gave under him. Falling to the ground, he stayed there, looking over at Lethian to make sure the other man was okay.

Lethian was also sitting. He looked pale and shaken but otherwise fine. When he glanced up, Kennick nodded in acknowledgement, but Lethian merely frowned at him. Then one of the healers turned their attention toward Kennick and shaped his knee and other small injuries. He was still tired, but his body was whole and sound. Pushing himself to his feet, he brushed some dirt off of his pants just before Meera threw herself at him. Kennick stumbled back, but he caught her and his balance, laughing.

Meera kissed him, and he kissed her back fervently, not caring if a stadium full of people was watching. "That was amazing!" she said, breaking away. "I'm so proud of you!"

Kennick glowed with her approval. "And the ending?" he asked.

"That was the best part!" she said, beaming. "Such showmanship! I hope Follaria was here," she added, glancing at the crowd.

Kennick laughed. Meera picked up his sword for him and shaped the blood from it. Together, they walked to where Endu awaited them. "Well?" Kennick asked his raek mentally, meeting Endu's large burgundy eye. He did not know what Endu would think of him forfeiting and feared he may have embarrassed his raek and possibly opened a chasm between them once more.

"I chose well," Endu replied simply.

Kennick grinned and continued to grin even when Meera had to more or less lift him onto Endu's back. Then he smiled the whole way back to the peninsula and all through the celebratory meal they shared with the rest of their family. He was so exhausted, he almost fell asleep at the table, but when Meera pulled him up to take him home, he smiled broader than ever.

29

SHAEL

Shael enjoyed watching Kennick's challenge and only experienced minimal jealousy upon seeing what his friend could do. However, he struggled to concentrate on the fight—he had been struggling to concentrate on much at all lately; the battle was always at the forefront of his mind. He'd been wanting to ask Meera what she was planning—assuming she would try to stop the battle and wanting to know what he could do to help—but he hadn't found the right time.

While Hadjal had welcomed Shael back to the peninsula with open arms, he wasn't sure he wanted to follow her and the other riders into war. He had no love for Terratelle's rulers or the soldiers who had captured him, but he had captained a crew of Terratellens who had been men and boys like any others. And when Shael pictured riding into the battle on Cerun and burning and hacking through the enemy, he couldn't help but picture the faces of his crew on the other end of his sword. If Meera had a plan, he wanted to be a part of it.

After Kennick's fight, they all returned to the peninsula for dinner. As much as Shael wanted to ask about the battle, everyone was in such high spirits that it never seemed like the right moment to discuss the war. Watching Meera heft Kennick from the bench and lead him into the woods, he decided he would ask them the next day what they were planning. Then he mounted Cerun to fly home and was struck by the thought that not long ago, he would have jumped at the chance to fight—he would have viewed the upcoming battle as an opportunity for him to prove his grit as a knell and his worth as a rider. He would've hoped it could make up for being captured and earn back some of the other riders' respect. He didn't feel that way anymore. Now it was his own respect he was concerned with. He had broken his oaths once to follow his conscience, and he would do it again.

"You have come a long way," Cerun agreed in his mind, making Shael feel unusually proud and gratified.

THE NEXT MORNING, Shael ran to Hadjal's house as he always did and found Isbaen sitting alone, staring out at the lake. "Good morning," he greeted his mentor.

Isbaen greeted him in return and smiled, but Shael could see that his mind was elsewhere. Isbaen hadn't quite been himself since Shael had left with Kennick to find Meera, and Shael couldn't tell if his mentor's change in behavior was directed specifically at him—was Isbaen disappointed in him for breaking his oaths? They hadn't actually discussed the matter since he had returned—they hadn't discussed much of anything. "Isbaen, are you disappointed that I left against Hadjal's wishes?" Shael asked, sitting across from him.

Isbaen looked up, blinking to dispel whatever had been on his mind. "No, Shael. I was glad to see you follow your own path. In fact, I have been thinking that your training is over," he replied, sitting up straighter and smiling.

Shael stared at him open-mouthed. "Really?" he asked in disbelief. When Hadjal had announced that Kennick's training was over, he had been envious, but now the thought of not having Isbaen's daily guidance made him nervous. Whether he was a full-rider or a rider-in-training, he was a rider, and he would rather have Isbaen as a mentor and guide than not.

"Yes, really," Isbaen said. "You have matured enough not to need my supervision. Of course, you will always have my friend-ship," he added reassuringly.

Shael smiled at him uncertainly. "In that case, friend, what's going on with you? You're not acting like yourself," he replied.

Isbaen met his eyes calmly and let his smile fade, showing Shael some of his sadness. "I searched my long life for love and have let it slip through my fingers," he replied quietly.

Gendryl, Shael thought, nodding. Of course, Isbaen's mood was not about him but about his break with Gendryl. Shael took a deep breath, thinking before he spoke. "Don't make the same mistake I did and wait until he is engaged to someone else before you tell him how you feel," he said finally, grimacing at his own folly.

"I knew you had become wise," Isbaen replied, blue eyes flash-ing. "I am not sure it is that simple, though."

"Why?" Shael asked. "What happened?"

"I could not reconcile myself to Gendryl's abortion," Isbaen admitted. "Even though it happened before I knew him and had nothing to do with me, I could not help but think about it at times and wonder if our values were too different. I found myself obsessing about the person that might have existed but does not and who they might have been."

"Did you tell him that?" Shael asked.

"I did, and he—rightfully—felt judged and said that he could not be with someone who was so bothered by a decision that he felt good about. I agreed—I agreed that we did not seem to be compatible—but I still love and miss him and wonder if it was a mistake ..." Isbaen replied. Despite the pain in his voice, he sat very still, and no lines creased his handsome face.

Shael leaned his elbows against the table and averted his eyes to think. He didn't know quite what to say to Isbaen's predicament. He wanted Isbaen and Gendryl to reconcile because they had clearly been very in love, and he wanted them to be happy. But Isbaen could not help how he felt about Gendryl's abortion—could he? "Did Gendryl explain why he made his decision?" Shael asked.

"He did," Isbaen said, not sharing the other man's private motivations.

"Do you think you love him enough to be glad that Gendryl did what was best for him, even if it was not what you would have done?" Shael asked.

Isbaen didn't answer at first. Then, after a few moments, he stood and said, "I will give it some thought," before walking down to the beach.

Shael watched him go. He didn't know if he had helped, but he hoped he had. When Hadjal came out of her house, she held two mugs of tea and handed him one. "I did not want to interrupt," she said. "But I did hear. Congratulations!" Reaching across the table, she squeezed Shael's shoulder.

Shael smiled at her, then looked down at the mug in his hands. "Hadjal, I don't think I can go into battle with you," he blurted.

He thought Hadjal would be upset—angry even that he was disobeying her again—but she continued to smile, the lines on the side of her eyes creasing slightly. "You, Kennick, and Meera have inspired me to go against Darreal's wishes. None of us will be fighting in the battle," she told him, a gleam in her golden eyes. "We will be trying to stop it."

Shael stared at her in disbelief for a second, then he grinned and lifted his mug in the human tradition, saying, "Cheers to that!"

Hadjal clinked mugs with him with a laugh.

WHEN EVERYONE GATHERED FOR BREAKFAST, Meera and Hadjal shared their plans for the battle. Shael was ready; he and Cerun would gladly stand at the border to delay fighting for as long as it took for negotiations to occur. Some of the others, however, were not as comfortable acting against Darreal's orders. "Rather than fight alongside our brethren, you would have us go against our queen and possibly forfeit our homes and lives?" Florean asked. "Even if we prevent the battle and Darreal manages to negotiate an end to the war, she may not allow us to return to Levisade."

"That is a valid point," Isbaen added.

Katrea and Soleille also looked torn.

"Is living on the peninsula in your houses really more important to you than the lives of thousands of humans?" Meera asked. "Not to mention the knell that might fall in battle—the raeken and riders, too."

"You do not know that we could stop the battle," Katrea said. "Then thousands would die, and we may lose our home, our families, and our country. Where would we go?"

"Kallanthea would take us in," Shael said, grinning. He didn't think Darreal would banish them for trying to prevent the battle, but if she did, he supposed they could all take a trip across the

Cerun Sea. Meera grinned back at him, but the others looked skeptical.

"I will not make any of you join us," Hadjal said. "But I agree with Meera that if we are to risk our lives, I would rather do so for peace than for victory."

Isbaen nodded at that. "I agree, but Hadjal, I think you should remain here. Someone must remain at the peninsula to teach future riders if we all perish."

"We won't die," Meera said confidently. "I won't let us."

"In that case, count me in," Katrea said, laughing.

"I will not let us die either," Soleille added, nodding her head.

Florean was the last holdout, but he, too, nodded. "My loyalties are with the riders above all else. If you will all go, then so will I," he said.

Once it was decided that they were all willing to follow the plan, they discussed logistics. Darreal had already told Hadjal when she wanted the riders to leave for the border and where they were to camp, and they decided to still follow those instructions. However, once the battle was about to begin, they would fan out along the border and use any means short of killing to prevent the armies from clashing. The strongest shapers were to be spread out with Meera in the center and Kennick and Hadjal at either end. Hadjal, it was decided, would fly with Florean.

Shael felt anticipation build in his stomach even though it would still be days until they left for the border and probably another week before the armies came close to converging. He was not the only one; they all immediately started making preparations: the raeken flew out to hunt, Soleille started dragging large amounts of herbs and other supplies from her house, Katrea left to visit family, and Meera and Kennick discussed methods for holding back the soldiers without hurting them.

Shael considered visiting his parents and godchildren in

Sangea, but he couldn't stand the thought of possibly saying goodbye to them for the last time. Instead, he helped Hadjal and Sodhu pack food and supplies, and he ran—not because it would help him at the border but because he needed to feel like he was doing something. Isbaen often ran with him, and while they didn't discuss it, Shael could tell he still felt conflicted about Gendryl.

Finally, the day before they were to leave, Isbaen beckoned Shael onto the beach. "Everything okay?" Shael asked, noting the unusually somber expression on the other man's face.

"I have been thinking about what you said," Isbaen started. Shael raised his eyebrows; had his words to his former mentor really stuck with him for so long? "You were right—I cannot value the person who might have existed had Gendryl not had an abortion over the man that I know and love. Gendryl already lives in this world, and his happiness and wellbeing are important enough to me to accept the decision he made. Perhaps a healthy baby may have been born and perhaps not, perhaps that baby may have grown into a quality person and perhaps not, but Gendryl is a certainty. Gendryl exists, and he matters," Isbaen said.

Shael nodded and smiled. He hadn't wanted to push Isbaen into anything, but he was glad that his friend had chosen love and acceptance over judgment. "Will you go to him?" he asked. They were to leave in the morning, but there was still time.

"I will go to him, and if I am not back before you depart tomorrow, know that I will meet you at the camp," Isbaen said before pulling Shael in for a hug. Such gestures used to embarrass Shael, but he was learning to enjoy the affection of his friends and hugged Isbaen in return.

30

MEERA

Meera rose early on the morning of their departure. She had already packed her bag to take to the peninsula and left out one of the outfits Follaria had made her. Dressing in the dim, new light of the day, she then stood still for Kennick to braid back her hair and tuck it under. Neither of them spoke; they were both contending with their own thoughts. Meera desperately hoped they would return to their house—both alive and still welcome in Levisade—but she had no idea how Darreal would react to their disobedience and found herself looking around like she would never be there again.

"All will be well," Kennick assured her, seeing the expression on her face.

She took a deep breath and nodded. She had more power than any one person should rightfully have, and she intended to use it to stop the battle and to get them home safely. She wouldn't let herself be captured or let her emotions control her; she wouldn't do that to Kennick again, she told herself. Then she released her breath in a woosh and watched Kennick strap his sword and other metal instruments to his body.

"That's not going to be comfortable for me to lean against," she teased. Shaya still hadn't returned. Meera could feel her raek in her mind and had tried to call her back, but it didn't seem likely Shaya would get to the peninsula before they departed. Meera was sure she would return in time for the battle, but in the meantime, she would fly on Endu.

Kennick grinned at her and shrugged. "Maybe you can sit in back for once, and I can lean on you," he suggested.

"You don't like when I'm in back because I lie down and go to sleep," Meera reminded him, smiling.

"What kind of person sleeps hundreds of feet in the air?" Kennick asked, dark eyes glinting.

"The part-human, part-knell, part-raek kind," she replied.

"That's my favorite kind," he said, leaning down and kissing her. "Are you ready?"

Meera looked around the room again, her eyes snagging on Aegwren's opal-hilted sword. She loved the sword and always felt closer to Aegwren when she carried it, but she had also seen what he'd done with it and hadn't touched it since. She wanted to do things differently than Aegwren had; she didn't want to fight or to kill, so why wear a sword? Shutting her eyes briefly, she sent a thought to Aegwren and his Uncle Fendwren to be with her, then she opened them and looked at Kennick. "I'm ready," she told him.

Kennick glanced at her sword where it leaned, sheathed, against their dresser, but he nodded, accepting her decision without argument.

As THEY WALKED to the peninsula, Meera felt Shaya's presence grow in her mind, and she picked up her pace, glad that her raek would carry her that day after all. "Shaya's coming!" she told Kennick excitedly, rushing forward until she was running to Hadjal's house.

Kennick ran after her even though he was more heavily burdened with weapons, and they both broke through the tree line in time to see Shaya and an even larger raek circling above. Meera's lips parted in surprise just before the raeken dove down and landed one after the other, rattling the slope and causing several flocks of birds to take flight nearby.

The wild raek with Shaya was the largest Meera had ever seen and a rich clay color. Across the slope, she could see the alarm and amazement on the faces of the riders who had already gathered. Hesitating a moment, she approached Shaya and the other raek—another female. "You made it just in time," Meera told Shaya mentally. She could sense that her raek felt frustrated but didn't think it was with her. "What is it?" she asked.

"I approached all of the wild raeken living in the mountains and could only convince one to join us. The others refused to get involved in human affairs. They do not believe the minds of the Terratellens can be changed after so long," she replied, radiating despair.

"One is better than none," Meera reassured her, glancing at the gigantic raek. If she were a human soldier, she would certainly not want to march up to such a spectacular creature.

The raek observed her in return through one great, golden-brown eye. Slowly, Meera approached her, unsure of what was polite in this scenario. The raek remained entirely still except for a nervous twitch at the very tip of her tail. Meera stopped ten feet from her head and said, "Thank you for joining us. I hope we can make this land better for humans, knell, and raeken."

The wild raek flared her nostrils, scenting Meera, before she replied, "For many years, I have done nothing to change the circumstances of my kind, and nothing has changed. I find it is now only logical to do something." Her mental voice was higher than Shaya's, and Meera noted, she spoke better than Shaya had at first.

She smiled at the raek, whose gentility she could feel in her mind. "I'm grateful to you for coming. You speak well—have you interacted with humans or knell before?"

The raek hummed at the compliment. "My ancestor was the very first raek to take a rider, and I have inherited some of her knowledge," she explained.

"Isabael?" Meera asked in fascination.

The raek merely hummed in response.

Meera stepped away to join everyone for a quick breakfast as the other riders' raeken converged on the slope. They appeared anxious about the newcomer, but the clay-colored raek kept to herself and didn't cause any issues. "Shaya brought Isabael's descendent to join us," Meera explained when she reached the table.

Everyone exclaimed in interest and amazement, but none looked more intrigued than Hadjal. "Do you think she would speak to me?" she asked, hope making the older knell woman appear even younger than usual.

"I think so," Meera replied, watching Hadjal leave her mug behind to approach the raek. When the raek didn't react adversely to the knell woman's presence, Meera focused on her breakfast, loading her plate and sitting next to Kennick to eat.

"Isbaen is back," Shael announced from across the table, looking into the sky.

Meera turned and grinned when she saw Hillgari's glossy

purple body descending onto the slope with two men atop her back. Isbaen had brought Gendryl with him, and she was beyond happy that the two seemed to have reconciled. When they approached the table, she stood to greet Gendryl with a hug and thank him for the crib he had made her. He hugged her warmly in return and offered his condolences for her loss before cupping her face and kissing her cheek. "Did you come to see Isbaen off?" Meera asked.

"Gendryl is coming with us," Isbaen interjected, attempting to sound exasperated but grinning at the same time.

"I will be perfectly safe at your camp and will keep Sodhu company when you fly to the border," Gendryl explained.

"I will be glad to have you," Sodhu told him, walking over to kiss his cheek in welcome.

After that, they all finished eating, strapped their bags and supplies to the raeken that crowded the grassy slope, and flew out of Levisade into the cold air of late fall. Despite Meera's protestations, Shaya flew faster than the other raeken, leaving them all far behind—except for the clay-colored raek, who kept pace easily. "The raeken in Kallanthea are the size of one of your feet," Meera told her, showing her a mental image of Adari's little orange raek.

She had thought Shaya would find the small raek humorous, but Shaya was downright appalled by the image. "If I did not already feel a burning need to resume breeding migrations to the north, I would now! How disgraceful! I thought the raeken of Levisade were small and absurd looking," she huffed in Meera's mind, radiating disgust.

Meera laughed and reclined along Shaya's back, blocking the wind and warming her bubble with raek fire. She hoped Kennick had worn enough clothing to keep warm on the flight. Then her mind drifted to their plan and the war camp they were joining.

Darreal, her council, and the warriors of Levisade had all left days ago—directly after the challenge—to camp near the border and Aegorn's other troops. The queen was expecting the riders that day, but she was also expecting them to follow her into battle. Meera's gut churned at the thought. She had defied a monarch before, but Darreal was her friend.

For the rest of the flight, she fretted about whether she should speak to Darreal or not. She wouldn't change her plans and join the fight, but she didn't feel right about surprising and possibly humiliating her friend. If she told the queen their plan, would she try to stop them? *Could* she stop them? Meera wasn't sure what Darreal would say ... She had wanted to negotiate for peace rather than fight, but she had also seemed reconciled to the battle the last time they had spoken. Knowing Darreal, Meera couldn't imagine she was having an easy time sending her people to fight and probably hadn't had anyone to lean on. Meera wished she had been there for her friend, but a part of her also wished Darreal had been there for her when she had been miscarrying in the negotiations tent.

It had not really occurred to her before to be upset with the knell who had left her behind in the tent. At the time, she had been convinced that she'd deserved it—convinced that she'd deserved to be dragged away and locked up for her mistakes. Now, looking back, she realized that if their roles had been reversed—if Darreal or Lethian had been in her position—she never would have left a friend or comrade on their knees in enemy territory. Meera's memory of those final moments in the tent were hazy—clogged with the swirl of ash—but surely Darreal could have paused for her or sent someone else to get her.

Rubbing her eyes, she sat up and released her shape-shield to let cold wind buffet her face momentarily and snap her out of her morose reverie. She had made mistakes that day, and maybe Darreal had too. Meera had forgiven herself and decided at that moment to forgive Darreal. They were friends—they loved each other—and she didn't want any part of the war to get in between them. She would go directly to Darreal to speak with her, she decided, relaying her decision to Shaya.

Shaya communicated their change in plan to the clay-colored raek and bid the other raek to land when they reached the outskirts of the camp where the riders were meant to remain. Then she kept flying, sweeping over the seemingly endless rows of tents that made up Aegorn's army. Humans and knell alike looked up at them in surprise as they flew low overhead. When they reached the center of the camp where Meera knew Darreal would be located, there was no room for Shaya to land, so Meera jumped from her back. "I will meet you at our camp," she told her raek as she fell through the air. "Please, let Kennick know!"

Shaya sent her a fleeting pulse of agreement before circling back to the direction from which they had come. Meera landed softly in a small clearing with a fire pit, surrounded by a gathering of knell. They were eating and looked surprised by her appearance but not as frightened as human soldiers would have been, at least. Meera nodded to them and asked, "Where is Darreal's tent?"

The knell warriors seemed suspicious and neglected to respond, then one of them walked away. Meera sighed and watched them go, waiting. She tried to sense for Darreal's shape, but there were just too many people and too many tents. After a few minutes of being stared at by the knell around the fire, the one who had walked away reappeared with Lethian. Lethian looked distinctly wary, which made Meera grin; she hadn't enjoyed watching Kennick's blade slice into the blonde warrior's shoulder, but she did find it amusing that Lethian now knew that both she and Kennick could beat him in a fight. "Meera, what are you doing here?" he asked without preamble.

"I'm here to see Darreal," she replied.

"About?" he asked.

"That's for Darreal to know," she said testily, crossing her chilled arms over her chest. She brought some raek fire to the surface of her skin to warm herself, and Lethian flinched at the sight. "I don't own a jacket," she told him, shrugging. Unfortunately, while Kennick and Follaria had thought to supply her with an abundance of useless shoes and dresses, they had not thought to get her a jacket.

Lethian frowned at her for several long seconds before relenting. "This way," he said.

Meera followed him to the outside of a tent, then pushed past him and walked inside without waiting for permission. Darreal was in the tent alone and looked up, startled, when she entered. The queen was fully dressed in one of her gowns with her gold circlet on her brow, but she appeared to be taking a much-needed break, wilting in her chair. She quickly straightened, however, when Meera appeared, and her brief expression of shock was replaced with calm assuredness just as rapidly. "Meera, what are you doing here?" she asked, repeating Lethian's question unknowingly and standing from her chair.

Meera knew Darreal well enough to sense how uncomfortable she was. "I came to talk," she replied quietly, taking a step toward her friend.

"What about? I know you will not fight with me, and you must know you will not convince me to let Terratelle invade our land," Darreal said, losing some of her diplomatic poise and radiating irritation.

Meera put her hands up placatingly. "I know you are only

trying to do what's best for your people, Darreal, but so am I—"
she started to say, taking another step.

Darreal's eyes widened ever so slightly, fixating on Meera's
raised palms. Suddenly, she jerked back, shouting, "Lethian!"

In an instant, Lethian was in the tent, forcing himself between
them, and Meera scarcely knew what was happening. She was
there for her people—all of her people: humans, knell, and
raeken—but Darreal seemed to think she was there for Terratelle
—seemed to think she was there to hurt her ... Meera took a step
back, gaping at her friend where she stood behind her well-
muscled champion. She couldn't believe Darreal could think that
she would hurt her—kill her even.

"Leave!" Lethian shouted at Meera. His sword was drawn, and
he was quivering, clearly itching to use it, as if she couldn't easily
shape it from his hand and incinerate him if she wanted to.

Meera took another step back, her disbelief quickly turning to
hurt and anger. How could Darreal think she would attack her?
Swallowing, she took a moment to compose herself. She could
explain, she thought—get on her knees and swear she wasn't
there to hurt anyone—but her pride wouldn't allow it. Instead, she
said, "Darreal, my friend, don't forget what we first set out to do
together, and—as you once told me—remember that fear and
respect are not the same." Then she turned and left the tent.

Shaya was gone, and Meera was both burning with emotion
and shivering from the cold, so she ran. She ran through the tents
toward the back of the camp, pushing herself until her clothes
were soaked in sweat and her breathing was ragged and shallow.
She ran so that she wouldn't cry because Darreal had been the
female friend she had always wanted—the one she had thought
would always see the best in her—and she had assumed the
worst, the very worst. Meera ran until, eventually, she reached the
other riders and found Kennick, all but crashing into him.

"Woah!" he said, catching her in his arms and cutting off her momentum. "What is it?" he asked, holding her away from him to look into her eyes.

She just shook her head. She had tried—she had tried to do right by her friend. Now the riders had a plan to enact, and she would not feel bad about it. She would not feel bad about disobeying and deceiving Darreal.

31

MEERA

For days, Meera and the other riders sat in their sad camp and waited for news. Winter took hold of Aegorn, and snow flurried down on them periodically. Soleille gave Meera one of her extra jackets, and Meera often warmed them all with her raek fire. Kennick had to keep reminding her to conserve her energy—that they might have to fly to the border at any moment—but she had a hard time sitting still and doing nothing. After her disastrous encounter with Darreal, she felt ready to go. There was not a single qualm left in her mind to hold her back from doing whatever she could to prevent the battle.

Now the only thing holding Meera back was waiting for the battle itself. The armies were still gathering and attempting to mobilize. While she understood that arming and moving thousands of men took time, the whole thing seemed ridiculous to her. All of Aegorn's troops appeared to be camped out along the border, waiting to defend their land, and she supposed Terratelle was still waiting for the Cesorean and Arborean armies to converge with their own. Meanwhile, they were all living out in the cold open, probably growing hungrier and weaker each passing day.

Meera certainly felt like she was weakening as she waited, but she supposed it was mostly in her head. As the days passed, the raeken took turns flying away to hunt, and every time Shaya left, she awaited her raek anxiously, hoping she would be back before they were needed. All she really did for days was wait, and her patience was wearing thin. She wished she could go for a run but wasn't willing to be away from the camp for any period of time, afraid she would miss something. Instead, she paced; she paced back and forth through their small collection of tents, the bulky forms of multi-colored raeken rising all around her.

"Meera, you are going to drive us all mad!" Hadjal finally snapped one day. The other riders were gathered around a fire, passing the time, but Meera was pacing once more.

"Sorry," she replied. Walking over to stand behind Kennick, she put her hands on his shoulders.

Kennick reached back and squeezed her cold hands, warming them in his own, and she looked down at the intricate braids in his hair. Everyone around the fire was bedecked in complicated braided hairstyles courtesy of Isbaen, who was keeping his hands busy to pass the time. Meera's hair, however, was still in her single, tucked braid; she couldn't sit still long enough for Isbaen's administrations. Looking around the fire at her friends, she almost laughed at the sight of them all with their hair done. "Even if we fail at the border, the bards will sing songs about your hair for years to come," she joked.

Katrea laughed, and Shael patted his head in embarrassment. "It looks good," Meera assured him, catching his eye.

"Are you hungry, Meera?" Gendryl asked. He had been taking his role at the camp very seriously and spent most of the day trying to ply them all with food—Meera especially—recognizing that her shaping would be critical for their plan to succeed.

Meera shook her head. She hadn't been doing enough to feel hungry. She kicked the tips of her boots into the dirt and probably would have continued pacing if Kennick weren't holding her hands. Instead, she jimmied up and down on the balls of her feet. She never felt more human around the other riders than when they were all sitting still. Knell had a knack for stillness and patience that Meera would never come close to mastering.

"If you need something to do, I have bone fragments stuck in my teeth," Shaya announced in her mind.

Meera could sense that her raek was also growing weary of her constant anxiety. "Fun," she replied sarcastically. Still, she kissed Kennick's cheek and pulled her hands from his to help Shaya.

Her enormous raek crouched side-by-side with the clay-colored raek. The two of them had been rather companionable, making Meera wonder how social wild raeken were. When she approached Shaya's muzzle, her raek unhinged her jaw, opening her mouth wide to give Meera access, and she began poking around Shaya's teeth and gums for bits of bone fragments. It was not an enjoyable task, but the raek's hot breath warmed her hands and arms as she worked.

Randomly, Meera sensed amusement from Shaya. "What?" she asked mentally.

Shaya flashed an image of the clay-colored raek into Meera's mind then continued the thought: "... asked what it has been like for me since taking a rider. I told her I have found training a human very tedious and trying."

Meera rolled her eyes in the mental sense. "Do you want my help or not?" she asked in irritation.

"I also told her that I now could not imagine continuing my

life without your company. I felt very desolate and alone when you were gone," Shaya admitted.

Meera was touched by her raek's words—which Shaya could undoubtedly feel in her mind—and she paused what she was doing to hug and scratch the side of Shaya's scaly face. "I would not trade you for any other raek," Meera told her, which was saying something because, for a time, she would have gladly traded Shaya for just about any other raek.

Shaya hummed affectionately, then she shoved Meera with her snout, sent her an image of her returning to what she had been doing, and opened her mouth again, blasting her with her smelly raek breath. "Alright, alright," Meera said, laughing and resuming her task.

When she was finished, Shaya closed her mouth and flicked her tongue around appreciatively. Then she flashed an image of the wild raek in Meera's mind again and said, "... wants you to bring over ..." She didn't finish her thought with words, instead showing Meera a mental picture of Hadjal.

"Really?" Meera blurted aloud, wondering if she was understanding what was about to happen correctly. She had noticed Hadjal occasionally interacting with the clay-colored raek and knew that Hadjal had always hoped to have a raek of her own again, but she hadn't considered that the enormous, clearly ancient wild raek might want to take a rider.

Shaya didn't bother answering her query; she didn't like unnecessary talking. Meera could sense her raek's anticipation, however, and took that to mean that she was, in fact, understanding the situation correctly. The battle and the need to preserve her energy forgotten, she sprinted for the fire pit and Hadjal. Everyone looked at her in alarm when she got there, but she was panting too hard for several moments to say anything. As she continued to catch her breath, she grinned at Hadjal.

"What is it?" Hadjal asked, perplexed.

"The wild raek wants to speak to you!" Meera told her, smiling so wide that her cheeks ached in the cold.

Hadjal blinked at her and raised her eyebrows, a small gleam of hope entering her eyes. Slowly and dreamlike, she rose, turned, and walked away in the direction of the clay-colored raek.

Meera bounced up and down, watching her go. She was so excited for Hadjal, she forgot her frustration and anxiety entirely.

"Meera?" Kennick asked, not bothering to express his entire question.

"I think the wild raek is going to take Hadjal as her rider!" she blurted in excitement, tearing her eyes from Hadjal's back to look at Kennick and the others.

Kennick appeared overjoyed, and Sodhu burst into tears. Gendryl sat next to the older knell woman and patted her on the back. Meera turned to watch Hadjal and the clay-colored raek, hoping she wasn't wrong and hadn't gotten everyone excited about nothing, and the other riders watched in anticipation as well. For several long minutes, Hadjal stood still in front of the raek, then she touched the raek's jaw and climbed onto her back. Meera shouted and clapped as the raek shifted and methodically rose to her feet before lumbering a few paces and lunging into the air to fly in circles over their camp.

She was so overcome with emotion, she didn't notice the knell man run into camp with a note in his hand. "I am looking for Hadjal," the man announced, approaching their circle. Meera turned in surprise at the unfamiliar voice, and her stomach leapt into her throat, their plan rushing back to her like the sudden burst of a dam breaking.

Sodhu wiped her face and took the letter from the man, who subsequently turned and ran away again. Without waiting for Hadjal to return, she opened the letter, which Meera saw bore

Darreal's familiar handwriting. "It is time," Sodhu said
seriously.

32

MEERA

The riders immediately snapped into action, hailing Hadjal from the sky and preparing to fly out. Falkai was hunting, so Soleille would fly with Katrea and Onyx until her raek could join them. So far, they still hadn't broken their orders, but Meera could sense the other riders' trepidation and guilt. "Darreal wanted to prevent more fighting when she thought it was possible," she reminded them. "Let's show her it's still possible!" It was about as close as she could get to a rousing speech, considering her own mind was buzzing with conceivable complications and the fear that she might accidentally hurt someone again.

Darreal wanted them to mobilize and circle above the marching army, ready to join the battle when fighting broke out, but instead, they planned to fly past the army and land at the border, creating a barricade. It was a simple plan, hinging entirely on the raeken's and Meera's ability to scare Terratelle's troops enough to prevent them from trying to cross the border to initiate a conflict. Meera's heart thudded in anticipation, and she did her best to stand tall and appear confident in front of the other riders, knowing how crucial her abilities were to their success.

"We can do this," Kennick murmured in her ear, kissing her goodbye.

Meera gripped his shirt and looked into his dark eyes. What if something horrible and unexpected happened? What if they never saw each other again? Should she say a real goodbye?

Kennick shook his head slightly and cupped her face. "We will go home together after this," he told her.

She nodded and swallowed. She had to believe that.

They all mounted their raeken, carrying with them enough food for several days. If the barricade was needed any longer than that, they would have to take breaks in turns. It wasn't likely, however; the human troops could not stand out in the cold without food or water indefinitely. Meera could only hope that Darreal would use the time they bought her to end the war for good. Otherwise, they might spend the rest of their lives holding the fight at bay. Swallowing, she directed Shaya to fly, leading her friends and family to war.

They reached the assembled army quickly and flew low over them. Meera took in the sight of Aegorn's ranks—some human, some knell, some on horseback, but most on foot. The knell warriors were clumped together behind a contingency on horses that Meera assumed contained Darreal. The knell were in the center of the army with human troops spreading out in either direction almost as far as she could see from up above. She marveled at how many more men were gathered now than Aegwren had collected for his battle and how much more carnage this fight could create. Then she rolled her shoulders back and looked straight ahead, channeling Aegwren and hoping to accomplish what he had not.

Gazing up at the raeken, soldiers and warriors cheered—no

doubt finding hope in the creatures' size and strength. But the raeken didn't remain with the army as they were meant to; Shaya led them past the front lines until Meera could no longer hear cheers or the dull cacophony of stomping feet and clanking weapons. They flew to where the border was no more than a vacant stretch of barren land—where, squinting into the distance, she could just make out the other army marching toward them.

Shaya circled and landed, choosing a spot on the top of a hill, so they would be able to see out around them. Then, once again, Meera waited. She waited while two armies closed in on either side of them. She waited to put her abilities to the test and to heed the calls of her fellow riders should they need her. Looking to her left, she saw Cerun's blue form land next to them some distance away. She checked to her right just as Hillgari descended to her position, purple feathers gleaming in the morning light. It was early in the day, and Meera suspected the rulers and generals all hoped to have the battle over and decided by the time darkness fell.

It was another hour before Aegorn's army came into view behind them. Meera was centered among the riders, so she turned around to see knell warriors on horses holding raised banners depicting Aegorn's tree symbol. Darreal was likely among them, and Meera didn't know how the queen would react to her presence. Shaya rotated her bulk to face the army as it neared, and Meera squinted at the mass of moving bodies until two figures on horseback disengaged and plodded toward them.

She knew it was Darreal and Lethian before she could make out their features. But when they drew close, she jolted in surprise to see that Darreal was riding Farrah. Of all the horses, she thought, rolling her eyes. She really needed to have a talk with Darreal about that horse at some point—assuming they both made it out of this situation and were friends afterward. Darreal and Lethian stopped when they were in shouting distance. "What is the meaning of this, Meera?" Darreal called, sitting tall and proud atop Farrah's sandy brown body.

"The riders will not allow this battle to take place!" Meera yelled back with as much dignity as she could muster. Darreal just gaped at her speechlessly, so she added, "We will not let either army cross the border, so do not try to pass us!"

Darreal looked affronted at that, drawing her thin shoulders back even further and rising to her full height in her saddle, but she did not respond. She and Lethian turned and rode back to the army, probably to discuss next steps with the Queen's Council and the human generals. Meera watched her friend go sadly; she wished they could have devised this plan together. But she was, at least, not alone in her efforts, she thought, glancing at Cerun's figure in the distance.

Shaya turned back around, and they waited once more. It was maybe another hour before Terratelle's army reached the border with Cesor's and Arborea's troops checkerboarded among them. The soldiers directly in front of Meera were from Terratelle's Royal Army, denoted by their red and black uniforms. Their general rode on horseback at their front with flag-bearing boys on either side of him. Shaya rose from her crouch and paced side to side, delineating the boundary she wouldn't allow them to cross, and the general stared at them in obvious horror. Meera only had eyes for the two boys at his sides, however. They were each holding red flags depicting Terratelle's bear and looked downright terrified to be there. She would not allow the war to claim the lives of any more children, she told herself, blinking and focusing her attention on the man in charge.

The general called a soldier forward and sent him running down the line, presumably to confer with some other general or maybe even King Otto about what to do. Meera watched, eyeing the army that reached out in either direction for signs of an impending charge. King Otto would have known that his soldiers might be facing raeken, after all, and probably expected them to plunge ahead, sacrificing themselves for whatever he thought this war might gain. Eventually, the runner returned, and Meera saw the whites of the general's eyes flash. She knew, then, that they had been ordered onward.

The general turned to his men, presumably delivering a speech about valor and victory—probably a better one than she had managed—and he turned back to face Shaya and lifted his arm, spurring his men onward around him. The men surged, running toward the border in the slow, ambling gait of humans burdened with weapons. Meera watched them approach for a moment, observing how the charge trickled down the line on both sides of the center troops. "Now!" she told Shaya in her mind.

Shaya lunged forward with a loud, menacing screech, unhinged her jaws, and released a sphere of swirling pale raek fire, whipping her head back and forth. The men at the front of the charge slowed to a stop in fear and were subsequently pummeled and trampled. Meera cringed, watching as the soldiers fell over one another, pushed forward by those behind them into a heap at the front of their line. Fairly quickly, the troops crashed to a stand-still.

The general was shouting orders to resume the charge, but the soldiers were tangled up in one another, slowly rising and finding their footing. Meera heard a raek screech in the distance and knew that other sections of the widespread army were attempting to breach the border. The men in front of her reorganized, but the momentary confusion seemed to have been enough to make them forget or rethink their orders. Shaya slashed her tail in satisfaction, clearly enjoying frightening the humans even though she was there to save their lives.

"Well done," Meera told her. Then she watched while the frantic general attempted to rouse his soldiers once more. She wouldn't kill the pesky man, of course, but she would rather prevent him from continually rallying his troops to action. Since she had been practicing her metal shaping with Kennick, she decided to use it; she shaped the point off the general's drawn sword and used the metal to crudely bind his wrists together so that he could no longer raise a hand to denote a charge.

Meera watched as the general squirmed and struggled in his saddle, eventually falling to the ground where nearby soldiers tried to help him remove the metal from his wrists. She heard him shout—presumably to charge—but his attempts were drowned out by fearful cries about magic. The soldiers near the front turned and started to weave and push into the ranks behind them, desperate to get away from the source of the magic, which clearly frightened them much more than the prospect of dying at the end of another man's blade. Meera used the moment to check to either side of her.

Hillgari and Cerun both seemed to be managing to keep the soldiers before them at bay with similar fear tactics, and glancing behind her, she saw that Aegorn's army was watching and waiting —at the ready in case Terratelle's troops crossed the border. Meera hoped Darreal was doing something with this time— something to end the war without a fight. She didn't know what that might be, but Darreal was smart, and Meera trusted her despite her friend's lack of reciprocal trust.

For a time, all was quiet, so she ate a snack, pulling dried fruit and some of Gendryl's cheese out of her bag. "If we are here longer than two days, I will have to eat at least one of the humans," Shaya informed her tonelessly.

Meera ignored her and continued to watch Terratelle's army while she chewed. She could only assume the other riders were managing in their locations. They were to send a message down the line if they needed her. When there was movement in the ranks before Meera, she put her food away and watched as a tall man on horseback took over for the general, but she could only vaguely make out his shape—he remained relatively far back from the front line. Reaching out, she tried to sense the metal sword in his hand, but he was out of her range.

Biting her lip, she debated between saving her magical energy and shaping some sort of wall to deter the men from charging again. She was leery of waiting until they ran to shape an obstacle before them, knowing they would crush one another against it, so after some consideration, she shaped a waist-high wall in front of the soldiers as far as she could see in both directions. She had hardly shaped in days, after all, and was feeling strong. The soldiers at the front lines jumped back again, causing a ripple effect as men fell over behind them and weapons clanked against one another.

Meera left the wall low so that she and the soldiers could still see one another, but if she needed to, she could raise it quickly. Then she pulled out her food to eat a little more and keep up her energy. It was at that moment that Cerun screeched to her left, and she jumped, turning to look toward him and Shael. They looked fine from what she could tell. "Onyx calls for help!" Shaya told her, leaping into the air at the same time.

33

SHAEL

S hael felt relatively useless sitting atop Cerun—unable to shape—while Cerun threatened the soldiers with his raek fire to hold them back. He saw Meera shape the wall and wished he could do something like that to help, but then he reminded himself that not having magic was nature's decision, not a testament to his character. He was there, ready to do whatever he could to help, and that was all that mattered. Just because he couldn't do what Meera could do, didn't mean he was useless.

Still, he didn't have much to contribute and mostly kept an eye on the soldiers and his surroundings. He could see Meera and Shaya to his right, but Onyx, Soleille, and Katrea were out of sight on his left, presumably just past the ridge that blocked his view. The riders had all agreed to keep their raeken grounded so they could store as much energy as possible to make raek fire. They all knew the fear of fire was their greatest weapon—that and Meera. Tempted as they were to fly and look around, Shael and Cerun remained in their position on the ground. That is, until they heard a sudden screech from Onyx.

"Onyx needs help!" Cerun informed Shael, shrieking his own cry to Shaya at the same time.

Shael knew Meera was to be the one to respond to cries for help, but he could not stand sitting on the ground not knowing what was happening. Cerun sensed his decision as he made it and lifted them both into the air, rising up a hundred feet just before Shaya also launched from the ground. Shael looked to his left, simultaneously instructing Cerun to focus on the soldiers before them and to the right, knowing Shaya's departure might spur the center troops into action.

From the sky, he viewed the enormous armies stretched out all around them and felt a shiver run up his spine. Squinting, he could see Onyx on the ground, the men before him unmoving. Shael only had a moment to wonder why the raek had called for help, however, before some sort of massive catapult in the distance released with a crack that made him jump. He watched helplessly as projectiles shot from the catapult over the heads of the Terratellen army, directed at Onyx—Soleille and Katrea on his back.

Onyx lunged to the side, avoiding most of the projectiles— Shael couldn't see what they actually were—but there was a whole row of catapults, and the next one over released just after the first, shooting out a mass that flew toward Onyx before spreading out into a heavily laden net that fell over him. Shael gaped in horror, but just then, Shaya and Meera flew behind Cerun on their way to help. The whole row of wooden catapults burst into pale flames all at once, and Shael's eyes widened as he marveled at the great distance Meera had managed to project her abilities.

His eyes quickly lowered to Onyx, however, as the black raek shrieked again. His wings were ensnared by the huge net, and Soleille and Katrea were struggling on his back underneath it, working to free themselves. A rush of Cesorean soldiers in gold uniforms ran toward the trapped raek. Onyx's head was free, but the soldiers skirted around the sphere of dark raek fire he emitted, their swords and spears raised and battle-cries emanating from their throats.

Katrea broke out of the net and met the soldiers on Onyx's right side, taking their spears from their hands and knocking them down, trying to incapacitate them without seriously harming or killing them. They had all agreed; they had all agreed that no matter what happened, they would not kill anyone. Shael had also agreed, knowing that they were there to stop the battle but also to show humans that raeken that knell were not monsters, but as he watched Katrea, he wondered if he would bother to be as careful as she was being if Cerun were in danger.

Soldiers reached Onyx's other side, tossing their spears at him and swinging their swords, but Soleille deflected the weapons from under the net, shaping them aside. Then the men before her suddenly fell to the ground. Shael didn't know what she had done, but she seemed to have shaped them all unconscious somehow. Shaya and Meera reached them soon after, and Shael released a puff of breath in relief, watching it fog in front of him in the cold air.

Shaya tore the net off of Onyx, shrieking her displeasure. Shael could see blood splattering to the ground from wounds the raek had suffered, but he knew that Soleille would quickly heal him. Katrea and Soleille waved to Meera and gestured to the soldiers around them in question. Some of the soldiers had run back to their troop when Shaya had appeared, but many were still strewn hurt or unconscious in the grass.

Suddenly, the two patches of ground to either side of Onyx raised, detaching from the rest of the land. Shael laughed as Meera shaped the chunks of land over to where the rest of the

Cesorean force was standing and slid the men onto the ground at their feet. He was delighted by the powerful display of nonviolence, but his smile faded when he sensed a shift in Cerun's thoughts. Before Cerun could even formulate mental words, Shael looked through his raek's eyes and saw that the soldiers Meera had previously been blocking had started to climb over her low wall and run toward the border.

Shael didn't have to tell Cerun what to do; the raek flew hard for the charging men. The line of soldiers was ragged and unevenly spaced as they poured over the wall, but those that made it to the other side ran quickly, making space for the troops behind them. By the time Cerun reached the charging soldiers, the front men had already mounted the hill Shaya had stood upon and were descending the slope on the other side. Shael felt a rush of panic, seeing the knell warriors in Darreal's army lift their weapons in the near distance, ready to fight.

"What should I do?" Cerun asked. He was flying for the front of the line even though he was unlikely to be able to pass them and scare them back.

"Call for Meera," Shael replied reluctantly, wishing he could do something himself. Cerun shrieked for help, and his cry drew the attention of some of the men running below who screamed in terror. "Keep making noise!" Shael told him, hoping to distract and slow the men running straight toward certain death. "Swoop low over them!" he added.

Cerun did as Shael suggested and the line of men scrambling over the rock wall slowed then stopped. Some of the soldiers who had made it over turned back and fled, while others kept running. "Quiet!" Shael told Cerun, and he cupped his hands around his mouth and shouted down to the men, "Stop! Turn back, or they'll kill you!" Most of the men were too panicked to even register his words, but several of them stopped and looked up at him in confusion. "Go back!" Shael shouted again, pointing across the border. He felt stupid, but it was all he could think to do.

One of the men turned and ran back for the wall, then several others followed. Cerun hovered in the air over them and shifted from trying to look threatening to trying to look harmless. Then Shael felt him make a decision, and the raek dropped down toward the closest man, gripping him carefully in his clawed feet. "I will show them that raeken do not kill for pleasure!" Cerun announced, before carrying the soldier into the sky.

The man emitted horrible, throaty screams even though Cerun wasn't hurting him, and those on the ground looked up, pausing in their charge to watch. Slowly, Cerun flew his struggling load toward Terratelle's army and dropped down just outside the rock wall to deposit the man gently onto the grass. He then raised quickly back into the sky before the army could get any ideas about shooting arrows; he could still remember the pain of the arrows that had penetrated his skin when he and Shael had been captured.

Shael looked down and watched the trembling man rise awkwardly to his feet and climb back over the wall to be welcomed by his fellow soldiers. Shaya and Meera arrived shortly after, and Meera hit the remaining charging Terratellens with an absurdly strong wind until they stopped trying to run forward and turned tail to retreat behind the wall. Shael waved to her in thanks, and she waved back, looking tired. He hoped she could now have a break, and he and Cerun flew back to their position.

"We did well," Cerun said.

Shael shrugged even though his raek couldn't see him. "We didn't stop them from crossing the border, but hopefully they will all tell the story of the raek that picked a soldier up and carried him back to his army unharmed for many months to come," he replied.

"And the pretty rider on his back," Cerun added with a rumble of raek laughter.

Shael figured Meera must have told Cerun about his nickname on the *Lady Emmaline*, and he laughed too. Then all was silent and still for a long time. If the Terratellen army had any other massive weapons designed for taking down raeken, they didn't use them, and if their generals tried to convince their men to charge again, they didn't listen. Shael watched as the confused, anxious soldiers before him grew weary and began resting their swords against the ground and shifting on their feet. He saw one man actually sit down, but it was not long before someone shouted for him to get back up.

The day passed slowly, and Shael longed continually to dismount from Cerun's back and get his blood flowing. But no matter how antsy he felt, he remained seated and ready to fly; he knew how quickly things could change. In the late afternoon, he finally pulled out some of his food and ate, beginning to feel sorry for the soldiers standing before him without food or water. He could only assume that the men in charge were conferring about how to proceed and hadn't made any decisions yet—that, or Darreal was negotiating with the king. Either way, the troops in front of Shael didn't make any attempts to cross the border or attack for the rest of the day.

There seemed to be an incident on Meera's other side that she left to address, during which time he and Cerun moved over to monitor her section of army as well as their own. However, the Terratellens located in the center of the army looked especially worn and disinclined to charge again, and they didn't move while Shael was watching them. About an hour later, Shaya and Meera returned, and Meera waved at him, letting him know that everything was okay.

As the day wore on and drew to an end, the sky darkened, and as darkness fell, the air grew bitterly cold. Flurries fell from above that Shael had to repeatedly blink from his eyelashes, and he rubbed his arms and wished more than ever that he could dismount and use his stiffening muscles. The army in front of him began to stir, moving around to keep warm and becoming agitated. He could hear their disgruntled whispers turn to shouts, and while he could not make out what they were saying, he assumed they did not think it right for them to have to stay in the field all night, hungry and freezing.

Shael turned and looked behind him, wondering how Aegorn's army was fairing. They were further away, but he could see that they appeared to be resting comfortably on the ground and seemed to have had food and blankets distributed to them, a clear sign that they would spend the night on the would-be battle-field. He waited to see what the Terratellens, Cesoreans, and Arboreans would do.

Despite the men's shouts of protest, they were ignored. As the sky darkened further, Shael breathed hot air into his palms, rubbing them together and watching the soldiers in front of him tuck away their weapons and huddle together for warmth. He hoped the night would not be cold enough to prove a threat to them; it was the riders' intention to wait-out the battle not to slowly starve and freeze the enemy.

34

SHAEL

When the sun eventually ducked beneath the horizon, it grew completely dark—eerily so. The moon was barely a sliver, hidden behind the clouds that continued to deposit floating snowflakes to the ground below. Neither army lit fires for fear of being easy targets in the dark, and Shael could no longer see the soldiers stretching out around him or even Shaya's bulk in the near distance. Unnervingly, while he knew he was surrounded, he felt entirely alone.

After an hour or two of darkness, Cerun rose from his crouch to shake collecting snow from his feathers and stretch his legs. Shael knew his raek was thirsty, but Cerun had to content himself with licking snow from the ground since there was no water to drink. Finally dismounting, Shael jarred his stiff, cold legs against the ground. He paced around a bit to revive his body, then he stared into the black surrounding him, wondering if anything at all was likely to happen that night. He didn't think so.

"I'm going to check on Meera," he told Cerun mentally, already starting to walk toward Shaya's hill, though he couldn't see even a vague outline of her in the pitch black. He wanted to make sure Meera was okay after all of the shaping she had done that day—that and he was curious to know what had happened on her other side. He supposed he was technically breaking protocol, but if she was mad, he could quickly walk back to Cerun; he needed the exercise anyway.

Shael knew based on Cerun's night vision that Shaya would be able to see him approach when he got close. Still, he wouldn't want her to think he was attacking and grew increasingly nervous as he began to ascend their hill. "Meera, it's Shael!" he called quietly, hoping she and Shaya could hear him.

He kept walking even though he got no reply, but a minute later, someone grabbed him from behind. He jumped, startled, feeling Cerun's simultaneous alarm in his mind. But the person attempted to tickle him of all things, and he relaxed—only Meera ... "Really?" he asked, shoving her hands off of him and turning to squint at her in the dark.

She grinned at him, her white teeth flashing brighter than the rest of her. "Everything okay?" she asked.

"Fine. I just wanted to make sure you were alright—you did a lot today," Shael replied, tucking his hands into his armpits to warm them. He wished he had gloves and a hat, but he hadn't needed such things since leaving Sangea for Levisade.

Meera bounced up and down to keep herself warm. "I'm okay," she said. "I'm tired, but I've been eating a lot, which seems to help replenish my energy after shaping. I'm starting to think nothing will happen in the night, and I might try to get some sleep."

Shael nodded, then realized she might not be able to tell. "I think that's probably safe," he replied. "Will you be warm enough?"

"Why? Are you offering to keep me warm?" Meera asked in a coy voice.

Shael opened his mouth and stuttered something incoherent.

"I'm kidding!" she said, shoving his arm.

He stumbled back a step because Meera still often forgot how strong she was, but he smiled. "Would you like some company?" he asked. He certainly wouldn't mind having someone to talk to and sit next to in the thick darkness.

"Come on," she said, taking his arm and leading him to Shaya.

The enormous wild raek always made Shael a little uncomfortable, and she was especially intimidating in the dark—her shape vaguely visible from the occasional beam of moonlight glinting off of her reflective feathers. Shaya didn't make any move to harass or even acknowledge Shael, however; she simply crouched on the ground, large eyes directed toward Terratelle.

"Shaya will keep a look out," Meera said. Then Shael felt the ground move and had to put out his arms to balance himself. "Come in," Meera told him, grabbing one of his outstretched hands and pulling him forward. She led him into a stone hideout she had just shaped into the ground. It had a swirling orb of raek fire burning in the center of it that quickly warmed the small space.

"Ahhh," Shael sighed, already feeling the heat of the fire penetrate his clothing and reach his bones. "No one will see the light?" he asked.

"No," she replied, tossing her bag against a wall and sitting down. "I can't keep it burning all night, but the stone should hold a lot of the heat."

"This is better than how I was expecting to spend the night," Shael replied. He felt bad for the other riders and for the soldiers all around them, but he was also relieved to be comfortable. Automatically, he judged his selfishness, but he quickly reminded himself that it was okay for him to want to be sheltered and warm.

"The others will survive," Meera said, clearly sharing some of his thoughts. "I need to sleep if I'm going to be much use tomorrow, and you might as well join me since you were here anyway."

"Do you know how everyone's doing?" Shael asked, suddenly feeling self-conscious for being alone with his best friend's fiancé.

"Florean and Cotarea dealt with some of those catapults earlier. Hopefully I've burned them all at this point—they weren't easy to ignite from so far away and took a lot out of me. I saw Endu at the end of the line, past the far side of the army, and can only assume he and Kennick are managing to prevent soldiers from going around our line and attacking Darreal's troops from behind. Hopefully Hadjal and Serene are managing on the other end as well," Meera replied, starting to sound exhausted.

"Go to sleep, Meera. You have done enough today," Shael told her, watching her eyes droop.

Rousing herself enough to pull her bag over, she laid her head down on it, curling her knees into her body. She looked so small all balled up, and Shael felt suddenly amazed by what her body was capable of. Her strength had once annoyed him and made him question his own worth, but now it just impressed and inspired him. He lay down as well, though he wasn't sure how easily he would sleep. Meera's fire went out, and Shael wondered whether she had fallen asleep already, but then her slight hand reached out for him, landing on his arm. He caught it in his, holding it to comfort them both, and he thought Kennick would be glad to know that Meera was not alone in her exhausted state.

THE NEXT MORNING, Shael and Meera both rose long before the sun. Meera shaped her cave back into the ground, and she and Shael hugged briefly before he ran back to Cerun, working his muscles before another dreaded day of sitting. Cerun had been dozing and rose to shake snow from his body and stretch his wings when Shael reached him. "Did you get any sleep?" his raek asked.

"Some," Shael said. He knew Cerun hadn't slept because he had been awake every time Shael had reached out to him in the night.

He continued to jog around in the shallow layer of snow on the ground until the sun peeked over the horizon and light flooded the battlefield. Then he leapt onto Cerun's shoulders to resume watching and waiting. As the light illuminated the army before him, he saw that the soldiers had slept—or at least survived the night—in dense clusters of bodies. Slowly, they disentangled themselves from their comrades and brushed snow from their uniforms and weapons, standing to the insistent shouts of their superiors to get back in their lines and be ready to charge.

Even so, when the men had arisen and reformed their lines, they were not led to charge; they once more stared uncertainly at Shael and Cerun and awaited orders. Shael shifted uncomfortably, hoping Darreal would negotiate an end to the war soon for all of their sakes. It had been a cold night, and he could see at least one man among the soldiers in front of him who hadn't arisen with the others. The soldiers around the man stared at him and didn't seem to know what to do about the strangely clean body on the unbloodied battlefield. Then, after conferring, they lifted the dead man and carried him away, forcing rows and rows of troops to part for them.

Shael hoped there were not any dead where Meera could see. He knew she would blame herself even though it was the king and generals who were to blame. Once the soldiers carrying the dead man returned to their lines, there was surprisingly little movement in the ranks before him. The men appeared weary and defeated after almost twenty-four hours of holding their positions, but they continued to stand. Shael supposed the adrenaline of an impending fight and the shout of a superior was enough to make any person endure for as long as they had to. He knew he would find the strength to maintain his current stance for as long as necessary.

35

LINUS

L inus rolled over and opened his eyes to Emmaline's pastel and lace-filled bedroom. The sight made him smile; waking up in her feminine space was still new to him. The Harringtons' servants had tried to prepare him his own bedroom, but he had declined it—Emmaline's room might have more flowers and frills than he ever would have thought he'd be comfortable with, but he actually liked it. It was like being surrounded by Emmaline. Not to mention, she was usually in there with him.

"Good morning," she murmured, lifting her head next to him and rubbing her eyes. Linus kissed her sleepy face in answer and rose to relieve himself in the adjacent room. "What do you want to do today?" she asked when he returned.

Shrugging, he started pulling on his clothes. "Whatever you want," he replied. Linus had married Emmaline and entered her world, leaving his previous life behind him. For the past week or so, he had committed himself single-mindedly to his wife's happiness and felt perfectly content to continue doing so. There was only one little thing nagging at his mind, but he pushed it aside as he had been doing each day.

"We could put my new skills to the test," Emmaline suggested as she stood from the bed, raising one of her thick eyebrows. She was referring to the card games Linus had been teaching her.

Linus didn't answer her for a moment as he gazed at her perfect, unscarred body before she could cover her nudity. "If you think you're ready for that, some of the crew meet for cards at a tavern in town," he replied. "That wouldn't be until late, though."

"We'll just have to occupy ourselves somehow until then," she responded primly, tugging on her many layers of dress. Linus watched her struggle with her clothes, knowing she didn't call in her maids because they made him uncomfortable. Pretty much everyone in the house made him uncomfortable except for his wife. Emmaline's mother had allowed them to marry—rightfully assuming her daughter would otherwise leave—but she had not accepted Linus, nor did she seem to like him.

At the thought, Linus scratched his beard and remembered that he really should write to his own mother. He knew he should contact his family—let them know he was alive and well—but somehow, writing a letter to his mother felt like going backward; he felt like letting any of his past reach him might spoil the perfect life he had found for himself in Harringbay with the beautiful woman who was studying him. "What is it? Tell me," she said, smoothing her dress and clasping her hands in front of her like she meant business.

"I should really write to my family, but—I don't know ... I don't want anything to change. I'm so happy for once," he replied.

Emmaline smiled and gave him a brief peck on the cheek before turning to her desk and pulling out a sheet of paper and a pen. "They will be glad to know how happy you are, and I do not want them to think I'm keeping you from them," she said, handing him the supplies and shoving him toward the desk. "Sit. Write," she told him.

Linus shot her a look over his shoulder, but he did as she bid, writing to both his mother and sister—explaining his circumstances as vaguely as possible. He then opened the bedroom window and whistled for the magic, letter-carrying bird Meera had sent him. It seemed to have made its home in a tree outside their window. Linus didn't know exactly what to tell the bird, but he assumed it would figure out where to go if he gave it a name and address. The bird observed him through its beady yellow eye as he struggled to try to tie the letter to its leg one-handed, then Emmaline walked over to do it for him.

Afterward, she pushed him back into the chair to tidy his hair. Linus didn't mind letting Emmaline do things for him because she never made a fuss about it. She never asked the servants to do it either. If Linus needed his meat cut like a child, she would cut it. If his boots came untied, she would bend and tie them. He appreciated the matter-of-fact way in which she helped him as well as the casual way she often touched his stunted forearm.

As she brushed through his hair and gathered it at the nape of his neck, Linus watched the carrier bird hop to the window and fly away. Staring after the bird, he couldn't help but be reminded of that which he'd been trying so hard to forget: Meera's letter. When he had first read that Otto was gathering troops from Cesor and Arborea and marching them to the border, he hadn't believed it. He hadn't thought that Otto would take such a drastic action all on his own. In the coming days, however, the news had spread all through Terratelle, even to the far-reaches of Harringbay.

Linus had been trying—as he now tried—to convince himself that the war had nothing to do with him anymore, that Otto had nothing to do with him anymore; he was Emmaline's and only Emmaline's. He hadn't been able to prevent atrocities as a general, after all, so what could he possibly do now that he had committed treason and was presumed dead? Why did the border pull at him when he was so damned happy for the first time ever?

"I wish you would tell me what's been bothering you," Emmaline said, staring at his face through the mirror over her little desk.

Linus blinked and met her gaze, smiling at the sight of her serious expression juxtaposed with her messy hair. Big, tousled waves framed her face. During the day, she always kept her hair perfectly pinned back, but at night, she took it out and let him touch it along with the rest of her. Linus sighed, feeling irrationally like sending the letter to his mother had already broken the enchantment over his life. "I keep thinking about the war," he replied sullenly.

"What about it?" Emmaline asked, twisting her hair away from her face.

"I keep thinking that maybe there's something I can do to stop it—like maybe I should go and talk to Otto, try to change his mind," he admitted, cringing. Saying it aloud felt like the last bit of paint crumbling off of a masterpiece to reveal bleak nothingness beneath.

Emmaline wrapped her thin arms around his neck and rested her pointed chin on the top of his head, still regarding him in the mirror. "That's because you are a good person—the kind of person who acts on his beliefs," she told him.

Linus knew she was throwing the words he had once used to describe Meera back at him, and he sighed again. He did want to be that kind of person ... But he also wanted to fully absorb himself in Emmaline and never think about anything else. "I'm your husband, and that's good enough for me," he replied.

Emmaline pursed her little lips at him and squinted her eyes. "My husband is a good man who does what he can to make the world a better place," she insisted.

"Emma, come on!" Linus objected, pulling gently out of her grasp to turn and face her for real. "I don't want to leave you."

"Then don't—I'll go with you," she replied.

Linus barked a humorless laugh. "Your mother would really hate me then. Emma, the border is no place for a woman," he said. Emmaline looked affronted at that, so he quickly added, "I mean, I wouldn't feel comfortable taking you there knowing you could get sick or put in danger. I would rather know that you were here, safe."

Emmaline stood very straight and very still, her poise betraying her inner turmoil, but she nodded her head stiffly. "Okay. You're right. I should probably stay here, but you need to come back quickly," she told him, touching his cheek.

"I'll come back as soon as I can," Linus agreed, only realizing in that moment that he really meant to go.

"But Linus, won't it be dangerous for you? Won't Otto be upset that you left?" she asked, nibbling her bottom lip.

He considered the question, then he shrugged. "I'll tell Otto whatever he wants to hear—that I was captured or forced away or something. He won't want to hang me and will believe whatever nonsense I tell him," he replied, confident that what he said was true.

Emmaline could tell that he meant it, so she relented. Then she took a deep breath, drew back her shoulders, and moved away from him, pulling out all of the clothes she and her mother had acquired for him and stacking them on the bed. "What are you doing?" he asked, smirking at her.

"If you're leaving, then I'll pack your belongings," Emmaline replied in a tone like she was addressing a moron.

"I'll just pack food and take a horse. It'll be the fastest," Linus said, standing and shoving the neat piles of clothes back into their drawers. "Besides, there's something I'd rather use the bed for before I leave," he whispered in her ear.

"We just got dressed!" Emmaline objected. She crossed her arms in front of her chest, but there was a smile in her eyes that betrayed her bluff.

"You're going to lose everything you own playing cards," Linus told her, laughing.

"Even my clothes?" she asked in a coy little voice, pushing one of her sleeves down past her shoulder and quirking an eyebrow at him.

Linus stopped laughing and quickly swept Emmaline against him and kissed her.

36

LINUS

L inus decided to leave the Harrington's house after breakfast. Emmaline and her mother stood in the foyer to see him off, and when he kissed his wife goodbye, her mother shot him a look, plainly stating that she hoped he wouldn't return. Linus ignored the duchess. He knew, in terms of a husband, he wasn't all that a woman could hope for her only daughter, and it comforted him to know that he wasn't leaving Emmaline alone; her mother would care for her in his absence.

He rode out of Harringbay at a brisk pace, but one he expected his horse could maintain for the rest of the day. He wanted to get his task over and done with and looked forward to the disappointment that would no doubt flash in the duchess's eyes when he returned to his new home. Emmaline had stood poised with dry eyes when he had left, but he knew she must ache for him as he already ached for her. He would ride out to the border, do his best to talk Otto out of the battle, and slip away and ride home.

Shifting uncomfortably in his saddle, Linus began to wonder what he might be able to say to Otto to convince him to withdraw his troops and end the war. He had trouble concentrating on his plans and his horse at the same time, however. Although he had ridden horses before, it wasn't something he enjoyed. Holding the reins with his hand left him incapable of scratching his beard or adjusting his genitals more comfortably against the rigid saddle. It was also growing cold, and he soon wished he had worn a glove.

While Emmaline had given him money, packed his saddle bags with food, and made sure he'd worn a warm jacket, she had forgotten a glove. Linus had too, of course, but Emmaline's forgetfulness made him smile; she had always worn gloves to defend herself from the world, but she didn't anymore—refusing to cover the ring Linus had given her. He had told her that he hadn't made the ring or even purchased it, but she hadn't cared, insisting she loved it because he'd given it to her. Emmaline never expected him to be anything other than what he was, which, he realized, was why he was traveling to the border: if she thought he was a good enough person to try to stop the war, then it must be true.

For days, Linus journeyed, sleeping in taverns and barns on his way west. No one questioned him or bothered him during his travels; the whole land seemed to be holding its breath, waiting to hear what would happen at the border—waiting to learn what had become of their fathers, brothers, and sons. Linus supposed his mother would be one of the only women in all of Terratelle who would know that her son lived once she received his letter.

By the time he and his horse—whose name he had never thought to ask—reached the outskirts of the war camps, they were both dingy with road dust. Linus hadn't bothered to bring extra clothes or to wash or trim his beard on his way there; he didn't much care what Otto thought of his appearance and knew that the king would probably appear just as grubby were it not for the servants in charge of washing and grooming him. As he entered the first camp, he sighed; despite the long hours he'd spent on his horse—and the bruises on his bony butt he had to prove it—he still didn't know what exactly he would say to his king and friend.

Nevertheless, he plodded on as darkness fell. He thought to join some of the troops for dinner and sleep beside their fire, but the tents he passed were empty—the firepits cold. Suddenly, his stomach dropped away with his plans; he was too late. If the soldiers weren't in their camps, they were on the battlefield or at least marching toward it. Linus pulled on his horse's reins gently to stop the beast, and for several minutes, they both stood among the eerily empty tents, watching their surroundings darken. If he was too late, maybe he should just turn around and return to Emmaline, he thought; why risk divulging that he was alive if there was no hope of him preventing the battle?

Standing there, he urged himself to turn around, but he couldn't do it. There was still hope until Otto told him otherwise, he decided, nudging his horse onward with his boots before stirring him into a gallop. Leaning forward, he breathed as quickly as the horse that raced beneath him. He didn't know exactly where Otto was, but he knew he would be close to the border. He rushed past acres and acres of tents—all empty—but he kept going. He had to see this task through.

Darkness descended quickly, and Linus slowed, knowing his horse would have to tread carefully. He had almost given up hope of finding Otto that night when a fire beckoned his eyes, and he turned his horse toward it. A group of young message-carriers stood huddled by the flames, keeping warm. "Where is the king's tent?" he asked bluntly.

The boys stared at him, eyes round and uncertain. They were boys no older than the ones Otto had brought into the negotiation tent and Meera had burned. Linus gritted his teeth and longed to keep moving; he hadn't stopped Otto then, but he would now if he could. The boys whispered to one another uncertainly, probably wondering if they should divulge their leader's location to a strange man. "My name is General Backer, and I demand to know the king's whereabouts!" Linus shouted in his best general's voice.

Collectively, the boys jumped, then one of them pointed and said, "That way, sir."

Linus nodded and turned his horse, pressing him onward into the dark even though he could sense the animal's exhaustion and hesitation. Not long later, they passed more fires, and Linus hid his stump and hung his head, not wanting to be recognized before he spoke to Otto. He knew, now, where to find the king; the camp's layout was the same as they always used. Linus rode straight to Otto's usual red tent, and he dismounted and ran forward, leaving his horse to fend for himself.

The startled guards at the tent's entrance tried to stop him, but he pushed past them, forcing his way into the familiar space. The guards quickly followed and snatched his arms, but Linus didn't struggle—he was already where he wanted to be: face-to-face with King Otto. "L—Linus?" Otto stuttered. He was wearing a robe and holding a bottle of alcohol, his hair disheveled and dark circles under his eyes. At the sight of Linus, however, his tired eyes brightened. "You're alive! Release him! Release him!" he cried, shooing the confused guards out of the tent with a wave of his royal hand.

"I'm alive," Linus agreed, studying his friend to determine just how drunk he was.

Otto swayed on his feet, and collapsed onto a cushioned chair behind him; he was pretty drunk. "I'll be damned," he said. "Drink?" He held his bottle out to Linus, who shook his head; he hadn't had any alcohol since marrying Emmaline, and as much as the golden liquid in the glass bottle beckoned to him after his long journey, he resisted that call.

"Otto, what are you doing?" he asked.

Otto laughed. "Drinking, of course!" he shouted.

"No—I mean, why did you gather more troops? Why are you still trying to fight Aegorn?" Linus persisted.

"*Trying* being the operative word," Otto replied, laughing even harder and slapping his knee.

Linus didn't know why that was funny. "Be serious, Otto! Thousands of men will die for no reason if you do this. Why not call them back? Has the battle started yet?" he asked.

"Have you come back from the dead to be my conscience?" Otto asked in return, blinking up at him.

"I came to be your sense, Otto. What good will this do?" Linus asked desperately. He knew the royals of Terratelle had always had their own reasons for waging this war, but he had never understood what they were.

"Nothing!" Otto cried, his laughter bubbling up again and becoming hysterical. "The people think we need this war because we have convinced them that we do—we convinced them that magic is evil so that they would not grow discontent and leave Terratelle for better places. We did it for ourselves—for our power! And do you know what's funny? I don't even want this! I don't even want power, but here I am!" Suddenly he broke off, no longer finding his words funny, and took another drink.

Linus ground his teeth in frustration. "Has the battle started or not, Otto?" he asked. He wasn't hopeful considering the time of day, but he thought maybe the troops had camped closer to the border to surprise the enemy in the morning.

"It has and it hasn't—your girlfriend has seen to that!" Otto replied.

Linus gaped at him for a moment, confused. He couldn't mean Emmaline—he didn't know about Emmaline. "Meera?" he asked.

"Righto! She has a raek! Did you know that? She and her raek and all of her little raek-loving knell friends are standing at the border, preventing the fight from happening," he said, chuckling again. "We have spent centuries convincing these men that they need to kill the evil raeken and knell that seek to destroy our way of life, and now—" he paused in a fit of giggles. "And now they are just standing there like docile ponies!" he shouted, bending over and slapping his knee with his sloshing bottle.

Linus knew Otto's drunken hilarity never lasted long, so he waited, gawking at his friend in confusion. Finally, Otto calmed, reached for a turkey leg sitting on his side table, and began eating it messily. "What are you saying? Meera and the other riders are at the border preventing the battle?" Linus asked.

"Righto!" Otto cried again.

"Then it isn't too late!" Linus said imploringly. "You can still call the troops back! You can still negotiate!" He knew Otto didn't actually want men to fight and die for him.

"The knell queen has tried," Otto replied, sobering slightly and pointing to a pile of letters on the desk in the corner. "But I'm only allowing the wheels that were already in motion to keep turning. Who am I to stop this war that has been so long in the making? The people want to fight! They want to destroy our evil neighbors once and for all!"

"You are their king, Otto," Linus told him in irritation. "You are the king, and the people only think they need to fight because your father told them so. You can still stop all of this!"

"I cannot," Otto said sadly, looking away from Linus and into his fire.

Linus clenched his hand and stared hard at his friend. Meera was holding off the fight while her queen tried to negotiate, but if

Otto wouldn't negotiate, it would all be for nothing. The one man in front of him would be the reason that countless others would die. So many of the empty tents he had passed on his way there would remain empty. So many mothers would never see their sons again. Linus wanted to be the kind of man who acted—the kind of man who did what he thought was best ... He knew what he thought was best, but he wasn't sure he could actually do it.

After a moment of hesitation, he lunged for a knife that sat idly on the plate where Otto's turkey leg had been. Then he stood in front of his king and friend, knife in hand, hand shaking. Otto tossed his turkey bone onto the fire behind Linus's legs and stared back at him. He didn't look scared or even a little upset. "Go ahead," he said, shrugging. "I never wanted any of this."

Linus squeezed the knife in his hand and took a step forward. His heart was beating rapidly in his chest, and the voice in his mind kept telling him to move—to strike—but his legs wouldn't budge any further.

"Do it!" Otto shouted, looking almost annoyed.

"I can't!" Linus shouted back, dropping the knife on the dirt floor. "Damn you, Otto!" Collapsing onto a chair, he folded forward and rested his face on his hand. He knew he probably should have done it, but apparently, he was not a killer. Linus felt a little relieved at the realization even as he grieved for the thousands that would die due to his inability to slit his friend's throat.

"Damn me! Cheers to that!" Otto cried, raising his bottle and once more offering the alcohol to Linus.

Linus stared at the bottle longingly, but he shook his head. The armies would not be able to attack on such a dark night, so he still had time; he could still try to convince his friend to call back the troops. Otto pushed the plate of turkey toward him, and he picked up a slice and crammed it into his mouth. It was going to be a long night, and he would need sustenance.

37

EMMALINE

Emmaline watched Linus leave and felt nerves pulsing through her veins with every beat of her heart. She tried to tell herself to calm down—that she was being silly— but the relentless feeling that something horrible was going to happen gnawed at her gut. "I should have gone with him," she said to her mother for the tenth time at lunch.

Duchess Kenna sighed and put down her fork to regard her daughter. "Emmaline, Linus may not be my favorite person, but he was right that you should stay here. I don't understand what it is he's going to do, but the roads of Terratelle are no place for a delicate young woman such as yourself," she replied.

Emmaline scowled at her plate but didn't object. She was sick to death of people telling her what she couldn't or shouldn't do. She had sailed with absolute strangers to Kallanthea and made it home safely, hadn't she? Gently, she put down her utensils, dabbed her mouth with her napkin, and rose, saying, "Please excuse me, mother," before leaving the dining room and shutting herself into her bedroom. There, she lay on her bed on the pretense of *resting* when really, she was smelling her husband's scent on her blankets and wondering if she should follow him.

Emmaline debated the matter all afternoon, shutting her eyes and feigning sleep when her maids occasionally poked their head in to check on her. At times, she rose and pulled out clothes, just to change her mind and pack them away again. As her indecision dragged on, so did the day, until one of her maids left her a tray of dinner, and the sun went down. Emmaline ate her dinner to keep herself strong, then she bathed and donned one of the nightgowns she hadn't bothered with since marrying Linus. Tucking herself into bed, she told herself she would decide by morning.

Without Linus under the covers with her, the bed felt unnaturally large and cold. She tossed from side to side, each time thinking of a new reason why she should or shouldn't try to find her husband. He had only just left, and she had agreed to stay behind ... He could be hanged for treason ... She could be attacked on the road ... He might be mad that she had not trusted him to go without her ... She might spend countless days and hours waiting for him to return ... Emmaline tossed again and again, until she finally swallowed the debate, urging herself to get some sleep.

That was when she felt it: it was barely a tickle, really, but it was there. She swallowed again, and the tickle felt a little like a scratch. She swallowed again and again, and terror gripped her. Rising from her bed, she quietly packed her trunk in the dark to avoid alerting her maids or mother to her activities. Fear cut through her mind with clarity like a splash of cold water: she was sick. She was sick, and she could die—she could die and never see Linus again.

EARLY THE NEXT MORNING, Emmaline carried her trunk to the stables and woke their coachman, Adam, to tell him she needed to go somewhere—immediately—and to prepare a carriage for a long journey. He was shocked, but he didn't argue; he had been one of the few servants she had trusted to aid her on her last journey. Emmaline waited in the stable while he got everything ready, swallowing and feeling the rawness in her throat like a riding crop to her back, urging her onward. She had packed clothes, bedding, and food and would not stop until she found Linus.

Finally, Adam carried her belongings into the carriage and offered her his hand to step inside. She didn't need the help, but she took it. Emmaline was used to being treated like she was weak and delicate, and she was used to playing along. This time, however, she would be strong, she told herself; she would do whatever she needed to do to reach Linus. "Adam, we're going to the war camps at the border, and I don't want to stop until we're there. Change out the horses if you need to, and pull over to rest when you cannot continue," she told him. The coachman looked even more alarmed than before, but he simply nodded his understanding.

Emmaline shut the carriage door and clutched her hands in her lap, willing herself not to fall to pieces. All day she sat in the carriage, and as it moved through unfamiliar streets, a headache was added to her sore throat. They stopped for the night to rest, and fever struck her. She spent the night alternating between rolling her window down to breathe in the cold wintery air and shaking, huddled under her blankets. The next morning, Adam could see she was not well and pleaded for her to let him take her back to Harringbay, but she insisted they keep going.

For days, they traveled, and for days, her sickness progressed in the back of the carriage until it finally reached her lungs. Emmaline felt like a heavy weight sat upon her chest, and each breath was accompanied by a dull, achy pain. Desperate to relieve some of her discomfort, she quickly pulled off her many layers until she reached her corset, ripped her corset from her body, and threw it to the carriage floor. However, by the time she replaced her clothes, jackets, and blankets, she was trembling violently from the cold and gasping for air—each gasp a club to her chest.

For a time, she rested her head against the side of the swaying carriage and waited for her body temperature and breathing to settle. Then she forced herself to sit back up and drink something. Her arms shook—sloshing water down her front—but she was covered in so many blankets, the moisture didn't reach her. Heart pounding from the exertion of drinking, Emmaline squeezed her eyes shut and thought of Linus, reminding herself why she was in the horrible little space and why she needed to keep breathing. Her breaths were not so difficult—yet—but she knew what was coming.

Bending over, she rummaged through what had once been the orderly contents of her trunk and was now a disastrous mess on the carriage floor. She found her bundle of papers and her pen and sat back up, resting her head for a minute or two after the effort. She knew she might die of this sickness; she had always known. Some of her earliest memories were of sickness and fear. She knew, too, that she might not make it to see Linus no matter how hard she tried, and she decided to write her good-byes to him as she had written periodically to her parents over the years.

Emmaline had written so many goodbye letters that the last few had hardly taken her any time. They all said more or less the same thing, after all: that she loved whoever they were written to and that she hoped they would go on to have a good life without her. This one wouldn't be any different. This one should be just as easy ... And yet, she stared and stared at the blank piece of paper clutched in her hand and couldn't seem to write a single word. She couldn't even write his name.

It was just another letter, she told herself; she had always known she would die, and nothing had changed ... Except that it *had* changed—everything had changed. She had changed. Linus had come into her life and told her to live instead of just waiting to die, and she had! She had lived, and she had loved, and she had dreamed of their future together ... Her letters to her parents had always been about them losing her, but now, for the first time, she stood to lose something—to lose everything. How could she possibly face that?

Emmaline threw the paper and pen back onto the floor and clenched her hands in her lap, forcing herself to sit up straight even though no one could see her. Tears pricked in the backs of her eyes, so she squeezed them shut and bit her lip. She wouldn't cry—she wouldn't. She could cry tears of joy when she saw Linus again, she told herself, and until then, she had to keep resting and eating and drinking and hoping that she would make it in time. She *would* make it in time, her mental voice insisted. Even if she was to lose the hope of playing cards with him and spending holidays with him and swimming in the ocean with him, she could not abandon the hope of at least seeing Linus one last time.

———

THE CARRIAGE CONTINUED to trundle onward, carrying Emmaline closer and closer to the war camps at the border, but she could barely register where one day ended and another began. Lying on her cushioned bench, she focused all of her energy on breathing. Her lungs filled with fluid, and each inhale was a gasping, wet rattle of effort, interspersed with fits of coughing that wracked her body and ejected thick mucus into her hands. She used one of her blankets to wipe her hands periodically, but she was too exhausted to do much about the state of her carriage, filthy as it had become.

Adam stopped at a farm and traded their horses for two fresh ones, promising her he would drive through the night. They should be there soon, he kept telling her. Hang in there, he kept telling her. He had given up asking if he could take her home or to a healer. Even when Emmaline could no longer speak, she had continued to shake her head adamantly in response to his pleas. He could take her to Linus, and that was all she would allow.

When the carriage began to move again, she collapsed, clutching her hands to her chest. Each breath was agony and every cough a flash of violent pain. Still, she kept coughing, knowing if she didn't, the fluid in her lungs would only build up and overtake her. She kept coughing and choking and breathing even when she fell to the carriage floor atop her mess. She didn't bother trying to get up again; she needed all of her energy to get to Linus. If she got to Linus, then she could at least die happy.

38

MEERA

After spending the night in the cave she had made, Meera felt relatively well-rested. Even so, nothing seemed likely to happen that day. Sitting atop Shaya, she stared at the soldiers on the other side of the low rock wall in front of her, wondering who the men were and whether they had families waiting for them at home. Most of them surely did, and she kept herself attentive by imagining the men's wives and children welcoming them home safe—reminding herself whenever her mind strayed that she needed to pay attention so that the soldiers would make it back to their families.

At some point, her eyes snagged on a man who seemed to be having trouble staying upright. He was in the third row, and while he appeared young and alert, he kept swaying and hopping around on one leg. Meera squinted and wondered if he had gotten hurt the day before. Would his superiors not let him go back to camp and get his leg splinted? What good would he be in battle if he could barely stand? She stared and stared at the man, watching him fight to keep his legs under him. She was mesmerized by his struggle and jumped when a shadow blocked out the sun overhead.

Looking up, she exhaled in relief to see Falkai circling above. The soldiers in front of her became restless and scared, but when the pale orange raek landed a little behind Shaya, they settled down. Meera waved to Soleille as she slid from Falkai's back and flicked her loose blonde hair over her shoulder. Then she watched her friend approach, grinning. It was always supposed to have been Soleille's role to fly between the riders, healing their injuries and carrying their messages down the row. Falkai had been absent hunting, and Meera was glad he had finally arrived at the border.

"Everything okay?" Soleille asked from the ground.

"All good here. What's going on with the others?" Meera asked.

"Hadjal is doing well—she unfroze the lake where the far side of the army was meant to cross the border, so unless they build boats, they should not cause any trouble. Katrea is burning for another fistfight, but the soldiers near her seemed to have learned their lesson. And Shael waved me on when he saw me fly over," Soleille reported.

Meera nodded, glad all was well to her left. She wished she had news of Kennick, but she would have to wait until Soleille made it to the other end and turned back.

"Have you spoken to Darreal at all? Do we know what is happening?" Soleille asked, sounding a little impatient.

"I haven't. We'll just have to wait. These men can only stand out here so much longer without food and water," Meera replied.

"Are you sure you do not have any injuries that need to be healed?" Soleille asked, backing toward Falkai to leave.

"I don't, but he does," Meera replied, remembering her injured soldier and pointing toward him.

Soleille tilted her head forward and gave Meera a look. "Seriously?" she asked.

Meera shrugged. "I've been watching him struggle all morning, and if he falls down, I might just go over there and help him up," she admitted, grinning sheepishly.

Soleille sighed at her and walked toward the army. As she neared the rock wall, the soldiers pressed back in fear, but they were packed in tightly and didn't have anywhere to go. When she was in range, Soleille stopped and held up her hands in a circle to focus her attention on the injured man's leg. A moment later, she turned back toward Meera, tossing her annoyingly shiny hair again. "Done!" she called, passing Shaya and leaping onto Falkai's back.

Meera smiled and waved, then she returned her attention to her soldiers and watched as the previously injured man tested his leg, exclaiming in confusion and wonder. Some of the soldiers crowded around him inspected it, and she saw a few point toward where Soleille had stood. "Maybe now they'll be less afraid of magic," she said to Shaya.

Shaya huffed a puff of smoke. "I do not find humans to be that logical," she replied tonelessly.

"Hey!" Meera cried aloud, smacking the side of her raek's neck half-heartedly.

———

AT SOME POINT, Meera couldn't take the waiting anymore, and she slid from Shaya's back. For several minutes, she paced around the top of her hill, sensing the soldiers watching her from below. Then she had a snack and shaped herself some water, wondering at how Otto seemed to expect his soldiers to stand there and possibly fight a battle after so long without proper rest or sustenance. It was only mid-morning, and some of them looked like they might pass out. Meera hated to think the men were all in for another cold night like the night before. She knew they couldn't have all survived it, though she had been glad to see all those before her had.

On a sudden whim, she walked toward the rock wall. "What are you doing?" Shaya asked.

"I don't know," she admitted mentally, but she had more power than any other knell and didn't see how these tired humans could pose a threat to her as long as she remained vigilant. "Hello!" she called to the men as she approached.

They appeared wary and pressed back once more. Meera stopped at the wall and put her hands on it, admiring the fine job she had done the day before. Then she looked into the faces of the soldiers before her, really looking at their features now that she could see them up close. She wondered if she might even know any of them from Altus, but she didn't recognize anyone. "My name is Meera!" she shouted. "I grew up in Altus and worked at the palace for a while!"

The soldiers nearest to her raised their eyebrows at her words and gaped at her, and those further away whispered to one another, passing along what she had said to those who couldn't hear.

"My raek's name is Shaya!" she called, pointing behind her where Shaya lifted a wing to wave as they had seen Isabael do in Aegwren's memories. Meera grinned at her and looked to see what the men thought of the display. They still appeared frightened and exhausted for the most part.

"Are you thirsty?" she asked before shaping a long stone trough on the other side of the wall from her and filling it with water. She knew she should save her energy in case she needed it, but she hated to watch the men suffer. The soldiers all ogled the water with wonder, but many of them seemed suspicious and none moved. "It's safe!" Meera yelled, casually hopping over the wall and plunging her hands into the water to drink.

The men all jumped when she breached the wall as if she hadn't been the one to put it there.

"Come on! Drink!" Meera called in exasperation. "I'm sure Otto's drinking his fill back at camp!" she shouted, knowing from Linus that the new king was a heavy drinker.

Some of the soldiers laughed then looked guilty for doing so.

Meera shaped a stone cup, filled it with water, and sent it floating toward one of the closest men, bumping it harmlessly against his chest as he quivered and pressed back in fear. "It's just water," she told him, looking into his eyes and smiling.

Tentatively, the man grasped the stone cup and took a sip, getting both curious and reproachful looks from the soldiers around him. After a sip, he took a gulp, then he drained the cup thirstily.

"Come get more!" Meera encouraged him. She shaped a whole row of stone cups along the edge of the trough for the other men to use.

The soldier took one step toward the trough, then another until he was directly across from her. "What are you?" he asked, his eyes wide. He had a typical Terratellen look of light brown skin and straight brown hair.

"I'm human, but my raek gave me abilities," Meera replied, still smiling, and trying to look harmless.

"Meera, what are you doing?" called Shael's voice from behind her. He must have seen her approach the army and followed to make sure she was okay.

"Making friends!" she yelled back, waving him over.

After a minute, Shael vaulted himself easily over the wall and stood next to her. "This was not a part of the plan," he reminded her, a note of amusement in his voice.

"I know, but I got bored," Meera admitted.

Shael stepped forward to take one of the stone cups, and the soldier that had spoken to Meera dropped his and scurried back to his line. Shael drank from the trough. "Any chance you can go make Cerun one of these?" he asked Meera.

She turned toward Cerun and shut her eyes, concentrating on where she could sense his shape even though she couldn't see him. She opened a hole in the ground right in front of him and filled it with water. The distance made her pant with effort, but she smiled to know she had quenched her raek-friend's thirst.

"You shouldn't tire yourself out," Shael admonished her, replacing the cup he had used on the trough.

The next thing Meera knew, Shaya was ambling down the hill to join them. The soldiers really looked afraid then, but they couldn't turn and run; they were too densely packed, and the men behind them were pushing forward to see what was happening. "It's okay!" Meera promised them to no effect.

Shaya walked up to the wall and reached her large scaly head over it, sniffing at the human soldiers. "They reek of urine and fear," she shared mentally with Meera, who ignored her.

"She says hello!" Meera yelled, making Shael laugh because he knew better. Meera patted Shaya's snout like she was a dog. "Raeken are dangerous, but they are very smart and honorable!"

All of the commotion seemed to have attracted the attention of a general, who waded through the ranks of soldiers on his horse. The general stopped and stared, open-mouthed at the sight of Meera, Shael, and Shaya, then seemed to consider turning around. Meera waved at him and smiled, and when he did lead his horse to turn and gallop away through the crowd, some of the soldiers laughed and called insults at him. "Alright, back to work everyone!" Meera yelled, pushing Shaya's head behind the rock wall and jumping over it herself.

Shael followed, and they climbed the hill together before he ran back to Cerun. Meera reassumed her position on Shaya's back and continued to watch her soldiers, grinning when they eventually stepped forward to drink the water in the trough and pass the cups around. She wished she could give the entire army water, food, and medical care, but she supposed she would have to settle for just trying to save their lives.

39

LINUS

Linus tried to coax Otto into calling off the battle late into the night, but the king only became more and more hopelessly drunk. Eventually, Linus nodded off in his chair, warm and comfortable next to the fire. He and Otto slept long into the morning and were finally roused by one of Otto's guards. "Your Majesty, there's a coachman here looking for General Backer!" the guard called into the tent.

Linus jerked awake at being referred to as such. He seemed to have wandered unwittingly back into his old life and old position, and the thought chilled him. Rubbing his eyes groggily, he got to his feet, searching the tent floor for his discarded jacket. Otto didn't bother to rise or respond to his guard; he simply waved a hand in the air in acknowledgement and rolled over, releasing a royal fart. Linus donned his jacket and spared a last look at his friend and king. He had not succeeded, and he doubted he would return to see Otto again. The first chance he got, he would ride home.

Warily, he left the tent, wondering who would be looking for him. At the sight of the Harringtons' carriage on the road that wound through the camp, his eyes widened, and he trotted over to it, simultaneously annoyed with Emmaline for following him and excited to see her. Adam, the Harringtons' coachman, intercepted him, looking gaunt and panicked. "My Lord!" he cried, making Linus cringe. That was another title he didn't much like.

"Adam, what is it?" he asked, studying the man's face.

"Lady Emmaline—" he started to say.

Linus didn't wait for his explanations; his chest clenched in fear, and he rushed for the carriage door, yanking it open. At first, he didn't see anyone inside. There was only a mess of clothes, bedding, and other detritus on the floor and a stale smell wafting from within. He started to turn back toward the coachman in question, when the pile on the floor jerked with the awful sound of a wet, hacking cough. Linus lunged into the carriage, pulling back blankets to reveal Emmaline's face.

Opening her eyes, she squinted into the light that hit them from the open door. They were cloudy and confused at first, but then she blinked and seemed to focus on him. Linus was horrified; his usually lively, pristine Emmaline was slack-faced with crust clinging to her mouth and cheeks. Her whole body trembled despite the weight of the blankets over her, and her breaths were short, painful rasps and gurgles. As he clutched her face and kissed her forehead, a single tear leaked from one of her eyes.

"Emma! What do I do? What do I do?" he asked over and over again, looking around the cramped space for some way to help her. One of her arms moved feebly under her blankets, so he scooped her into his lap and held her, leaning protectively over her even though he knew it wouldn't help. He had to do something, but what?

"We need to get her to a healer!" Adam called from outside the carriage door. "I tried before, but she insisted I bring her to you. I really tried ..." he stammered.

Of course—they needed a healer, Linus thought. Putting Emmaline gently back onto the floor, he backed out of the carriage. "Otto! Otto!" he shouted for his friend, not caring how he was addressing the king or who heard.

A moment later, Otto came stumbling out of his tent, still wearing his robe and looking around in confusion. "Who's here? Do they want me?" he asked, clearly still drunk but trying to pull himself together.

"My wife needs a healer!" Linus shouted desperately, his voice cracking like it hadn't in years. He couldn't believe this was happening. It didn't feel real. Emmaline in a war camp—Emmaline struggling to breathe and move; it was all so ridiculous. Why was she here? How had she gotten so sick so fast? She had always told Linus she was ill, but he had never listened—she had always seemed so well, so young and full of life. Why hadn't he listened? Why had he left?

"Wife?" Otto asked in shock. Then he started shouting for a healer to be brought. Seeing the panic on Linus's face, he stepped forward and gripped his arm. "What can I do? What else can I do?" he asked.

Linus looked up at his friend, feeling like it was he who could not breathe. He put his hand to his chest and doubled over. He had to do something—he had to help Emmaline—but he really couldn't breathe. Otto grasped his upper arms and shook him. "Look at me!" he demanded.

Linus looked at him in surprise; he had never heard Otto sound so kingly. Focusing on his friend's eyes helped, and he found he could draw in air again. After several deep breaths, he could also think. "You said Meera is at the border?" he asked, shaking off Otto's hands.

"Uh ... yes," Otto replied, looking confused and glancing toward the open carriage door.

"I need my horse! Where's my horse?" Linus shouted, looking around. He had forgotten about the horse the night before, and it seemed to have wandered off.

"Linus, what—" Otto started to ask him.

"I need to get her to the knell!" Linus cried desperately. He didn't care what Otto thought of that; if anyone could save Emmaline, it was the knell and their magic. Meera would help him.

"Ready my horse!" Otto shouted to no one in particular.

Linus nodded at him in gratitude and paced back toward the carriage. "I'm going to take her to help," he told Adam, sounding more confident than he felt. He felt like he might be sick.

After a few minutes of pacing, Otto's fine horse was led to him, saddled and ready to ride. Linus looked at the animal with trepidation, but it had to be a horse; the carriage would not fit through the tight ranks of men. A horse would be faster. He approached the white mare and climbed awkwardly into her saddle. "Can you hand her up to me?" he asked Adam.

The coachman had been pacing with him and looked relieved to have a job to do. He pulled the blankets off of Emmaline's body and picked her up, carrying her over. She looked so small and limp in the man's arms that Linus had to fight back tears. He just had to get her to the knell, he told himself; their magic would heal her. Adam held her up to him, and Linus struggled to pull her onto his lap. His stunted left arm held her torso upright against his chest, and his right hand clutched the horse's reins.

"Your friend has been positioned in front of the center troops," Otto told him from the ground.

Linus nodded his understanding and his thanks, too overwhelmed to speak. He was about to kick his heels into the horse when Otto held up a hand, "Wait!" he cried, turning to go back into the tent.

Linus waited, but it took all of his willpower. Emmaline's breathing was loud but short and stunted, and the prolonged pause before every new inhale stopped his heart in dread. Otto returned quickly and thrust some things up at him. Linus had to drop the reins to take them and found himself holding the king's uniform jacket, sword, and signet ring. "What—" he started to ask.

"Just take them! No one will stop you if you have these, and I don't want them anyway! I don't want any of it! Take them and go!" Otto shouted, waving his hand dismissively.

Linus did as he was told. He threw the jacket over his shoulders, pushed the ring awkwardly onto one of his fingers, tucked the sword under Emmaline and left, spurring the horse forward. He rode at an even pace at first—not wanting to jostle Emmaline —but at some point, he realized that she hadn't coughed in a while ... Fear dug its nails into his skin, and he, in turn, dug his heels into the horse's side, pushing the mare into a gallop.

Emmaline bounced in his lap, and Linus struggled to hold her to him with his weak, disused left arm. For a time, they passed only more empty tents, and he wondered if the war camp would stretch on forever, trapping them in endless limbo. Eventually, however, the tents gave way to men. Linus reached the confused, disgruntled back of the army and flew heedlessly into its midst, scattering soldiers with his charging horse. In theory, he should be able to ride between the troops up orderly aisles, but there was nothing orderly about Terratelle's army at the moment. "Move!" he shouted in desperation as his horse had to slow to pick around soldiers.

The men saw his horse and his jacket and quickly started to reform their lines, probably sending word through the ranks that the king was among them. Linus didn't care what they thought; he only thought of Emmaline. Her head bounced against his bony chest limply, and her hair—falling out of its pins—bounced as well. Linus's left arm was shaking and cramping, but he would not drop her. Finally, his horse found a clear path through the army, and they flew—kicking up dirt in the faces of the men they passed.

The ranks of soldiers stretched on and on, and eventually, Linus's left arm gave out. He dropped the reins in his right hand to grab Emmaline and keep her in his lap. Otto's horse kept going regardless, knowing their direction and holding her pace. Linus gripped the saddle with his legs, thighs trembling, and leaned forward into the horse's gallop to keep himself in his seat. "I'm getting help, Emma. You're going to be okay—I'm getting help," he kept telling her, wishing he could hear her ragged breaths.

Finally, the horse broke through the front of the army, stopping short at some sort of stone wall. Linus stared at the wall in confusion, then looked past it, searching for Meera. He could see the large shape of a raek in the distance, but he didn't know if it was hers—he had never asked what color her raek was. For a moment, he wasn't sure what to do, then he just started moving again; he had to do something. He picked up the reins, turned Otto's horse around to retrace their steps for a time, and had the mare face the wall again. He could sense the alarm and confusion of the men all around him, but he ignored them.

Heart racing, he stared at the stone wall and let the horse take it in, too. Then he kicked the mare into a run and leaned his body forward as much as he could with Emmaline in his lap, willing the animal to jump. Otto's horse leapt and cleared the high wall, landing in the grass on the other side with a self-satisfied whinny. Linus released his held breath in relief, and turning the mare toward the raek in the distance, he coaxed her back into a gallop.

40

MEERA

The morning wore on as Meera sat atop Shaya's back, staring at the army in front of her. When the sun reached its peak, she turned around and glanced at Aegorn's gathered forces, wondering if she should try to find Darreal. Terratelle's army didn't seem inclined to attack or to leave, and Meera hoped it was because Otto and Darreal were still coming to terms. However, despite her curiosity, she didn't leave her position; she knew she shouldn't become overly complacent and also hoped that Soleille might return soon with news from Kennick.

It was still cold, but the sun was strong, and she tilted back her head to let it warm her face, closing her eyes to rest them briefly from her endless staring. When she returned her gaze to Terratelle's army, she rolled her shoulders back, stretching and thinking of Aegwren. Would he be proud of her for what she was doing? Had he ever found happiness after his own battle? She thought maybe one day she would return to his cave to see if she might learn more from his memories, but all she wanted to do in that moment was go home and live her life with Kennick.

Suddenly, she saw movement among the army and squinted to her right, trying to discern what might be happening. There appeared to be someone on horseback moving quickly through the lethargic troops, and she and Shaya both tensed, wondering if he was trying to lead a charge. The soldiers didn't charge with him, but when the white horse reached the wall, it turned and doubled back to jump it. Meera didn't know what to make of this new development and grew even more confused when she saw that the horse's rider seemed to be holding a woman.

Shaya didn't like that the white horse was charging toward them and rose to her feet, building her raek fire in the back of her throat. "No!" Meera told her, suddenly recognizing the rider on the horse with a thrill. "It's Linus!" Sliding from Shaya's back, she ran forward, stopping herself from descending the hill so that she could still see out in all directions.

"Meera!" she heard Linus shout, bouncing awkwardly atop the galloping horse.

Meera's stomach dropped when she heard the fear in her friend's voice and saw that it was Emmaline clutched in his lap. The white horse reached the top of the hill, sweating—eyes wild to be so near a raek—but she didn't bolt, and Meera lunged forward to grab her bridle and settle her. "Meera, it's Emma! She needs help!" Linus panted, his own eyes as wild as his horse's.

"Get Falkai and Soleille!" Meera shouted to Shaya.

Shaya shrieked loudly enough to startle the soldiers and make Linus wince. Meera held the horse's bridle in her unnaturally strong knell grip and didn't let the mare balk, releasing her when Shaya quieted. Then she reached up and scooped Emmaline's small form into her arms. Meera could hear her breathing, but each breath was just a tiny rasp. Her body felt limp and cold and was still—unnervingly still. The thin layer of snow that had graced the ground that morning had already melted in the sun, and she laid Emmaline down in a patch of grass, burning small raek fires all around her to keep her warm.

Linus half slid and half fell from his horse's back, trembling all over. Then he staggered over to her, falling on his knees at Emmaline's side. "Help is coming," she told him, looking up into the sky and hoping Falkai would appear that second. He didn't.

Linus didn't look at Meera; he only had eyes for Emmaline and stared and stared at her like he could will her to suddenly rise and shake off whatever illness gripped her. He held her hand and brought it up to his cheek where his beard was scraggly and unkempt. "She should be coughing," he said. "Her lungs are full of fluid—she should be coughing it up."

Meera's own throat constricted at the sound of his strained voice. She bent over and tried to sense the fluid in Emmaline's lungs, but she didn't know how to shape it out of her and didn't want to risk hurting her. Frustrated, she settled for burning the crust and gunk that coated the young woman's face and clothes, and she twisted back and re-pinned Emmaline's hair, knowing she always liked to look polished. Then she rose and paced, gazing up hopefully at the sky.

"She's not breathing!" Linus choked suddenly.

Meera flew to her friend and fell to her knees at his side, wrapping him in her arms and staring down at his wife's still face. How could she have so much power and feel so helpless? Clutching Linus, she bit back her tears, looking once more into the sky for Falkai. Come on, she thought, willing him to appear. "She's here!" she cried, seeing Soleille's pale orange raek appear in the distance. "Help is here!" she told Linus, trembling along with him.

Terratelle's army could have been charging toward them, and Meera wouldn't have even noticed. All of her concentration was on the small woman in front of her and her still chest. "Help!" she cried to Soleille as Falkai landed.

Soleille leapt from her raek's back and sprinted to them. Without asking any questions, she crouched and put her hands on Emmaline's chest, sensing into her body.

"Please, please!" Linus begged, swaying where he knelt. Meera squeezed him tighter to hold him upright.

Soleille looked at Meera with a sadness she had never seen in her friend's sky-blue eyes before and shook her head. "She is gone," she told them.

"No!" Linus keened, falling forward over Emmaline, touching and kissing her face, leaving tears and snot behind on the skin Meera had just cleaned.

Meera kept her hands on Linus, trying to hold him together even as she crumbled apart. Her face scrunched with her sobs— grieving for the beautiful young woman who had been so alive, so full of joy that last time she had seen her. While Emmaline had never really let Meera in, Meera had loved her—she had loved her for bringing Linus so much happiness and for offering her the forgiveness she had so desperately needed. Now she was gone. How could that be? Why did the young and innocent die?

Soleille put a comforting hand on Meera's back, but it was not nearly enough. Meera bent forward and buried her face in Linus's shoulder, clinging to him as he clung to Emmaline. She couldn't bear his grief—it was too much. It reminded her of her own losses and all of the pain she was still destined to feel as the people around her died. She wanted to curl in on herself and disappear; she wanted Shaya to remove her crumpled figure from the ground and fly her away—away from death and loss and all of the love that may one day turn to grief.

Shaya was ready, too, hovering behind her—prepared to be there for her in whatever way she needed. Meera could sense her raek's presence and her willingness, and she was tempted to succumb to her instinct to flee. But she didn't. She held onto her friend, and she reached out mentally for Kennick—something she didn't know she could do until she did it.

Suddenly, Kennick's consciousness was around her, the familiar loving embrace that she needed. "Meera?" he asked in alarm, feeling her chaotic grief and not understanding what was happening.

Meera showed him through her eyes—she showed him what had happened and sent a wordless plea for him to hold her. She couldn't do this—not alone. Linus continued to sob and beg with Emmaline to return to him, but eventually, his body softened enough for Meera to pull him into her lap. She cradled him and leaned to press her face into his, letting their tears mingle. Then Shael was there, putting his hands on both of them, offering them his wordless comfort.

After a time, Kennick was there, too. He sat behind Meera and supported her weight while she and Linus cried until they were too tired to continue—until their shaking and sniffing subsided, and they both went still. Slowly, Linus pulled away from Meera, wiping his face—still staring down at Emmaline—and Meera finally tore her eyes from the young woman and turned to hug Kennick, who held and rocked her for a moment, kissing the side of her face.

Kennick was alive, she reassured herself over and over. Linus's grief had felt like her own, but she still had the man she loved, she reminded herself, giving Kennick a brief kiss before pulling away to pull herself together. Meera quickly tidied Emmaline again and placed her hands over her abdomen how she had always clasped them, making her look as poised in death as she had been in life. As she did so, she noticed paper poking out of Emmaline's jacket pocket, and she pulled it out.

There was a letter for Linus and one for her. Meera touched Linus's arm gently to get his attention and handed him his letter. Then she opened hers, too weary to even wonder why Emmaline had written to her.

Meera,

Thank you for bringing Linus into my life. If you are reading this, then I am dead, and he will need you now more than ever. I know that you will take care of him, not to make up for my father's death, but because Linus was right about you. I wish we could have been better friends.

With Love from Beyond,
Emmaline

Meera smiled at the letter. She found it oddly comforting that Emmaline had foreseen her death with such acceptance and clarity. She glanced at Linus where he stood reading his own and hoped he found his comforting as well. Then she tucked hers in the pocket of the jacket Soleille had given her and reached out for Kennick, taking his hand. Looking into his face, she could see light glinting in his dark eyes despite their sad circumstances. "What?" she asked quietly.

"You finally ran toward me," he replied, his pointy canine showing over his lower lip. He kissed her knuckles beside her ring.

Meera huffed a little laugh that felt like an unforgivable crime with Emmaline's cooling body on the ground before her. "I guess that's one thing I accomplished today," she replied.

"Someone is coming," Shael said, interrupting her thoughts.

Meera looked around until she saw two horses approaching

from Aegorn's army. She knew who would be riding them before their faces came into focus. "It's Darreal and Lethian," she said.

"Meera, our line is breaking down. We should spread back out!" Soleille called anxiously.

Meera sighed and rubbed her eyes. As much as she didn't want to think about the battle trying to take place around her, she had to. Now that Emmaline's life couldn't be saved, she had to focus on the lives that still could be. "How was it at your end?" she asked Kennick.

Kennick's lips compressed, which was enough to tell Meera how it had been before he even replied. "The soldiers at the end are still putting up a fight and trying to find a way around. I have been taking their weapons from them. Florean moved over to guard the weapons, but he and Cotarea are now alone at that end," he explained.

"Let's just see what Darreal has to say before you go back," Meera replied warily. She broke away from Kennick and approached Emmaline to pay her last respects to her before truly turning her mind to the war. She hated to see Emmaline lying prone on the ground and shaped a stone platform under her to lift her up. Linus had stepped off to the side and was still staring at his letter, so she left him to himself.

"What is going on?" Darreal asked as she and Lethian rode quickly up the hill.

Meera turned to find the knell queen studying Emmaline's body. When Darreal met her gaze, she immediately dismounted and walked toward her. Suddenly, Darreal was hugging her—her light, intricately decorated armor pressing into Meera's body. "I am so sorry for everything," she said with emotion. Then she pulled away and cupped Meera's face. Meera was doing her best not to start crying again. "You have done so well," her friend told her.

She just nodded in response, swallowing her emotions.

"What is happening, Darreal? Are you still negotiating with King Otto?" Soleille asked.

Darreal stepped away from Meera and quickly donned her queenly demeanor. "There have been no negotiations," she replied simply. "I have tried, but King Otto has not responded to any of my missives."

Meera's heart plummeted, and she gripped the stone table on which Emmaline lay to prevent herself from sinking back to the ground. Was it all for nothing? Would the troops retreat long enough to rest and eat before coming together again? Would she spend the rest of her life on that hill trying to keep an inevitable battle at bay? She wanted to go home! How long could she live for other people and not for herself? Was she doomed to be more than just a person as Aegwren had been? Would their stories end the same way even though she had taken her own path?

Meera peered around for answers and for hope and found everyone looking just as tired and hopeless as she felt. Lethian had dismounted from his horse to put a comforting hand on Darreal's shoulder, and the queen didn't even push him away. Shael and Kennick made brief eye contact with one another that told Meera what they both thought, and Soleille looked ready to fly back to the peninsula that second. Linus walked toward Emmaline and took one of her delicate hands in his. "I'll do it," he said quietly, looking down at his dead wife.

Meera averted her eyes at first, thinking he was talking to Emmaline, but then Linus looked up at her. "I'll do it," he repeated.

"Do what?" she asked, confused.

"I'll recall the troops and send them home," he replied, slouched like the weight of the world sat upon his shoulders.

Meera gaped at him, speechless.

41

LINUS

For a long moment, Meera just stared at him. Then she asked, "How?"

Linus released Emmaline's hand reluctantly to hold his up and show her Otto's signet ring. Then he turned and found where he had unceremoniously dumped the king's uniform jacket and sword on the ground. Feeling like he was assuming a destiny he didn't want, he pulled on the jacket and fumbled awkwardly with the sword's belt until he got it buckled around his waist.

He would do this, he told himself; he would prevent the battle and end the war so that his journey and Emmaline's death would not be in vain. He would do whatever he could to be the man she had thought he was. He had already memorized her letter, and Emmaline's last words to him swarmed repeatedly through his mind:

My Beloved Linus,

You once told me that we all die, most of us in horrible ways. If

you are reading this, then I have died in my own horrible way.
Don't be sad. I wish I could stay alive if only to make sure that you
continue to bathe and don't drink yourself into your own grave.
Well, there are so many things I wish I could stay alive to do with
you, but we will both have to be content with the time we had
together. Wasn't it amazing?

I need you to know that I'm not sorry for following you, and I
hope you will not regret your own actions. You needed to go to
Otto. You needed to do what you thought was right because that is
the kind of man that you are. Don't ever forget it, and don't ever
forget me. I wish you a long and happy life and would not
begrudge you a new wife or even children. You taught me to live,
and I want you to keep doing so without me.

Love,
Your Emma

Linus didn't want to go on without Emmaline, and he didn't
want to be responsible for the lives of so many men. But he would
do it—he would do it all for her. Otto's white mare was eating
grass on the hilltop—having apparently decided that the present
raeken were no threat to her—and Linus stepped up and took her
reins once more in his hand. He put his left foot into the stirrup
and vaulted himself into the saddle before looking once more
toward Emmaline's body. "Take care of her while I'm gone," he
told Meera. He didn't wait for her reply—he knew she would.
Instead, he guided the horse's head around and descended from
the hilltop.

Linus had seen Kennick look to the east, concerned about the
army there, so that was where he would start. He spurred Otto's
horse to a gallop and rode all the way down the length of the army
to the very end where a bright green raek stood looking menac-

ing. Then he cut into the ranks, searching, until he found the nearest general—the only other man in the vicinity on horseback. "Ho!" Linus told his horse, pulling his reins in when he reached the general.

The general was not one that he knew, and the man gaped at him in confusion, clearly recognizing that he was wearing the king's jacket but was not the king.

Linus didn't care; Otto had told him to go ahead and take his place, so he would. "Orders are to turn back!" he shouted. "Let the men rest, then send them home!"

The general continued to eye him suspiciously, but he nodded. Linus didn't need to show him Otto's signet ring or provide his name or anything. These men wanted to go home—the generals included. Turning away, he spurred his horse back into motion, moving toward the back of the army. He spent most of the day zigzagging through Terratelle's forces, commanding the generals to lead their troops back to camp then send them home. Occasionally, he faced questions and reluctance and had to flash Otto's sword and ring around, but for the most part, the generals accepted the news with relief.

Some of the soldiers Linus passed recognized him and exclaimed in surprise to see him alive, but he ignored their surprise and kept moving. He also ignored his thirst and hunger and head-pounding exhaustion. His wife was dead—his beautiful, lively Emmaline would never rise again—and nothing else seemed nearly as important. Even so, he kept riding—kept commanding the men to turn around. He needed it all to mean something.

Eventually, Linus reached the other end of the army, and he finally looked behind him to watch the soldiers slowly gather themselves and trudge back to food and shelter. He watched the troops start to retreat, and he thought of his brother Sam for the first time in a long time. Sam had been about his age—Emmaline's age—when he had died. He had fallen to Shael's raek trying to feed the beast, doing what he had thought was right for his king and his land.

For a time, Linus had needed to believe that Sam hadn't died for nothing. He had needed to believe that raeken were evil and that the war sought to protect them all. Then he had joined the war and learned that it really was all for nothing—that every soldier who fell, fell for no good reason—and he had thought Sam's death had been a waste; he had thought his brother had been a fool and that he had, too. Now Linus wasn't so sure.

He still didn't think the war was being waged for a good reason, but he supposed the men fighting had at least believed in something ... He supposed his brother had believed in something —been living for something rather than just surviving. Linus knew what that was like—just surviving, just living for the sake of living. That was what he had done as a general. Then he had met Emmaline, and he had lived for her and for joy.

As he watched the soldiers before him hang their heads in defeat and walk back toward their beds and dinners, Linus thought maybe everyone just needed something to live for and it didn't matter much what it was—any purpose was better than no purpose. Sam had died unnecessarily, but he had died believing in his cause. Maybe that was all any of them could hope for: to live and die *for something.*

Emmaline had died trying to get to him, and as much as Linus wanted to rage about her decision and shout that he wasn't worth it—that seeing him wasn't worth dying for—she had at least had her own purpose. She had believed in what she'd been doing, and Linus took comfort in that. In that moment, he realized that he hadn't had to end the war to justify Emmaline's death because she had already done that for herself; she had chosen to live for him as he had lived for her, and she had died doing it. The trouble was, Linus had lived for Emmaline, and now he was moorless—a ship without anchor and a man without purpose.

Slowly, letting his horse have her head and take her time, Linus wandered back toward Emmaline's body. The mare became nervous at the sight of so many raeken gathered together, but she was a well-trained warhorse; when he urged her on, she lifted her head and plodded up the hill. Linus looked around and supposed the knell he was looking at were the other riders, all gathered together. Then his eyes snagged on where Emmaline had been.

Where her slight body had lain motionless on Meera's stone table, there was now a statue of her standing over a stone coffin. The statue looked just like Emmaline and depicted her as Linus imagined her: standing very straight and poised with a steady expression on her face. Ignoring the other people on the hill, he dismounted to get a closer look. The stone coffin beneath the statue was intricately decorated with flowers just like the ones on Emmaline's wedding band, and the epitaph read: *Here Lies Emmaline Harrington Backer, Beloved Wife, Daughter & Friend.*

"Well?" Meera asked, coming up behind him and putting her hand on his back.

Linus knew she was asking about the memorial, but he didn't want to talk about it—it was beautiful, but he couldn't handle breaking down again. "I did it," he said. "I sent them back."

"I see that," she replied. "Well done." She gave him a brief hug and kissed his cheek, but Linus remained motionless, appreciative of her love but unable to respond to it.

"Now what?" a massively muscular woman with short red hair asked.

"With any human luck, King Otto will sign the peace treaty I sent him," the knell queen responded.

"What are the odds of that?" a slightly older knell man asked, looking grim.

"I'll make him," Linus said quietly. He might as well finish what he had started; he didn't know what else to do with himself. He would send a letter to Emmaline's mother, of course, but he didn't want to return to Harringbay. There was no longer anything for him there.

"Then what will you do, Linus?" Meera asked, wondering the same thing he was wondering.

He shrugged.

"You could come with us," she offered, not for the first time.

"To Magicland?" he asked, skeptically.

She smiled and nodded.

"I have a spare room," Shael added.

Linus peered at the knell man where he sat atop his raek, looking ready to leave. He was surprised by the offer and to read in the man's face that it was genuine. Linus had thought Shael hated him—or at least strongly disliked him. But Shael reached a hand down toward him, offering him a place behind him on his raek—a place in his life. Linus stared at the hand and considered the offer, but he shook his head. Not this time, he thought.

⸻

LINUS EVENTUALLY RETURNED to Otto's tent with his friend's horse and belongings. He found the king dressed and groomed but otherwise in much the same state as he had left him. When he looked up at Linus's entrance and raised his eyebrows in question, Linus shook his head. Otto merely held up a bottle in response. The amber liquid sloshing within seriously tempted Linus, but alive or dead, he didn't want to disappoint Emmaline. He shook his head again, then he unceremoniously threw Otto's jacket, ring, and sword onto the ground at his feet.

"How'd you like being king for the day?" Otto asked with a grin. He obviously knew that the troops had been sent back to their tents—presumably on his order—and he didn't seem particularly upset about it.

"Sign the treaty, so we can get out of this hell hole," Linus replied.

———

IT TOOK ALL EVENING, but in the end, Otto signed the treaty when Linus promised to return to Altus with him. Linus figured he needed a new purpose, and it might as well be protecting his land from his friend—the king. He went to Altus with Otto on the back of his horse from Harringbay, but he didn't return to his old room in the palace. Instead, after what felt like an almost insurmountable time, he moved home with his family.

He hadn't lived with his family since he was fifteen—since before he'd joined the palace guards. It was undeniably strange for him to be home after so much had happened, but it felt good too. His parents hardly believed the stories he told them, but his sister did. Linus was shocked to find that his sister, Kathleen, had grown from a girl into a young woman—talking of dances and boys instead of dolls. He was even more shocked to find that she seemed to have missed him while he was gone. Though Linus went to the palace each day to make sure Otto wasn't burning Terratelle to the ground, he spent most of his time with Kathleen.

He grieved for Emmaline every second of every day and never expected to be truly happy again. But he had never expected to find happiness before meeting Emmaline, and she had proved him wrong. She had been so many things to him and still was even though she was gone. Over time, Linus found himself wishing he had something of hers and was surprised that when he wrote to her mother from Altus, she actually wrote back and sent him some of Emmaline's things. Duchess Harrington even thanked him for bringing her daughter joy and reminded him that he was the heir to Harringbay, inviting him to visit—or move back in—at any time. Linus wasn't ready to return to the Harringtons' house yet, but he thought maybe he would be one day.

After a while, his pain dulled as pain usually does, and the wound of Emmaline's death became more or less like the wound of his mutilated arm—it no longer burned in agony every second of every day, and slowly, he learned to live with it. Spending time at home with his family—with Kathleen, especially—helped remind him of who had been before he had ever entered the palace. He even started to remember that he was young—much younger than he usually felt—and that he had a long life full of possibilities ahead of him.

42

MEERA

Meera awoke and reached for Kennick next to her, but he wasn't there. Disentangling herself from their covers, she pulled on one of Kennick's silk robes—she had never bothered to get one of her own and probably never would—and left their bedroom to find him making breakfast in the kitchen. She smiled at the sight, then positively beamed when she saw the bag of pastries on the table. "Mmmmmm," she intoned happily, biting into one that oozed with jam.

Kennick grinned at her and walked over to kiss her good morning. Meera didn't stop chewing to kiss him back, which made him laugh. "Are you still going to the estate today?" he asked, leaning down to steal a bite of her pastry. He still didn't eat many sweets, but Meera felt like she was wearing him down to her ways bite by bite.

She nodded in answer, her mouth full of flakey, buttery deliciousness.

"Will you be back tonight?" he asked.

"Probably tomorrow," she replied, swallowing. She didn't like to rush her visits. Besides, Shaya would be migrating north soon with Hadjal's raek, Serene, to show the wild raeken it was safe to pass over Terratelle. Meera wanted to visit the estate as much as possible before then.

"Are you going to sleep in your own room or challenge Lethian for the honor of sleeping beside the queen?" Kennick asked, his dark eyes glinting.

"I'll challenge him if I have to, but I think you and I have already put him in his place—he'll stay out of my way!" she replied, laughing and picking up a plate to load with food.

After breakfast, she gave Kennick a proper kiss. Then she went outside to find Shaya. "Hello! We're flying to the estate today, remember? Here, girl!" she called to her raek mentally, reaching out to wherever she was nearby.

"I am a raek, not a puppy," Shaya retorted, swooping down from the cloud cover above and battering Meera with an abundance of wind before snorting a puff of smoke at her.

Meera waved the smoke away with her hand, not bothering to shape a gust of air. "And you're a good raek!" she said. "Yes, you are! Yes, you are! Who's a good raek?" she asked, patting Shaya's scaly snout condescendingly.

Shaya lashed her enormous, tufted tail at her, and she jumped it easily. "Do you want a ride, or do you want to be eaten?" the raek asked.

"Please, Your Majesty, may I have a ride?" Meera asked, giving Shaya her very best curtsy.

Her raek merely snorted, but Meera could sense that she was amused and leapt onto her back to get going.

When Shaya settled into a steady rhythm in the sky, Meera reclined, enjoying the sun on her face and the air that was slowly warming with spring's arrival. It would be the equinox soon, and she looked forward to going to the celebration with Kennick and dancing all night—well, until they didn't feel like dancing anymore and disappeared to do other things. She made a mental note to give Kennick some human dance lessons since they had both promised Shael's mother that they would attend her next ball. That, or Shael was going to have to give them both lessons, she thought smiling; that would be a fun day at the peninsula.

When they reached the estate, Shaya circled but didn't bother to land. Meera jumped from her back and soared through the air, enjoying the heady sense of free-falling before gradually catching herself with a swirl of wind. Some of the knell on the back patio glanced up at her, but none of them looked overly alarmed; Meera was becoming a common sight at the estate. She walked inside and moved purposefully through the halls to her father's research room. They had made plans to have lunch, but she knew he had likely gotten caught up in his work and forgotten.

"There you are!" he exclaimed the moment she entered the room, having—apparently—not forgotten her.

"Here I am!" she replied, catching Ned as he barreled toward her for a hug. Meera was growing increasingly fond of her new brother and couldn't believe how quickly he was growing. Sometimes it made her sad to know that she would likely outlive all of the humans she knew by hundreds of years, but then she would remind herself that she was lucky to know them to begin with. Luck was a human concept, after all, as Darreal would remind her.

"I have something for you!" her father cried, coming toward her with a sheet of paper.

"What is it?" Meera asked, extending a hand.

Her father quickly snatched the paper out of reach. "This is the original, so be careful," he admonished, as if she'd just spat on her hand.

"Okay ..." she said, suppressing a laugh. "What is it?"

Her father finally handed her the document, explaining: "It's Aegwren's Last Will and Testament."

"Really?" Meera asked, squinting at the paper. The writing was sloppy to begin with and also smudged and ancient, so she couldn't make out many of the words. "What does it say?" she asked, knowing her father was an expert in deciphering such documents.

"It essentially says that he wished to leave all of his wealth and possessions to his beloved wife and all of his chores and responsibilities to his sons," her father said, laughing. "It is not so much a legal document as the loving joke of an old father," he added knowingly.

Meera gazed down at the illegible script before her and felt her throat constrict; Aegwren had found his happiness, after all. She didn't know how and possibly never would, but knowing Aegwren had loved and married and had children brought her immeasurable joy. She was glad to have this final bit of information about her long-dead friend—and it would be the final bit, too, unless her father uncovered more documents. Meera had decided never to return to Aegwren's cave. She had gone one last time to return his sword, but she had not stayed the night and had decided it was time to live her own life and only her life. Aegwren was in the past, and she wanted to look toward her future.

"Let's eat," she said, handing the paper carefully back to her father. "I have my own silly old father to be getting on with."

Orson Hailship grinned at his daughter and replaced the paper carefully on the table before putting a hand on each of his children's backs to guide them from the room. Meera enjoyed their meal even though they ate the kind of light, fishy food the knell favored for lunch. She enjoyed it because she loved seeing her father happy with his new wife.

Doreen often seemed uncomfortable with Meera, but Meera

just smiled and hoped that the woman would grow accustomed to her with time. She knew she should probably stop lighting things on fire when in the presence of humans, but her raek fire was such a habit that she just couldn't help it; it was really no wonder she made Doreen uncomfortable. Even so, they had a lovely lunch all together.

Afterward, Meera went in search of Darreal, deciding to check first in her friend's bedroom. She pushed open the door without knocking and walked inside before quickly slapping her hands over her eyes when she saw what Darreal and Lethian were doing in the bed. "It's the afternoon!" she exclaimed. "Don't you have important queenly things to do?" she asked, laughing. Darreal and Lethian had been all but attached since the war had ended, and Meera was still waiting for this phase of their relationship to simmer out a little. Leaving the room, she dawdled in the hallway until Lethian finally exited, looking annoyed.

"She's mine, and don't forget I can beat you in a fight," Meera whispered to him on his way past. Then she entered the room and found Darreal dressed and laughing on one of her chairs. "I'm going to need those sheets changed before I sleep here tonight," Meera told her, making a face.

"You make demands like a queen—a human queen, that is," Darreal told her.

"Yes, because *clearly* as a knell queen, you spend all day toiling for your people," Meera replied, giving her friend a pointed look.

Darreal lifted one of her narrow shoulders and sipped delicately from the water glass in her hand, the vision of elegance and serenity. "What am I supposed to do now that you have ended the war?" she asked.

"I didn't end the war—Linus did," Meera replied, taking a seat.

Darreal rolled her eyes, a gesture Meera had taught her. "The riders prevented the battle because you made them believe that they should, and Linus did what he did because you inspired him to be a better person—he told me so," she said.

Meera waved her hand dismissively. She had played her part, but she hadn't been alone; they had all ended the war together. "What else did Linus say, and when did you start writing to him? He rarely answers my letters!" she complained. It wasn't strictly true; Linus did answer her, he just didn't seem to feel the need to write weekly like she did.

"I have given up trying to correspond with King Otto and write directly to Linus now. It saves us all time," Darreal responded.

"Are you still trying to arrange a visit to the palace?" Meera asked.

"I am if you are still willing to accompany me," Darreal said.

"Only if we fly. I'm not traveling all over on horseback again—especially not one of your horses," Meera replied. She would feel strange visiting Altus and the palace again, considering she had fled from there—twice—but she thought it would be good for her to return in peace. She also wouldn't miss an opportunity to visit Linus or taste Cook's food again.

"Then what?" Darreal asked her. "What will you do now that the war is over, and everything is settling peacefully?"

Meera smiled and leaned back in her chair, resting her head and sighing in contentment. "This," she replied. "Keep the peace and be with my people." She looked forward to a long life of doing both.

Milton Keynes UK
Ingram Content Group UK Ltd.
UKHW040133130324
439347UK00003B/50

9 781963 256048